THE DUKE AND THE LADY GARDENER

The Grantham Girls
Book One

By Alissa Baxter

© Copyright 2023 by Alissa Baxter
Text by Alissa Baxter
Cover by Kim Killion Designs

Dragonblade Publishing, Inc. is an imprint of Kathryn Le Veque Novels, Inc.
P.O. Box 23
Moreno Valley, CA 92556
ceo@dragonbladepublishing.com

Produced in the United States of America

First Edition May 2023
Trade Paperback Edition

Reproduction of any kind except where it pertains to short quotes in relation to advertising or promotion is strictly prohibited.

All Rights Reserved.

The characters and events portrayed in this book are fictitious. Any similarity to real persons, living or dead, is purely coincidental and not intended by the author.

ARE YOU SIGNED UP FOR DRAGONBLADE'S BLOG?

You'll get the latest news and information on exclusive giveaways, exclusive excerpts, coming releases, sales, free books, cover reveals and more.

Check out our complete list of authors, too!

No spam, no junk. That's a promise!

Sign Up Here

www.dragonbladepublishing.com

⇾⇾⇾✕⇽⇽⇽

Dearest Reader;

Thank you for your support of a small press. At Dragonblade Publishing, we strive to bring you the highest quality Historical Romance from some of the best authors in the business. Without your support, there is no 'us', so we sincerely hope you adore these stories and find some new favorite authors along the way.

Happy Reading!

CEO, Dragonblade Publishing

Dedication

For my parents

CHAPTER ONE

THE DOOR OF the carriage jerked open, and a coated figure on horseback, wearing a wide-brimmed hat and black face-covering, leaned into the coach with pistol drawn. "Stand and deliver!" The coarse cloth mask may have muffled the voice, but not the force of the command behind it.

The occupant of the vehicle, a dark, elegantly attired gentleman, raised his quizzing glass and inspected the highwayman through it. "I think not."

"Stand and deliver!" The highwayman's eyes narrowed behind the slits of the mask. "Your money or your life."

The gentleman lowered his quizzing glass and leaned back against the seat cushion. "My guarded retinue follows me and will come upon us at any moment. I suggest you depart forthwith and play your childish games with someone else."

"I play no games with you, sir, and you are foolish to challenge me. Stand and deliver, I say!"

The gentleman gave a weary sigh. "My dear fellow, you may think it great sport to masquerade as a highwayman, but you have surely had your fun. Take that beast back to your father's stable forthwith, or you may leave me with no choice but to unmask you."

The highwayman scoffed. "You cannot unmask me, sir. I am the one pointing this pistol at you."

Quick as a flash, the gentleman moved, knocking the pistol out of the thief's hand and into the verge. Leveling his own pistol, which he had kept hidden beside him, he drawled, "I think you find yourself mistaken."

The bandit's hands shook as the reality of this sudden reversal settled in. A second, larger thief, who held a pistol to the coachman's head, shouted to his accomplice, and, in an instant, both highwaymen wheeled their horses around and galloped away.

The thieves rode swiftly across the countryside, saying not a word to one another as they sped away. Finally, they came to a secluded copse where they drew up their horses and silently dismounted beside an open carriage, which had been carefully concealed amongst the bushes. The leader picked up a bundle from the conveyance and slipped away behind some trees while the larger highwayman harnessed the horses.

He went about his task efficiently, muttering to himself as he put the animals in their traces. Finally, the man raised his voice: "Our escape this time was too narrow, Miss Grantham. When I saw the barrel of that gun in your face—. Your brother would have my blood if he knew I aid you in such foolishness."

"It isn't foolishness, Ben, and we managed to escape, so don't fuss. Is my appearance tidy enough?"

Ben scowled at the young lady who emerged from behind the bushes. "Aye, miss, you look tidy enough. But that wouldn't be the case if a bloodstain happened to mark those pretty clothes of yours."

"You concern yourself far too much over me. I admit our plans went slightly awry today, but Lady Luck has smiled on us—as she always does." She laughed up at him as he assisted her into the carriage.

Ben continued to frown. "Well, in my experience, miss, it don't pay to tempt fate. We'd be mad to continue this for much longer."

Alexandra Grantham opened her eyes very wide. "Continue

what?" Her voice was innocent. "I am a perfectly respectable lady enjoying a perfectly respectable drive in the countryside."

Ben merely grunted as he lowered himself into the driver's seat. He clicked to the horses and set them in motion along the deserted country lane, which led to the main road a couple hundred yards further on.

Alexandra settled back against the seat, grateful for the swaying motion of the vehicle, which calmed her a little. Although she refused to admit it to her henchman, she *was* rather unnerved at how close they had come to discovery.

A cold shiver ran through her body, and she rubbed her hands over her arms as she brooded over the gentleman who had so successfully turned the tables on her. He had appeared almost indifferent to the attack, failing to exhibit any of the signs of fear and anxiety she had come to expect in the countenances of the people she waylaid.

Perhaps he had recognized the quality of her mount and presumed she was a young gentleman playing at being a highwayman on the road. Alexandra's brow wrinkled. It was commonly known that the horses used by highway robbers were often stolen from the stables of the nobility and gentry. A good, speedy beast was essential for a highwayman's survival, and the best place to find such a horse was, of course, in a gentleman's stable.

Her mount could very easily have been stolen from such a stable. Yet the coach's occupant had told her to take her horse back to her *father's* stable, which suggested that he had believed her to be the son of a gentleman. Something in her appearance must have alerted him to the fact that she wasn't a member of the lower classes. But what could it be? She had been convinced her disguise was impenetrable.

Alexandra straightened her spine as her coachman directed the horses onto the main road. Soon they would be home, and she could put this unfortunate incident behind her. However, as they came around the bend, her eyes widened in horror as the coach she had just waylaid came into view. "Slow down, Ben! The horses! He may recognize them." Her voice was urgent.

Her coachman glanced back at her. "Nay, miss, he won't. They're in their traces, and I disguised their markings for the attack. Besides, he'd never suspect a lady of being a highwayman, so he oughtn't to look at your horses with a leery eye."

"Of course you're right. Yet the impression I received of him was that he is an uncommonly perceptive gentleman. I hoped he would have been well on his way by now" She chewed her bottom lip. "We must stay as far back as possible until we turn off to Grantham Place." Even as Ben drew on the reins, the carriage in front of them came to a halt, blocking their way on the narrow road.

As Ben halted as well, a groom jumped down from his perch to open the coach door and let down the step. Alexandra held her breath as the dark gentleman emerged. He stood immobile in the road for a while before bowing politely in her direction. Alexandra inclined her head in response. He was very tall, well over six feet, and his shoulders were uncommonly broad, filling out his well-cut jacket impressively. Her wary gaze came to rest on the strong line of his jaw and the uncompromising set of his mouth and chin.

All in all, it was a thoroughly disagreeable face.

"Do I pass muster, ma'am?"

Her eyes met his. Perturbed at the mocking gleam in their green depths, she said the first thing that came into her head, "I am afraid, sir, that I have never considered dark-haired men to be particularly attractive."

The gentleman's eyes narrowed at this daring remark, but then he laughed softly as he looked at her hair. "For my part, I have often found red-headed young ladies to be uncommonly impertinent."

Alexandra raised her brows. "I am returning home, sir, and find it disconcerting that I have been forced to stop my carriage by a complete stranger. Indeed, given the fact that we find ourselves alone on a deserted country road, I consider my natural wariness toward you not impertinent but imperative!"

A corner of his mouth lifted. "Forgive me, ma'am. Robert Chanderly, at your service." He bowed again.

Alexandra nodded in a regal fashion. "I am Miss Alexandra Grantham of Grantham Place, daughter of the late Sir Henry Grantham."

"I am honored to make your acquaintance, Miss Grantham." A smile hovered about his lips. "And now I shall allay your very natural feminine fears at being asked to stop your carriage by a stranger." He paused before continuing in a brisker voice, "A few miles back, two highwaymen accosted me. Not very skilled thieves, admittedly, yet highwaymen nonetheless. They could still be very close to the road and may attempt to strike again. When I saw your carriage turn onto the road, I indicated to my coachman that we should stop to warn you of the danger."

"Highwaymen, sir?" Alexandra's eyes widened. "Here? How shocking! I have heard talk that there are highwaymen at work in the district, but to be so close to the scene of a crime—!" She cleared her throat. "What do you mean by saying they were not ... er ... skilled?"

Mr. Chanderly shrugged. "They bungled the hold up. I don't think they are the most experienced of thieves. More than likely, they're a couple of youths out for a lark."

"Oh." Alexandra clenched her teeth together at this disparagement of her recent performance.

"Nevertheless, it does not pay to take risks. I may be underestimating the danger of these scoundrels, and you—a lady on your own—could prove to be a far easier target for them. May I escort you home?"

Alexandra shook her head. The last thing she wanted was to spend any more time with the man she had so recently held up. "Thank you, sir, but no. Ben is perfectly able to protect me. He carries a pistol with him, you know."

He frowned. "Nevertheless, I would prefer to escort you

home."

Alexandra's cheeks heated at this apparent disregard for her assessment of her own safety. "Indeed, sir, I am not afraid to continue on my own."

"Your intrepidity does you credit, Miss Grantham. I had expected you to succumb to an attack of the vapors upon hearing about my experience," he added drily.

"Not all ladies are weaklings, sir. I have never suffered from an attack of the vapors in my life."

"You are to be admired then, Miss Grantham, to be sure." He turned to look at her servant. "Lead the way home, Ben. I shall follow behind you to ensure your mistress's safety."

Her coachman bent his head. "Aye, sir."

Alexandra drew in a sharp breath. "Sir, I have made my wishes quite plain to you. I shall continue on my own."

Mr. Chanderly studied her impassively. "You have no choice in the matter, ma'am."

Before she could utter another word of protest, he turned and climbed back into his coach.

Alexandra sank back against the squabs. What a nerve he had to impose his will on her in this manner. She had a strong mind to order Ben to take the longest route home, merely to inconvenience the imperious Mr. Chanderly. But, after considering this delightful idea for a moment, she set it aside. The less time she spent in the vicinity of this man, the better.

She only hoped Mr. Chanderly didn't look too closely at her horses as Ben drove around the other carriage to lead the way toward Grantham Place. Even though he had disguised their distinctive markings for the attack, it was impossible to hide the general conformation of an animal from the experienced eye.

Highwaymen were frequently betrayed by their horses. Even the notorious Dick Turpin had once narrowly escaped the arm of the law when someone recognized a bay mare he had stolen, resting in a stable. But although Alexandra risked discovery every time she held someone up, she felt bound to continue her highway activities for the sake of the people who depended upon her.

She had first come up with the idea of playing at being Robin Hood several months ago when the vicar's wife, Mrs. Simpson, had informed her of the terrible conditions in which many of their parishioners lived. The older lady had shaken her head and said with a sigh, "He that has mercy on the poor, happy is he. But it seems the local landowners have no such desire. It is a shame indeed."

Alexandra had visited a few of the families Mrs. Simpson mentioned and was horrified by what she had seen. The people seemed to live in utter penury, and the misery on their faces had struck a compassionate chord deep inside her.

On a wave of righteous indignation, had she sought out her brother. John was one of the few landowners in the district who looked after his tenants well, living by the proverb that one should not withhold good from those who deserved it when it was in one's power to act. Although her revelations about living conditions had angered him, he had not approved of her stated wish to personally confront their heartless neighbors. On the contrary, he believed it would do more harm than good as they would not take kindly to a young woman reprimanding them.

Alexandra had reluctantly agreed not to approach them. But she felt the need to do something practical to help the poor families and had asked John to sponsor food baskets. He had been happy to oblige her in this, but Alexandra realized that their indigent neighbors needed more than just food to survive. They also needed other material provisions.

If it had not been for the fact that her money was tied up in a trust fund until she either married or turned one-and-twenty, Alexandra would have helped the poor from her own pocket. But her money was not hers to do with as she willed until she attained her majority. After thinking the problem over, she decided that justice would be best served if the funds the poor needed but weren't receiving could be obtained from the very people who had failed in their responsibility to look after them—the privileged classes.

Alexandra had recently enlisted the help of her faithful coachman and so had begun their series of daring highway robberies. They had succeeded in inspiring fear in the hearts of all the local gentry and nobility with their robberies. Well, nearly all of them. Alexandra grimaced as she thought of Mr. Chanderly. He hadn't looked afraid or concerned, only somewhat displeased!

When they reached the gates of Grantham Place, she instructed Ben to halt. As she waited for Mr. Chanderly's conveyance to draw up alongside them, dread gripped her stomach. It was incumbent upon her to thank him for escorting her home—the dictums of propriety required it, however much she wished she could ignore them in this instance. So when Mr. Chanderly descended from the coach once again, Alexandra formally thanked him for his assistance.

"The pleasure was all mine, Miss Grantham." His tone was polite, but Alexandra had the uncomfortable feeling he was amused at her belated efforts to be civil.

"May I offer you some refreshment, sir, before you continue on your journey?" She was determined not to be betrayed into incivility again by her emotions. It only set her at a disadvantage in the face of Mr. Chanderly's good manners.

"Thank you, but no, Miss Grantham. I must continue on my way."

Alexandra smiled sweetly. "As you wish, Mr. Chanderly. Good afternoon."

"Good afternoon, ma'am." He made to move away, then turned back. "I hope we meet again sometime, Miss Grantham. Your charming attempt at politeness has reassured me of the fact that you may not be a complete baggage. Perhaps you will even improve upon further acquaintance."

Alexandra stared at his back as he re-entered the coach, unable to believe the man's arrogance. It was only when the coach moved off and disappeared round the bend in the road that she recovered her breath sufficiently to direct Ben to continue up the drive. Alexandra released her pent-up breath as the seventeenth-century manor house came into view with its ashlar dressings and stone-tiled roof. About a hundred years ago, one of her ancestors had remodeled the Tudor structure upon more elegant lines, and it stood now like a gracious old lady within its beautiful and well-maintained gardens.

On returning home, Alexandra hurried through the oak front door and made her way upstairs to her bedchamber to bathe and dress for dinner. Never before had anyone upset her equilibrium to the extent Mr. Chanderly had. There was something about him, a perceptiveness and a steadiness of purpose, which quite unnerved her. She shook her head at her reflection in the mirror and ran a comb through her tangled hair. The best thing she could do was put him from her mind as he was probably just passing through the district. She would most definitely have heard about it if he were visiting one of the local families in their small community, so there was no reason she should be concerned about him.

No reason at all.

CHAPTER TWO

SUNLIGHT SHONE THROUGH the bare branches of the old oak tree, warming Alexandra's skin as she knelt by the stream at the bottom of the vegetable patch tucked away on the grounds of neighboring Durbridge Hall. She dipped a bucket into the water and then leaned back on her heels as she recalled the contents of the letter she had received from her esteemed grandmama earlier that day, a letter that seemed destined to change the course of her life forever. At least it would if Grandmama had her way.

Her usually placid grandmother had written to her in the strictest terms that she would no longer accept Alexandra's excuses for not being presented in London in the upcoming Season. "Because in all truth, my dear child," she wrote, "I cannot possibly imagine why you wish to remain in that rural place—unless you imagine yourself in love with the squire's son or some such nonsense. But rest assured, my love, that if that is your reason, then the attentions of the polished London gentlemen you will meet will make you forget any young man on whom you may have set your heart. And I am quite determined to find you a most eligible husband."

Alexandra blotted the unpleasant words from her mind as she bent forward once again. The bucket was nearly full when a barking dog ran up and jumped hard against her legs in greeting. Her knees buckled just as she heard a shout from behind. She tried desperately to retain her balance, but the friendly dog knocked against her again, causing her to lose her footing and topple headlong into the depths of the icy water.

She came up sputtering and fuming. As she dragged her thick copper hair away from her face, her gaze rested on a pair of shiny brown leather boots directly in her line of vision. Raising her eyes, she took in the well-cut buff-colored breeches, the form-fitting coat, and the perfectly tied cravat of the gentleman standing before her.

"Why are you trespassing on my land, Miss Grantham?" Mr. Chanderly's voice was even icier than the water.

Impeded by her wet skirts, Alexandra climbed out of the stream with difficulty and tried to gather her wits as he glared down at her. "I am in no way trespassing."

Mr. Chanderly folded his arms. "Aren't you?"

"Indeed, I am not. When I was a young girl, Sir George Durbridge gave me permission to care for this vegetable patch, which I have done ever since. I came here today to water the cabbages as it has been so dry of late. I grant you, I will need to confirm that agreement with Sir George's heir when he arrives at Durbridge Hall, but whatever distant cousin that may be has not yet come to take possession of the estate." Alexandra raised her chin. "I would like to know, sir, on what authority you address me in such terms."

"The authority on which I speak is that I happen to be that 'distant cousin,' and I now own this estate."

"Oh! Well, you took long enough to get here. Sir George died all of six months ago. And, although I admit I don't yet have your express permission to work here, you had no right to sneak up on me and shout at me in that appallingly uncivil manner." She placed her hands on her hips. "Really, sir, it was too bad of you."

"I wasn't shouting at you. I was calling Bruno away." He glanced around. "Where has that dog got to?"

"Oh, he's probably deep in Grantham Woods by now, looking for rabbits."

"Ah." Mr. Chanderly's gaze traveled over the shabby gown Alexandra always wore when she gardened. It was in the style of another era, low-waisted with full skirts. Alexandra usually donned it because it was comfortable and loosely fitted, but now the wet cloth molded to her frame, outlining her figure. Warmth crept into her cheeks. She must look a complete sight.

His lips twitched. "I realize it is now the trend for ladies of the more daring set to dampen their skirts to show off their figures, ma'am, but you seem to have taken this fashion to the extreme."

"Sir, you . . . you go beyond the bounds of what is seemly. A gentleman would not comment on—"

"The fact that your gown is clinging to your form?" His eyes glinted in a most disturbing way.

"Precisely." She turned away, ostensibly to pick up her fallen pail, but in reality to regain her shaky composure.

"But clearly, my dear girl, I am no gentleman."

She whirled around to stare at him. This man's handsome face had haunted her dreams for the past week, and she found herself thinking about him at the most inopportune moments. A painting of Apollo hung in the library at Grantham Place, and Mr. Chanderly reminded her very much of the Greek god of archery, poetry, and the sun, with his classical features, which seemed to have been hewn from stone, and his cool demeanor. Now he was here before her again, even more disturbing in person than she remembered. "May I say that it is *not* a pleasure to renew my acquaintance with you, Mr. Chanderly."

"Now, now. A *lady* would not comment on her true feelings about a new acquaintance."

Alexandra's face burned at Mr. Chanderly's turning her own words against her. Several less than polite responses sprang to her lips, but she valiantly bit her tongue. The best course of action open to her now would be to retreat in haste with dignity. She had no desire to continue arguing with this man while standing before him in a wet gown. It placed her at too great a disadvantage. "The wind is quite chill, and I am catching cold. I think it is time that I returned home." Her voice was carefully neutral.

"Of course." Mr. Chanderly glanced at Alexandra's horse, tethered to a nearby tree. "Why are you unescorted?"

"I always dispense of a groom's services when I am out riding because I know the countryside very well and see no need to burden myself or the groom."

"I beg to differ. It is not at all the thing to ride unescorted. You may encounter an unsavory character and have no protection from him."

"Yes," Alexandra mused. "I think I discovered that today."

A dangerous light appeared in his green eyes. "Careful, my dear."

Alexandra backed away from him and went to untie Starlight, her chestnut mare.

He followed her. "Tending a vegetable patch is an unusual occupation for a young lady. Do you often work here?"

"Not as much as I once did. This field borders our land, though, so I occasionally check on it. It has been rather neglected of late."

"Let me escort you home."

Knowing from previous experience that it would be futile to argue with him, Alexandra, with a somewhat ill grace, consented to be thrown up into the saddle.

Mr. Chanderly then mounted his own horse, tethered nearby, and inclined his head. "The way, madam?"

"My home is about a mile down the lane which borders this field, Mr. Chanderly, although, truly, I see no reason for you to accompany me. I sincerely doubt I will encounter any 'unsavory characters' in this area. Why, most of the people who live here have known me from my babyhood."

"Nevertheless, I would be remiss in my duty as a gentleman to allow you to ride home unescorted."

Alexandra opened her eyes very wide. "But, sir, not ten minutes back, you informed me most succinctly that you were no gentleman."

He gave a crack of laughter as she nudged her horse toward home, taking advantage of her preoccupation with the animal to allow his gaze to rest on her dainty form appreciatively. Robert had to admit she was uncommonly beautiful. Creamy skin and sapphire-blue eyes provided a striking contrast to her long copper-red hair, which tumbled around her sloping shoulders after her dip in the stream. And although she was dressed in an outmoded gown, the proud cast of her face indicated she was no country bumpkin. Her features were too fine to fit that description, and her temperament far too fiery. "Touché, Miss Grantham. Now I am properly put in my place."

A blush rose in her cheeks. "Er... don't you think the weather is unseasonably temperate for January, sir?"

Robert smiled at her obvious discomfiture, but he merely said, "It has been warm. Many of the London hostesses are hoping for mild temperatures during the Season so the al fresco parties and other events they are planning will not be ruined by inclement weather. Do you, Miss Grantham, go to London for the Season?" he asked abruptly.

"In all probability, yes. My grandmother, Lady Longmore, wants me to participate in all the social activities."

"The prospect does not please you?"

"It does not."

His eyes narrowed. "How extraordinary. In my experience of young women, most are inordinately eager to take the Polite World by storm and snare themselves eligible husbands. You must be the one remarkable exception, Miss Grantham."

"I am beginning to think so as well."

"Forgive me for being vulgarly inquisitive, but what are your reasons for not wanting to go to London?"

She gave a tiny shrug. "I am loath to leave my brother behind while I go gallivanting off to Town. We have been constant companions and friends all our lives, and since our father's demise, our friendship has grown stronger, especially as my younger sisters are now at school." She paused before continuing.

"As a child, John was unwell, so we grew up very close. If I go, I am afraid he will be lonely, and I—." She looked away, leaving the sentence unfinished.

"You do not have the heart to leave him," he said. "Your sentiments do you credit, Miss Grantham, but you must also think about your own future. I am sure your brother would not wish to stand in the way of your going to London to find an eligible husband."

She threw a decidedly disdainful glance in his direction as they rode through the gates of Grantham Place. "It is not the intention of every unmarried female to saddle herself with a husband. I have the means to be independent, and I have no intention of getting married now, or ever for that matter."

Robert looked at the young beauty riding alongside him with a skeptical expression on his face. He knew very well that although she may have no intention of entering the Marriage Mart, once she arrived on the London scene, she would be actively pursued by every buck and dandy in Town and collect her share of marriage proposals. Because, apart from her sizeable portion, to which she had so pertly alluded, Alexandra Grantham was also a diamond of the first water who would stand out from the mass of pale blondes and lackluster brunettes who had dominated the London ballrooms for so long.

The only factor against Miss Grantham being a resounding success was her outspokenness. She had actually dared to challenge his opinions, and some of her comments were positively scandalous. And, although he found her brand of conversation highly amusing, he knew that many members of the *ton* would not view her frankness with such leniency.

He remained silent as they passed the woods Miss Grantham suspected Bruno had disappeared into. He narrowed his eyes but could see no sign of the animal. No doubt the dog, who had followed him when he had ridden out to begin the inspection of his recently inherited estate, would find his own way home.

As a charming manor house came into view at the end of the

drive, Robert spoke again. "Even if you have no plans to marry, my girl, if you travel to London and wish to be accepted by Society, you must take care to temper your speech and conduct. Hoydenish behavior like riding about unattended will not be accepted."

"I would appreciate your not addressing me as 'my girl' in that patronizing manner," she snapped. "And you have absolutely no right, no right at all, to stricture my conduct and cast aspersions on my character. Hoydenish behavior indeed!"

"You seem not to realize it, Miss Grantham, but your unruly tongue could cause the members of the *ton* to ostracize you. Simpering misses are the order of the day, and red hair and the fiery temperament that often accompanies it have not been fashionable for some time."

His companion stared straight ahead. "I refuse to change who I am merely to fit in with Society."

He remained silent until she turned her head to look at him, and then he said calmly, "I am afraid you will need to bow to convention if you wish to be accepted in polite circles. Try to behave more maturely in future, Miss Grantham, and take your groom with you when you go riding."

A stable boy ran up to take Miss Grantham's horse and help her dismount. She stood on the first of the shallow steps that led up to the front door and tilted her head up at him, seething in silence.

"Your servant, ma'am." He raised his hat and bowed from the saddle before cantering off down the tree-lined drive.

Alexandra glowered at his serenely retreating back for a moment longer then stormed up the stairs to the front door. "Insolent, insufferable, interfering man," she muttered just as their faithful family butler, Higgins, opened the door.

At the hurt expression on his face, she hastened to assure him that she did not—would never—speak of him in such a way. But, although evidently relieved that her vituperative words were not directed at him, this did not prevent Higgins from scolding her soundly for her wet appearance. "Because truly, Miss Grantham, you could end up with an inflammation of the lungs if you do not have a care for your health."

"Thank you, Higgins, but I am perfectly well."

She swept up the stairs to her bedchamber, which was decorated in calming shades of blue and white. She did not find her surroundings soothing at all as she stepped out of her gown and rang the bell violently for her maid. When Hobbes entered the room, Alexandra pointed at the wet dress on the floor. "Take that and burn it. I never wish to see it again."

"You wish me to—to *burn* it, miss?" Hobbes's mouth was agape.

"Yes. Take the horrid thing away. But please help me change first."

After replacing her gown, Alexandra hastened from her room and made her way downstairs, via the servant's staircase to the kitchen, and through the door to the kitchen garden. As she stepped along the path to the hothouse at the end of the enclosure, Alexandra drew in a lungful of the soil-scented air. She slowed her pace as she walked, allowing her favorite refuge in the world to work its magic on her. The walled garden teemed with neat beds containing an array of vegetables and herbs, while the pear and apple trees, trained along the walls, welcomed her like old friends. She had spent many a happy afternoon perched in their branches as a little girl, watching the gardeners at work.

She never failed to feel at peace in this secluded space. It was a place of promise, where the past came to life for her in a tangible as well as a metaphoric way, as it was also a place of memories. Before her father's death, she had spent many hours with him here as he imparted his horticultural knowledge to her.

When Alexandra had demonstrated an interest in his particular field of scientific expertise, Henry Grantham, who had been an esteemed member of The Horticulture Society of London since its inception in 1804, had been pleased to teach her everything he knew. Her papa advised her that horticulture could be divided into two distinct branches, the useful and the ornamental. It was the first branch that occupied the principal attention of the members of the Society, although they did not neglect the second.

And although Alexandra appreciated a beautiful garden as much as anyone, her attention, of necessity, was focused on the useful at present, as she ensured sufficient fruit and vegetables were grown at Grantham Place to fill the food baskets she distributed to the destitute.

When Alexandra was a young child, her mother had spoken to her many times about the importance of caring for the weak and penniless. "It is our duty, my love, to plead the cause of the poor and needy and to visit the fatherless and widows in their affliction." And Alexandra had always held that instruction close to her heart, seeking out every opportunity to live up to the high standard her mother had set.

⸻

ALEXANDRA FROWNED AT her breakfast plate the following morning as she thought of all the crushing replies she should have made to Mr. Chanderly when he told her to behave more maturely. It was such a pity that one only ever thought of those clever responses when it was too late to utter them. Her brother's exasperated voice finally penetrated her brown study, and she looked up with a start.

"Alexandra! I have asked you the same question three times without a response. You haven't heard a word I have said. You were the same last night. You left me to converse with Aunt whilst you sat in your chair, scowling. What ever is the matter with you?"

"Forgive me, John." Last night, Alexandra had given her brother a brief recital of her unfortunate tumble into the stream, but she had refrained from mentioning her unpleasant encounters with the heir to the Durbridge estate. Instead of enlightening him now, she seized upon her grandmother's letter to explain her unwonted fit of the dismals. "It is only that Grandmama has written to me. She insists I go to London for the Season, but I don't want to leave you here, all alone."

John was only two years older than Alexandra and very like her, possessing the same blue eyes and fair skin. But his hair was a shade lighter than his sister's, and constant ill-health had left its mark on his face, etching lines of strain around his mouth.

A certain gentleness of expression and a humorous look in his eyes endeared him to all who knew him. Now, however, his bearing became stern. "I won't let you sacrifice your future for me. No matter what you may think, I am sure to get on exceedingly well here without you. I shall certainly miss you once you are in London, but I won't repine. Even though Grantham Place is isolated, I have my books and the running of the estate to keep me occupied."

Alexandra shook her head. "But you will only have Aunt for company!"

"It is past time you were presented. Father particularly wanted Grandmama to manage your coming out, and if we had not been in mourning for him this past year, you would already have had your first Season. You are nineteen years old already. You must go to London."

Alexandra studied her brother in consternation. "But John! I thought you would be averse to the idea of my going."

"You cannot think me so selfish that I would begrudge you a London Season. Besides, I plan to visit you in Town—once you are settled in, of course. I am feeling in prime form at the moment, and it will be enjoyable to visit the Capital."

Alexandra hid her dismay with difficulty. John had suffered from a bronchial complaint his whole life, which condition would only be exacerbated by the city air. When he was younger, Alexandra had regularly made a cough remedy for him from the milk of sow thistle. She also created a mixture of sweet almond oil and the syrup of violets along with a plaster of candle wax, saffron, and nutmeg, which John had applied to his stomach every night. It had provided some relief for his symptoms, though he still lived a much less active life than a typical young gentleman.

Alexandra remained silent on the subject now, knowing her brother disliked more than anything to be reminded of his ill-health. Although he had never said so in as many words, she was well aware that her brother's illness was a source of despair for him. Resenting his weak chest, which had robbed him of the opportunity to attend Eton or study at Oxford, John preferred to ignore its existence in the rather naïve hope that the malady would simply disappear. And although his physician, Dr. Wainfleet, had cautiously indicated that his patient's bronchial complaint might improve with maturity, he still needed to be careful of his health.

But now, as she studied his profile, her spirits did lift somewhat. John's color was much improved of late, and he hadn't had a coughing fit in months. Perhaps he was finally outgrowing that dreadful childhood ailment. In spite of this hope, she was still relieved a short while later when he added, "I shall only stay in London for a few weeks. I enjoy the country far too much to endure the rigors of city living for long." A mischievous grin lit up his face, erasing the lines of strain. "But that doesn't mean I don't plan to sample some of the entertainments the Metropolis has on offer."

The door of the breakfast parlor opened, and at the sound of rustling skirts, Alexandra looked up to see her Aunt Eliza walk into the room.

Her aunt had been widowed young. Having no real prospect of receiving another marriage proposal, she had agreed to look after her brother-in-law's household and children at his request when Alexandra's mother had died tragically in a carriage accident six years ago. Not having been well acquainted with his late brother's wife, Papa had only realized the magnitude of his mistake after his sister-in-law came to live with them. He had quickly come to regard her as a decidedly foolish creature, remarking to his children that their aunt had more hair than wit and that her incessant babbling would send him to Bedlam. He had managed to escape this terrible fate by retreating frequently to his library and adjuring Higgins that under *no circumstances* was he to allow Mrs. Grantham to disturb him.

Aunt Eliza bid them good morning. However, the amiable smile faded from her lips when her gaze came to rest on Alexandra's plate. "My dear child, it is positively indecent the amount of food you manage to consume every day. A lady should never pile her plate. I, myself, never eat more than a slice of bread and butter for breakfast."

Alexandra glanced at her aunt and barely contained a most undutiful giggle. While Alexandra was slim to the point of thinness, her aunt was a woman of generous girth. She was a lady of middle years, with a pleasant, somewhat plump face, and when she spoke (which was often), her audience was wont to lose the line of her discourse in favor of staring in increasing fascination at her wobbling double chins.

Alexandra was on the verge of making a most mischievous reply to her aunt's admonition when she intercepted a reproving frown from John. Therefore, she nobly refrained from commenting on the number of sweetmeats her relative consumed daily and said instead, "Aunt Eliza, I engage in activities of an energetic nature and need a large breakfast every morning to sustain me."

Her aunt threw her hands up in the air. "And that is yet another grievance of mine. Your way of life is far too vigorous for a young lady. Why, I am sure I have told you countless times that you are ruining your complexion by being forever outdoors fishing, riding, and tending that garden of yours. No, I insist you press crushed strawberries on your face. I read recently in the *Ladies' Monthly Museum* that your grandmama so kindly sent us that this remedy keeps the complexion wonderfully pure and reduces the danger of getting freckles."

Aunt Eliza sat at the table and took a roll from the breadbasket. "Speaking of your grandmama, my dear, I have just received a letter from her wherein she advised me you will be going to London for the Season. I must positively insist that you practice singing and playing the pianoforte this morning. Why, I believe that you have not set foot in the music room this month past. Fie on you, child! I don't know what your grandmama will think of me if you are called to play and sing in London and have forgotten how!"

"But I have absolutely no musical talent whatsoever. In fact," Alexandra's expression was meditative, "I cannot differentiate tones at all."

"That is all the more reason why you should practice, you foolish girl! Before you do so, though, you must accompany me on a visit to Mrs. Hadley."

Alexandra grimaced at the thought of having to converse with the squire's gossiping wife, but before she could voice an objection to this scheme, her aunt carried inexorably on. "Truly, I am all agog. Yesterday afternoon when I was shopping in the village and received Mrs. Hadley's invitation to tea, she told me she had some most interesting information to impart to me. I assure you, she was fairly swelling with news. I wonder whether she has finally found a suitor for Jane. Poor girl, she is most plain, but at least *she* applies crushed strawberries to her complexion every night, which is more than one can say for you, my love."

Alexandra glanced up from her breakfast plate. "My dear aunt, if I were so unfortunate as to have Jane's perpetually supercilious expression, I assure you I would not only put strawberries on my face every evening, I would also walk around with them all day long to hide my face."

John gave an amused laugh, which he quickly turned into a cough upon encountering a frown from his aunt. With an apologetic look in Alexandra's direction, he excused himself from the table. His sister gave a tiny shake of her head and compressed her lips, but John merely shrugged as he left the room. Alexandra released her breath in a sharp puff. If only she could escape from Aunt Eliza as easily as her brother could.

Chapter Three

A LEXANDRA SMOTHERED A yawn behind her hand as she listened with increasing abstraction to Mrs. Hadley's insipid conversation. However, her attention was caught and held when her hostess said in an excited voice, "My dear Mrs. Grantham, I have discovered who has inherited Sir George Durbridge's estate—a Mr. Robert Chanderly. And what a distinguished-looking gentleman he is, to be sure. I have even heard rumors that he is connected to one of the most influential families in England—the Beaumonts!"

Aunt Eliza's eyes brightened with interest, but before she could comment on this stranger in their midst, Mrs. Hadley gazed meaningfully at her daughter, who sat across from her. "Mr. Chanderly is only here for a short period of time to set the estate in order before he goes to London for the Season." She cleared her throat. "I am sure I can rely on your discretion, and your niece's, of course," she bowed her head in Alexandra's direction, "but my hopes are high in regard to a match in that direction for Jane."

At Aunt Eliza's gasp, Mrs. Hadley swelled in satisfaction. "You may well look surprised. Indeed, so was I when Jane and I encountered Mr. Chanderly yesterday afternoon. We were on our way to the village when he came toward us on a most impressive-looking stallion. I had met him a few days earlier when Mr. Chanderly came across to ask Mr. Hadley's advice on a farming matter. We stopped to exchange pleasantries, and he was the soul of amiability and kindness and seemed most taken with Jane. And I can assure you, my dear, that I am not speaking with the bias of a fond mama! When I commented to Mr. Chanderly that Jane was most accomplished at playing the harp, he looked very impressed. And when I further told him, most subtly—because, naturally, one does not wish to boast about these things—that Jane had more beaux than she knew what to do with, he said with a charming smile that she must lead the country gentlemen a rare dance. I admonished him for this piece of playful banter and assured him that Jane was an extremely modest girl and that she would never dream of, let alone be capable of, enslaving helpless males. And, my dear Mrs. Grantham, when I said this, Mr. Chanderly said most kindly that he was sure that I was right!"

Alexandra suppressed a burst of horrified laughter. How could Mrs. Hadley fail to perceive the blatant sarcasm in Mr. Chanderly's remark? Positively exuding self-satisfaction, the older woman smiled condescendingly at Alexandra. "My dear Miss Grantham, you must be aware that Jane and I are exceedingly fond of you. Indeed, we quite dote on you, don't we, Jane?"

"Indeed we do, Mama." Jane's lips curved into a deceptively sweet smile.

"Which is why when Mr. Chanderly informed us that he was not acquainted with anyone in this district but that he had heard that you, Miss Grantham, were a lady of considerable beauty, Jane and I made haste to relate to him exactly what you have told us on numerous occasions. I assured him that you are much more interested in book learning than in marriage. And Jane went on to tell him about your passion for horticulture."

At Aunt Eliza's groan, Mrs. Hadley stretched out a hand. "My dear Mrs. Grantham—what ever is the matter? Jane, the smelling salts!"

"I am in no need of salts, Mrs. Hadley, although I am nearly overcome. Alexandra is to go to London very soon, and if Mr. Chanderly allows it to be known that she is interested in books and horticulture, she will be shunned by all the gentlemen!"

Mrs. Hadley appeared taken aback. "My dear Miss Grantham, if Jane and I had known you were to be presented in London, we would never have told Mr. Chanderly about your little idiosyncrasies that we ourselves find so charming. Had we known, we would not have mentioned to him that you are far more interested in fishing and riding your horses than in learning feminine accomplishments like embroidery and playing the pianoforte."

Upon hearing this, Alexandra's aunt succumbed to the vapors that had been threatening and had to be revived with smelling salts and burnt feathers waved under her nose by her solicitous hostess. "Ruined, ruined, Alexandra! All my plans for you have come to naught."

"My dear Mrs. Grantham, do not distress yourself so." Mrs. Hadley's smile was benign. "There must be some gentlemen in London who will be so kind as to overlook the fact that your niece is a scholarly female. There are sure to be a few who will even condescend to pay their addresses to her. And Jane will be perfectly agreeable to taking your niece under her wing once we arrive in London. As the prospective bride of Mr. Chanderly, who is rumored to be connected to a ducal family, no less, she will have some standing in polite circles and will be able to influence social opinion." Glancing across at her daughter, she said in a bright voice, "You will aid Miss Grantham—won't you, dear?"

"Indeed, Mama." Jane tilted her head to one side. "And my mother and I will be careful not to mention your lack of feminine accomplishments when we arrive in London."

"*Indeed.*" Alexandra met Jane's limpid look full on, and she clasped her hands in satisfaction when the other girl was the first to look away.

"Yes, and when Mr. Chanderly singles us out, I shall ask him—in a most delicate fashion—to forget my thoughtless words," Mrs. Hadley said. "Rest assured, my dear, that he will oblige me in this."

Alexandra's amused gaze swung from Jane to Mrs. Hadley. If nothing else, she admired their tactics. She rose from her seat. "I think we should take our leave of you now, ma'am."

"Yes, it is probably for the best. Your poor aunt looks quite overcome. I recommend that she spend the rest of the day in bed with her vinaigrette at hand. And I do hope you are not vexed with us. As I said before, Jane and I did not know that you were about to enter London society. You should have told us! Then we would have been far more discreet about your unconventional behavior." She cleared her throat. "I feel I must issue you a friendly warning, though. If you are considering casting your eye in Mr. Chanderly's direction, for he is a most handsome gentleman, I assure you, you are bound to be disappointed, my dear. Men with his connections do not marry beneath themselves, and although you are a most charming girl, you are only the daughter of a baronet. Jane, on the other hand, is the great-grandniece of a viscount on her father's side! She will, in all likelihood, be married before you and Emily—unless my stepdaughter has somehow managed to secure an offer of marriage in the last few weeks, which I sincerely doubt."

Alexandra pressed her hands together. "Rest assured, Mrs. Hadley, that I am not interested in securing an offer of marriage from Mr. Chanderly—or any other man for that matter. I wish your daughter joy of him." She paused. "Have you had word from Emily, ma'am?" Emily Hadley, who was only two years Alexandra's senior, had been her closest friend in the district until her stepmother had sent her away to live with her godmother in Bath nearly two years ago.

Mrs. Hadley pursed her lips. "Emily is not a very good correspondent. The child writes occasionally but has made no mention of any potential suitors. I am of the opinion that her godmother indulges her far too much. And now, Mr. Hadley says that Emily must accompany Jane to London in order to find a husband."

Alexandra's lips twisted into a wry smile at Jane's poorly-disguised scowl. The younger girl clearly resented the idea of sharing her London Season with her far prettier stepsister, almost as much as Mrs. Hadley resented the duty of chaperoning her.

Alexandra sighed as she considered her friend's unhappy situation. Emily was, in actual fact, an excellent correspondent and wrote to Alexandra almost every week. But she would never admit this to the squire's wife. No doubt, Emily had very little to communicate to her stepmother, who had always treated her as though she were a poor relation.

Alexandra returned her attention to her hostess. "Please send Emily my regards when you write to her next." She took her leave of the ladies then and helped Aunt Eliza outside, the sorely tried lady leaning heavily on her arm.

When they were in the carriage and safely out of earshot, Alexandra gave way to the mirth bubbling inside her, much to her aunt's disgust. Chuckling deeply, she said, "Oh, Aunt. Thank you for insisting that I come with you this morning. I have never been more royally entertained."

She stared at Alexandra in outrage, for once at a loss for words. Finally, with a longsuffering sigh, she settled back against the carriage seat and closed her eyes.

Chapter Four

"Bless your heart, Miss Grantham."

Alexandra smiled at Mrs. Hind as she placed the basket of food she had brought with her on a table in the small room. The elderly widow was confined to her bed and lived alone, but a niece came in every day to attend to her basic needs. Yet the cottage still felt neglected. Alexandra shivered a little at the chill in the room. She would bring extra blankets and bed linens with her the next time she visited.

"Are you feeling any better since that attack of influenza, Mrs. Hind?"

The older woman bobbed her head weakly. "That I am, Miss Grantham. That mutton soup you brought set me to rights. It warmed my insides, that it did, what with that hole in the roof keeping things chilly."

Anger rose in Alexandra as she glanced up at the gaping aperture. The state of the cottages on the Durbridge estate was truly a disgrace. Due to poor management on Sir George's part, his property had ailed for many years. Their neighbor had never had a good head for business, and John had told her that Sir George had invested most of his fortune in a number of risky ventures and had lost most of it. The shortness of funds meant the estate had deteriorated rapidly over the last few years.

Upon his death six months ago, news had spread that a

wealthy cousin of Sir George had inherited the estate. The tenants and farm workers had dared to hope their living and working conditions would soon improve, but their hopes had been short-lived. The steward sent to take charge of the property in its owner's absence had allowed things to deteriorate even more, and many of the cottagers were now in a desperate way.

Alexandra sighed as she prepared to depart. Although she did her best to make the lives of the Durbridge estate workers more bearable, there was only a limited amount she could do to help them. As a result, she came away from her charitable expeditions feeling as if the burdens of the world rested on her shoulders.

She forced a cheerful smile to her lips as she bid the widow farewell and pressed some coins recently obtained from an unwilling and unhappy coach occupant into her fragile hands. The look of delight on the older woman's face was imprinted on her mind as she left the cottage, reigniting her desire to help those who had been dealt such an unkind hand by fate.

Poverty was a widespread problem in England these days. In their county, the process of the enclosure of common land in the last century enabled significant advances in agricultural practice. But it also meant lesser landowners had been forced to sell their smaller strips of land to the owners of larger estates and give up the right to graze their animals on the common.

Papa had told her that many of England's cottagers and petty yeomen, bereft of their traditional employment, had been forced to seek work in the cities or as laborers for the remaining landowners. In past years, her father had hired many of these men and looked after them well.

However, not all the landowners were as generous as her father and, now, her brother. Many people found themselves wholly at the mercy of employers from whom they could not always wring a living wage. They were also at risk of being laid off in bad weather or during slack periods. And, being landless, they could no longer save for sickness and old age. Mrs. Hind was just one of the many victims.

Alexandra turned back to look at the tumbledown cottage. Hopefully, Mr. Chanderly would make some improvements. Mrs. Hadley said he had come here to set the estate in order, but Alexandra was skeptical about the truth of this statement. If he were serious about making changes, wouldn't he have sent a more capable custodian to take charge of the property in the first place?

She set her troubled thoughts aside as she strolled along the deserted country lane, concentrating on the beauty of the day instead. Thomas, the groom who had helped her carry the food baskets to the cottagers, followed a few feet behind, leading her horse.

As she breathed in the pungent scent of wood smoke and newly turned earth, her tensions drained away. The first tiny snowdrops peeped through the soil beneath the green hedgerows, and she stopped to observe them, her lips curving upwards. Walking in the countryside never failed to act as a balm to her spirit.

Rounding a bend in the road, Alexandra spotted a squirrel crouched under an oak tree, holding an acorn between its furry little paws. She halted again and gestured to Thomas that he should do the same. The tiny creature hadn't seen them, and Alexandra stood very still so as not to scare him away. She had always been charmed by the funny little creatures, and she frowned with disappointment when the sound of another approaching horse quickly alerted the squirrel to the fact he was not alone, and he dashed away into the undergrowth.

Alexandra turned to see who had broken the peaceful silence, and her heart sank as Mr. Chanderly himself rode up. He reined in his horse and inclined his head. "Good morning, Miss Grantham."

"Good morning, sir." Alexandra eyed him warily, their most recent encounter fresh in her mind.

He studied her for a few minutes. "May I ask why you are trespassing on my property again?"

He said this in a civil enough tone, but Alexandra had the distinct impression he was not well pleased to find her on his estate. For a moment, she hesitated. Should she bring up the subject of the welfare of his tenants? As she looked into the face of the man seated on the horse, she made her decision. Any censure she might suffer due to her outspokenness would be a small price to pay if Mr. Chanderly paid heed to what she said.

"I have been delivering baskets of food to some of the cottagers. Many are barely scraping a living and desperately need outside help."

A frown descended on his brow. "My tenants are not in financial straits, Miss Grantham. Your charitable works are not needed here."

"I hate to contradict you, sir, but they are. The steward you put in charge of the estate in your absence has allowed the living conditions of your workers to deteriorate at an alarming rate, and there was already much that required repair and improvement before that. The wages paid to them in the last six months have truly been a disgrace, and many of them go to bed hungry at night." Alexandra paused before continuing in a quieter tone. "If you would take the trouble to visit some of them, you will see that what I say is true. The roofs are leaking in many of the cottages, and some are all but derelict. Walls are even crumbling in places."

The stallion jumped skittishly, and Mr. Chanderly turned his attention momentarily to bringing his horse back under control. "I was abroad when Sir George died, but I instructed my man of business to send a suitable person to oversee the estate. Although I have noticed there is much room for improvement here, I was under the impression that things have been sufficiently well managed in my absence."

Alexandra met his gaze squarely. "Once you have inspected the state of the cottages, you will realize that your man of business was duped. I dare say Mr. Bailey certainly gives the impression of competence, but he is nothing but a fraud. Anyone on this estate will tell you that."

"I shall be sure to investigate the matter." Mr. Chanderly still frowned. After a moment, his brow cleared. "Although on the whole I object to any interference in my personal affairs, Miss Grantham, I thank you for your interest in the well-being of my tenants. I must ask you to desist in future from your self-appointed duties on their behalf. They are within my care now."

"I am afraid, sir, I cannot agree to your request until I am reassured they will be well looked after."

"You speak out of turn, ma'am." His voice was cold, and Alexandra flinched at the forbidding expression on his face.

Too late, she realized her mistake. By questioning Mr. Chanderly's word, she had made a direct attack on his integrity, something a man of honor would find it difficult to forgive. "I—I apologize, sir. I spoke without thinking."

He continued to stare at her, his face like thunder, and Alexandra began to feel like a prisoner in the dock, awaiting sentence. Eventually, his stern features eased a little. "I shall excuse you this time, Miss Grantham, since your concern for those in need led you to speak out of turn. However, let me speak equally plainly." He paused and studied her for a long moment. "This is my estate, and you will never question my word again."

She swallowed. Mr. Chanderly's anger was no less frightening for being so well controlled.

He tightened the reins in his gloved hands. "Good morning, ma'am. You will hear more from me concerning this matter." With a slight nudge from one knee, he turned the stallion around and cantered back along the track in the direction of the cottages.

When Alexandra returned to Grantham Place, she sought out her brother and told him what had transpired between her and Mr. Chanderly. He shook his head. "Really, Alex. You must learn to put a guard on that tongue of yours or at least say things in a less forthright manner. I only hope you haven't severely offended Mr. Chanderly. He is our closest neighbor, after all. And I, for one, do not wish to be at odds with him."

Alexandra bit her lip. "I did apologize, John, and he appeared to accept my apology."

"Well, I sincerely hope this is the end of the matter."

"He . . . he did mention that I would hear more from him regarding this."

"Sometimes, I despair of you, Alex! You are always rushing headlong into situations without weighing up the consequences of your actions. Please try to be more careful in the future."

"I shall do my best," she promised and then felt an upsurge of guilt as she remembered the secret part of her life about which her brother knew nothing. But she couldn't give up her activities yet. Not when so many people still relied on her help.

Later that afternoon, Alexandra and John were seated in the library together, discussing the merits of Byron's latest offering, when Higgins entered the room to inform them that a Mr. Robert Chanderly of Durbridge Hall had called.

John raised his brows. "Has he indeed? Well, show him in here, Higgins."

"Certainly, sir." The butler padded softly from the room.

Alexandra looked across at her brother with wide eyes. "Well! I did not expect to see him so soon." She trailed off as the butler opened the door again and ushered their visitor inside.

"Mr. Chanderly," he intoned before leaving the room.

Their visitor, who had paused in the doorway, made his way across the room and bowed gracefully.

John rose from his chair and bowed in turn. "John Grantham, at your service, sir. I believe you have already made the acquaintance of my sister?"

"I have." Mr. Chanderly studied Alexandra with an inscrutable expression on his face. "Good afternoon, Miss Grantham."

Alexandra's cheeks warmed at his detached appraisal and the memory of her recent blunder. "Good afternoon, sir."

The gentlemen sat, and Alexandra rang for the tea tray to be brought in. As her brother conversed with Mr. Chanderly about the state of agriculture in their county, Alexandra's mind spun in a fever of speculation. She was grateful when the arrival of Higgins with the tea tray gave her something corporeal on which to focus her attention.

Alexandra handed the men their cups of tea before pouring her own. She had just taken a sip of the refreshing brew when Mr. Chanderly said, "I must thank you, Miss Grantham, for informing me about the state of the living conditions of my estate. I have done a thorough investigation of all the cottages and agree with you that they are in an execrable state." He paused to take a sip of tea. "Needless to say, Mr. Bailey is no longer in my employ."

Alexandra replaced her teacup in the saucer. "I am pleased I was able to bring the matter to your attention, Mr. Chanderly."

"And the manner in which you did so was most enlightening," he murmured.

She glanced away in embarrassment. Her predominant sensation was of having had the wind taken out of her sails. She had been ready to fight Mr. Chanderly on behalf of his suffering tenants, but before the battle had even begun, he had conceded to her wishes. Feeling his gaze still upon her, she looked across at him again.

As she met his eyes, she felt suddenly suspended in time, caught in the spell of that bold green gaze. It challenged her while at the same time seemed to draw her magnetically closer. But, for some reason, she could not bring herself to look away, and it was only John's voice, asking for another cup of tea, that brought her back to her senses.

She placed her cup and saucer on the side table with a shaking hand and turned her attention to her brother, blinking as if she had just come out of a trance. John repeated his request, recalling her to her sense of duty as a hostess. She hastened to refill his cup, all the while avoiding looking at Mr. Chanderly again. He was too distracting an influence by far, she decided crossly as she handed the teacup back to John.

With a tremendous sense of relief, she bid their visitor goodbye shortly thereafter. She did so in her most formal manner, hoping to win back some of the ground she felt she had lost to him over their encounters.

A faint smile curled his lips as she finished her civil little speech. "I said you could well improve upon acquaintance, my dear, and I believe I was correct. You are not, I am happy to see, a *complete* baggage. Good afternoon, Miss Grantham. Sir John."

And upon these words, he took his leave of them.

Chapter Five

"Dearest!" Aunt Eliza hastened into the drawing room where Alexandra was seated. "I have the most exciting news. Indeed, I am sure you will be overjoyed when you hear it."

Alexandra glanced up from the novel she was reading, her brows raised in query. Her aunt, needing no further encouragement, plunged into speech again. "Mrs. Hadley has decided to organize a little evening party this Saturday to welcome Mr. Chanderly to the district. It should prove to be a most enjoyable affair with only the best families in the neighborhood invited. And I have already received our invitation. Are you not pleased?"

Alexandra's brow creased. "But I haven't attended a party since Papa died, Aunt Eliza. Surely, I cannot be expected to attend?"

"Your year of mourning is up now, Alexandra, and you need to mix in Society a little before you go to London. Your grandmama expects it." The older lady sat on the sofa across from Alexandra, her face animated. "There is to be no dancing or anything of a formal nature. It is merely a local gathering intended to welcome Mr. Chanderly amongst us. I am sure it will be delightful."

"Oh." Alexandra's tone was distinctly unenthusiastic, but her aunt seemed not to notice. And she did not have the heart to dim her enthusiasm for the affair by asking to be excused. So, with a resigned smile, she listened with one ear as her aunt rambled on about who she expected would attend the gathering and what fashions the ladies would, in all probability, be wearing.

A while later, John came into the room and received the news of the gathering with even less interest than Alexandra had exhibited. He grimaced when their aunt bustled out of the room to ask her maid to add some lace to her new evening gown. "I suppose there is no way we can avoid it? Having to converse with all those fusty people is liable to give me a headache."

Alexandra winced in sympathy. "We must bow to the inevitable. As you might have noticed, Aunt is quite set upon the idea."

"I would have had to be both blind and deaf not to notice." He studied his riding boots and sighed. "Oh well, I suppose we must do our duty." His face brightened a little as he looked up again. "At least I shall be able to converse with Mr. Chanderly. He has a fine head on his shoulders, you know, and spoke with some authority on agricultural matters when he paid us that call."

"Yes, he did," she murmured before quickly turning the subject. "I have decided to write to Grandmama, John, and ask her to allow me to stay at home instead of going to London for the Season."

"But, Alex! I thought we had agreed you were to go. I shan't have you remain at Grantham Place purely on my account."

Alexandra shook her head. "That is not my principal reason for wishing to remain here."

"Then what is?" A puzzled frown creased his forehead.

She lifted her shoulders. "So many of the poor who live in this area rely on me for my charitable works. You know how I feel about helping them. It would be selfish of me to leave them to their own devices and gallivant off to London. My conscience would not allow it."

"Well, I can tell you that Grandmama's conscience won't countenance your remaining here. She has just written to me, as well, and I can tell you she is quite determined to see you presented this year."

Alexandra's eyes widened in dismay. "Do you think she will relent if I tell her the real reason I wish to remain here?"

"Somehow, I doubt it, Alex." His voice was grave. "Besides, I don't see why you cannot delegate your duties to someone else. Surely Aunt Eliza could take over some of your work?"

Alexandra gave her brother a speaking look. "Can you really imagine Aunt Eliza visiting a cottager who is ill? She would probably give the poor person a setback with her nonsensical chatter about this and that and nothing. No, John. It simply would not do."

Her brother's smile was understanding. "You are right, of course." He paused for a moment, pressing his lips together. "I shall give the matter some thought. There must be a suitable person in the neighborhood who could take over your duties." He glanced at the mahogany clock above the mantelpiece. "Unfortunately, I must go now to meet with my bailiff. But let us discuss this matter later. I am sure we will be able to come up with a solution to the problem."

He strode quickly from the room, and Alexandra leaned back against her chair, staring into space. She was in no doubt that a suitable person could be found to undertake her charitable duties. But it seemed unlikely such a person would be willing to take on her more dangerous activities, as well. John permitted Cook to make up the various food baskets Alexandra delivered every day to the poor, but he did not know his sister also gave the families money, money obtained illicitly from the very people who refused to pay their laborers a decent wage.

The arrival of Mr. Chanderly in the district, though, would hopefully make a difference in how the other landowners treated their workers. However objectionable she personally found him to be, she had to admit that Robert Chanderly had an aura of authority that was difficult to mistake. His concern for his laborers the other day had seemed genuine enough, and the local gentry, who would not listen to a man of John's tender years, might take the advice of an older, more knowledgeable man, experienced in the ways of the world. Though Mr. Chanderly couldn't be more than thirty, he was certainly no green youth to be easily dismissed.

Alexandra nibbled her lower lip. She was still mystified as to what had originally alerted Mr. Chanderly to the fact that, despite her disguise on the road that day, she was from the upper classes. She must be very careful in future not to accidentally waylay him again. But his carriage had been fairly anonymous—black, plain, with no crest—and therefore not easily distinguished from any other. Her stomach clenched at the thought of being unmasked by him, but she put the disturbing notion aside.

She would not allow that green-eyed gentleman to unnerve her.

❧

ALEXANDRA SURVEYED HERSELF in the glass, twisting this way and that as she studied her reflection with a critical eye. She wore the white muslin evening gown her aunt had picked out for her, delicately embroidered with colored borders and cut low and square in the neck. The dress outlined her figure very prettily, but the style was a bit revealing. She had no desire to draw attention to herself this evening at the party, but she had a nasty suspicion that if she went attired like this, she might well do so.

She was fiddling with the strand of pearls that adorned her neck when the door opened, and Aunt Eliza entered the room. As Alexandra turned around to face her relative, the older lady clasped her hands together. "My dear! You look quite charming."

Alexandra's forehead puckered. "You don't think, perhaps, that this neckline is cut a bit low?"

Aunt Eliza clicked her tongue. "Now, now, Alexandra. Do not fret about that. I assure you it is quite à la mode." She advanced further into the room. "Hmm, let me look at you more closely." She fussed around her niece, straightening a flounce on the hem of her gown and rearranging a slightly wayward curl in Alexandra's coiffure.

She gritted her teeth at these ministrations but endured them. Finally, Aunt Eliza stood back with a satisfied smile on her face. "There we are, my love. You look quite lovely, you know." Her smile faded as her eyes welled up. "It quite oversets me to see my young niece all grown to maturity." She sniffled a little, and Alexandra's eyes widened in dismay as her aunt began to cry. "So young and beautiful. And you are to leave me so soon."

Pressing a lacy handkerchief into Aunt Eliza's hand, Alexandra racked her brain for something that could distract her aunt from launching into one of the sentimental soliloquies for which she was renowned. Fortunately, Hobbes stepped into the room at that moment and saved the day by informing them that their coach awaited them.

Her aunt's tears miraculously dried up at this news, and she hurried to the mirror to check on her appearance before following Alexandra out of the room and down the stairs to the hall where John stood.

Alexandra shot her brother a warning look as she whispered, "Be careful what you say. Aunt Eliza is in her sentimental mood."

John's eyes widened at the import of this statement, and he turned with a nervous smile to greet his aunt. But fortunately, she seemed to have her emotions more under control and only smiled up at him in a slightly misty fashion. "Dearest John! Are we not fortunate to have such a dashing young man as our escort?" She glanced across at her niece. "Do you not agree, Alexandra, that our dear boy is splendidly turned out?"

"I certainly do," Alexandra's voice was solemn, but as her aunt turned to walk through the front door, she giggled. "Don't look so pained, John. At least she didn't weep all over you!"

An hour later, Alexandra tried to concentrate on the discussion around her in the Hadleys' overwarm drawing room. She had just remembered that she had neglected to water her favorite camellias.

She did not, as a rule, allow any of the gardeners to fulfill this particular task as camellias needed to stay moist but not wet, as too much water in the soil could cause the root to rot. Too many of the gardeners at Grantham Place had overwatered her camellias in the past, so Alexandra had taken on this specific duty herself. Now she was guilty of the opposite crime—of allowing the roots to dry out. Her brow creased. She had been far too distracted of late by her highway activities. The minute she returned home, she would water the camellias, even if it meant going out to the hothouse with a lamp.

She stood amongst a group of young people she had known since her childhood. Although she usually enjoyed speaking to her old friends, the conversation had turned to the upcoming London Season, and Jane Hadley was expounding at some length on the number of gowns her mother's dressmaker had made up for her.

Alexandra glanced at the gentlemen in their party and stifled a grin. Thomas Gibson and Edward Henry regarded Jane with ill-concealed irritation, while poor Oliver Keaton had the look of a man who has suddenly found himself trapped in a most unpleasant place with no means of escape.

Jane finally seemed to exhaust the subject of her clothes, and Thomas Gibson jumped into the lull in the conversation before she could begin speaking again. "I say! Have you heard that a couple of Bow Street Runners are to be sent down here? They are going to try to apprehend those two highwaymen who have been terrorizing the region."

Oliver Keaton nodded his head. "My father told me about that. He is confident that they will soon be arrested."

Alexandra looked at Mr. Gibson inquiringly. "Do you know when the Runners will arrive?"

"They should be here in about a week, I think."

Jane Hadley placed a shaking hand on her forehead. "Oh, let us not speak of such horrid things. Those highwaymen quite terrify me. My father was held up by the rogues only a few weeks ago."

"He was?" Mr. Gibson said. "Well, rest assured, Miss Hadley, that they will soon be apprehended."

At this moment, Mrs. Hadley came up to the group with Mr. Chanderly in tow. "Ah, Jane, dear. I have brought Mr. Chanderly across so that you can introduce him to your friends."

"Certainly, Mama," Jane murmured. Her mother moved away, and Jane smiled coyly up at their guest of honor. "May I make my friends known to you, sir?" She performed the necessary introductions, leaving Alexandra till last. "And finally, Miss Alexandra Grantham."

Mr. Chanderly bowed in her direction. "I am already acquainted with Miss Grantham."

"You are?" Jane said sharply, forgetting to be sweet.

"Yes. I recently paid a call on Miss Grantham and her brother. They are my closest neighbors."

"Oh, yes. Of course." Jane glanced across at her. "You will know then what a charming eccentric our dear Miss Grantham is."

The words hung uneasily in the air. Then, finally, Mr. Chanderly said softly, "She is indeed charming."

He smiled warmly at Alexandra, and she lowered her eyes in some confusion. She was accustomed to Jane's barbed comments and usually took little notice of them. She had to admit, it was unexpectedly comforting to have Mr. Chanderly come to her defense in this way. She looked up to see Jane scowling at her. The other girl masked her expression quickly, but Alexandra knew she could not be happy with Mr. Chanderly's gallant support of her.

Jane batted her pale lashes as she again turned her attention to the man standing beside her. "On behalf of my friends, Mr. Chanderly, I would like to welcome you to the district and wish you a pleasant stay."

"Thank you, Miss Hadley."

Oliver Keaton spoke. "We also hope that your stay will be a safe one, sir. My father informed me that you were waylaid on your journey here?"

Mr. Chanderly nodded. "I was. But the thieves were unsuccessful in their attempt to rob me."

"They were?" Mr. Keaton's jaw slackened. "You were fortunate then. Many others have escaped less favorably."

Jane shuddered. "I shall only sleep peacefully in my bed when I know the Bow Street Runners have arrested those scoundrels. It is a scandal that we should live in fear of our lives on a daily basis!"

"I have not heard that those highwaymen have ever killed anyone," Alexandra said quietly.

Jane shuddered again. "No, but they might well do so if provoked. I do hope that they will be apprehended soon. It is ridiculous to have so many thieves on the rampage. My papa says there are at least three other highwaymen at work in the wider district, as well. Imagine if they were all to descend upon us at once!"

"The Runners will see to it that they are apprehended, Miss Hadley," Thomas Gibson said. "Soon, they will soon be hanging in chains for their sins. That you can be sure of."

A chill ran down Alexandra's spine. It had been news to her that the Bow Street Runners had been called in to investigate the highway robberies. And alarming news at that. Never before had she allowed herself to dwell on the real possibility that she might be captured one day, but now the prospect of discovery loomed large in her mind's eye, making her feel slightly ill.

Alexandra drew in a deep, calming breath. She was foolish to feel so nervous. The Bow Street Runners would never suppose a lady to be a highwayman, so there was no possible way suspicion could ever fall on her. While the Runners were in the district, she would simply cease her activities.

The conversation had now turned to the hard frost that Thomas Keaton expected on the morrow, but Alexandra couldn't attend to it. Unbidden, an image of herself and Ben, hanging in chains, flashed before her eyes, and she felt the blood drain from her face. She blinked to clear her mind of the disturbing picture and looked around at the group of people amongst which she stood, trying to pick up the thread of the conversation. How horrified they would all be if they ever found out she was one of the notorious thieves of whom they had just spoken.

Feeling someone's gaze upon her, Alexandra turned her head, and her eyes met Robert Chanderly's. As she stared up at him, she had the strangest feeling he was looking straight into her soul and that he knew her secret.

She broke eye contact first and looked away, scolding herself for allowing her imagination to play such tricks on her. Mr. Chanderly would surely never suspect her of being a highwayman. There was no reason why he should. It was only because the man set her all on edge that she felt so exposed in his presence. She glanced at him again and was relieved to see that he no longer looked at her but instead was listening to Mr. Keaton, who was now describing a new farming method he had employed on his estate.

However, as Alexandra studied Mr. Chanderly's strong profile, a cold shiver ran through her body again. She had not imagined the arrested expression on his face, and she sensed now, beyond a shadow of a doubt, that she was not mistaken in her earlier instinctive belief.

He knew.

Chapter Six

"No, Miss Grantham, I simply won't do it," Ben said in a low voice, even though they were alone in the stable. "The danger is too great."

Alexandra retreated a step, taken aback by her coachman's s refusal to help her. "But this will be the last time for a long while, Ben. When the Runners arrive, we shall naturally cease our activities until they leave the district again. They only arrive at the end of the week, so there is no danger we shall be captured."

Ben lowered his brow. "I have a bad feeling in my bones about this, miss. What with the Runners coming and all." He shook his head. "Nay, miss. I'm that sorry, but my conscience will never allow it. If something was to happen to you, I'd never forgive myself. And your brother wouldn't forgive me either for aiding you in this madness."

"But nothing will happen to me, nor to you, and he need never know. Please, Ben." Alexandra's expression was beseeching. "I visited Mrs. Smith yesterday, and she looked quite desperate. With seven children to support and no husband, she is in a terrible way. I promised to bring her some money."

Ben stood irresolute for a moment. "Nay, miss, I cannot help you, and that's my final word on the matter."

He deliberately turned his attention back to the wheel he had been repairing before Alexandra interrupted him, and she stared at him in dismay.

She had wanted to carry out just one more robbery before the Runners arrived in the district. But, with her accomplice refusing to aid her, the chance of her being able to do so successfully was much less likely.

Seeing that Ben was not to be moved, Alexandra lifted her shoulders and left him. She hesitated outside the stable doors for a moment. It was time for breakfast, but, even though her stomach rumbled loudly, she turned to walk down the hill to the stone wall that served as the eastern boundary of the estate. Leaning her arms on it, she sighed as she gazed at the surrounding meadowlands, hardly feeling the rough stone digging into her elbows.

Sheltered by a spinney on the one side and a wood on the other, the meadow looked peaceful and still in the mid-morning light. Several sheep grazed in the distance, and nearby a brook gurgled happily on its way.

Alexandra spotted a pretty blue kingfisher perched on a low-hanging willow branch at the water's side, and for a moment, she forgot her troubles as the elusive bird swooped down to seize its prey from the water. But as the kingfisher flew away, her problems came to the fore again.

It wasn't often that the peaceful sights and sounds of the countryside failed to console her, but today not even nature could soothe her downcast spirits. She was tired and frustrated by her seemingly fruitless efforts to help the needy around her because, although she gave them food and money as regularly as she could manage, this was only a temporary measure of relief.

Dramatic reforms were needed to enable the people to become more self-sufficient and less reliant on charitable handouts. But with the landowners in the surrounding area being so reluctant to implement changes, the chance of things altering for the better was minimal.

Alexandra sighed, thinking of Mrs. Smith's difficult predicament, and suddenly her resolve hardened. Even if Ben refused to help her, she would do what she could to help the poor widow. And if that meant undertaking a robbery on her own, then that was simply what she would do. Though she had gone back later and scoured the hedgerow until she found her pistol, Alexandra had not attempted an attack on a coach since their last failed effort, and now she was down to her last few coins. The need in the district was so great that she had already spent most of the stolen money on provisions and clothes.

Pushing herself away from the wall, she began to walk up the hill to the manor. Her brow creased as she considered the finer details of her newly forming plan, and she tried not to let nervousness overtake her. The best thing she could do was to take a suitable saddle from the stables and carry it with her to a secluded copse situated a little distance from the road when she went riding early this afternoon. She would change into her disguise and replace her sidesaddle with the ordinary saddle before riding closer to the road and remaining hidden there until a likely victim came along.

After the robbery, she would return to the thicket, change back into her riding habit, exchange saddles, and ride home again, with no one the wiser. The plan was risky, but there was a reasonable chance of its success if she remained careful.

The only thing that concerned her about undertaking this final robbery was her uneasy conviction that Robert Chanderly had somehow guessed her secret. Taking a deep breath, Alexandra put him from her mind. Mr. Chanderly could never conclusively prove that she was a highwayman, so for her to continue worrying about him in this manner was not only unproductive but also ridiculous.

Alexandra entered the manor's front door and smiled in response to Higgins's greeting before hurrying upstairs to her bedchamber to wash her hands. A few minutes later, she made her way down to the breakfast parlor and joined her brother at the table.

His perceptive gaze searched her face. "Is anything the matter, Alex? You look rather out of sorts."

Alexandra glanced down at the piece of toast she was buttering. "I do have a slightly dull head. But I plan to ride this morning, so that will hopefully clear away the cobwebs."

"Fresh air is always a good remedy for that. Perhaps I shall join you."

She scraped more butter onto her toast. "Actually, I would prefer to ride alone today. I have a few things on my mind." She took a bite of her toast but could hardly taste it.

"Of course, Alex, if that is what you wish." He studied her for a moment. "Are you still concerned about going to London?"

Glad of the excuse her brother offered, she quickly agreed. "Yes. But I doubt that there is anything I can do to change Grandmama's mind."

"No, she is quite adamant." He frowned slightly. "You must not feel that you alone are responsible for solving all the problems in the world. You cannot help everyone."

At this moment, Aunt Eliza walked into the breakfast parlor, so Alexandra made no response. But as she rode out of the gates of Grantham Place a short time later, John's words played through her mind again. She knew he was correct in what he said, but she still could not help feeling responsible for the laborers who had come to rely upon her so much.

She rode cross-country, keeping away from the main roads and any people who might consider it odd to see a young woman out riding for pleasure with an extra saddle and a bundle of clothes. Reaching the copse without mishap, Alexandra dismounted and changed into her men's clothes with the ease of long practice. After placing the black mask over her face, she carefully tucked her copper curls out of sight under her hat and pulled it low.

Alexandra then set about changing the saddle on the carriage horse she'd chosen for her ride, knowing Starlight was too recognizable as hers, and darkening the animal's distinctive white markings with a small piece of charcoal. Several minutes later, her tasks successfully completed, she mounted her steed again and left the sheltered enclosure, riding toward the main road where she hid behind a small band of trees.

The minutes ticked slowly by until Alexandra eventually heard a telltale clip-clop. But when the horse and rider came into view, it was only a farmer riding a cob. She immediately dismissed him as a likely target, and the farmer passed on his way unharmed.

Alexandra waited impatiently for someone else to come along, but no one else appeared for an age. She calmed her restive horse, who seemed to have picked up her agitation, by stroking his satiny neck while time ticked by interminably. Finally, she heard the sound of approaching horses and carriage wheels. Drawing in a deep breath, she rode a little closer to the road but remained hidden amongst the shadows of the trees so that her quarry did not become prematurely aware of her presence.

She peered out at the road as a gentleman, driving a curricle and two, came round the bend. As a lone traveler, he was the perfect victim.

She quickly rode free from the cover of the trees and brandished her pistol. "Your money or your life! Stand and deliver."

She almost dropped the pistol when the gentleman turned his head, and she found herself staring into the face of Robert Chanderly. She remained motionless, quite unable to believe the perversity of fate that had led her to hold up the only person in the whole county who might suspect her. The silence between them stretched to an eternity as Alexandra waited for him to do or at least say something.

And then everything seemed to happen at once. There was a thunder of hooves, and within an instant, even as Alexandra looked frantically around her, she was surrounded by three men on horseback, wearing the distinctive red waistcoats of the Bow Street Horse Patrol.

One of the men carried a wooden tipstaff, in the form of a short mace, with a metal receptacle on the top where his papers were kept safe. He rode closer to her and, in the stern voice of the Law, declared, "I carry with me here a warrant for your arrest."

Alexandra's gaze flew wildly from the tipstaff the man held in his hand to the truncheons the other Runners carried. If she fired a shot in the air, could she somehow distract them and make her escape? But before she could do anything, Mr. Chanderly spoke evenly. "I am afraid, my good man, that you have made a somewhat regrettable mistake."

Four pairs of eyes turned to look at him. Finally, after a strained moment, the man carrying the tipstaff, who seemed to be the most senior, said, "I don't understand your meaning, sir."

Mr. Chanderly gestured in Alexandra's direction. "The person you see before you is not, in fact, one of the thieves you are looking for but my tiger, intent on playing a practical joke on me. That horse he is riding belongs to me. Unfortunately, of late he has developed an . . . unhealthy obsession with the idea of being a highwayman, having heard about the thieves at work in this district. I forbade him to try his hand at it when he expressed a wish to do so recently, but as you can see, he has outrightly disobeyed my orders."

The Runner's eyes narrowed as he glanced from the man in the curricle to the small figure crouched on top of the horse. Finally, he said, "Is this true?"

Gathering her wits together, Alexandra tucked her pistol away and said in a broad accent, "Aye, guv'nor. Right sorry I am to have worried you, guv'nor."

The Runner shook his head in disgust. "I can see now that you are just a boy. I hope your master punishes you severely for pulling this prank and wasting the time of the Law."

Mr. Chanderly inclined his head. "Rest assured. He will be dealt with appropriately."

The chief Runner grunted before he turned his horse around. "Wasting the time of the Law," he muttered again before setting his horse in motion. The other two Runners followed shortly after him.

When they were out of sight, Mr. Chanderly said quietly, "Get down from that horse, Miss Grantham."

She started, causing her mount to jump skittishly. Then, tightening her hands on the reins, she stammered, "I—I don't want to."

Mr. Chanderly descended from his curricle. "Very well, then."

He secured the ribbons to the overhanging branch of a tree and strode across the road to her. Looking down at his formidably angry face, Alexandra swallowed nervously and sent up a silent prayer of thanks that she had been wise enough to stay safely on her mount, out of harm's way. But she had prayed too soon. Without warning, Mr. Chanderly reached up and, in none too gentle a fashion, plucked her from the saddle and swung her down to the ground.

Alexandra's heart quickened as his arms closed around her. She attempted to push him away, but her efforts were to no avail. Holding her with one arm, Mr. Chanderly removed her hat and mask and stared down into her eyes.

"Little fool." His voice was harsh as he lowered his head to catch her lips in a hard kiss. Tears stung Alexandra's eyes at this sudden onslaught on her senses. But then Mr. Chanderly gentled the kiss and ran his hands soothingly over her back. Sensations she had never felt before raced through Alexandra, making her body come alive. Her head spun at the warmth of his lips moving over hers and his arms holding her close.

But as abruptly as Mr. Chanderly began the kiss, he ended it, drawing back. Alexandra blinked up at him in a dazed fashion, completely mesmerized by the fire smoldering in his eyes. He pushed her away from him, the glittering expression fading from his face to be replaced by the mask of impassivity he usually wore.

Alexandra drew a deep breath, then exhaled slowly. Her heart still pounded, and a curious weakness seemed to have pervaded her limbs. She bit her lip, not knowing quite what to say. As an unmarried woman, her sensibilities ought to be outraged by the liberties he had dared to take. But Alexandra's innate sense of fairness precluded her from primly reprimanding him for his ungentlemanly conduct when she herself was attired in far-from-ladylike breeches and had just attempted to rob him.

It was Mr. Chanderly who finally broke the silence. "We need to discuss a few things, Miss Grantham, but this is hardly the time or place for a discussion. I shall call on you later this afternoon."

"You—you do not intend to tell my brother about this, do you, Mr. Chanderly?"

He raised an eyebrow. "About our kiss? No, Miss Grantham, I don't." His voice was dry.

Alexandra flushed and averted her gaze. "No. No, I mean about my being a highwayman."

"I shall wait until I have heard what you have to say for yourself before taking any action," he replied slowly.

Alexandra cleared her throat. "Ah—my aunt will insist on chaperoning us, so it won't be possible to have a private conversation. Could . . . could we not meet elsewhere?"

He frowned at her. "I don't intend to put your reputation at further risk by meeting with you clandestinely, Miss Grantham."

"But if my aunt finds out about this—."

Mr. Chanderly sighed in the manner of a man whose patience had been pushed too far. "When I arrive, I shall profess an admiration for the fine grounds of Grantham Place, and you will offer to show me the gardens. We shall talk then."

Turning away from her, he freed the reins from the branch and climbed back into his curricle, taking his seat. Alexandra mounted her steed again and arranged her feet in the stirrups. When she turned her attention back to him, he met her gaze squarely. "I expect you to be at home when I call later, Miss Grantham. Don't try to avoid me."

Setting his horses in motion, he drove off down the road, leaving Alexandra staring after him, her mind a mass of confused, unhappy thoughts. How—and why!—could he have kissed her in that manner? And how mortifying that she had responded to the urgency of his lips. It was as if her body had become completely disconnected from her mind when his lips touched hers. She inhaled deeply in an attempt to calm her still-racing pulse.

No wonder chaperones were so protective of their charges if a gentleman's kiss could be this potent.

CHAPTER SEVEN

Mr. Chanderly called at three o'clock that afternoon. After he had paid his respects to Aunt Eliza and accepted her invitation to join them for tea, Alexandra led him on his requested tour of the grounds.

She showed him the greenhouse first. When they entered the sizeable, glassed structure, Alexandra came to a halt and breathed in deeply of the warm air, drinking it in. She had been in a state of heightened anxiety since returning to the house, but as usual in this special place, peace began to flow over her. She spread out her arms as she gazed around. "We grow flowers, vegetables, and force fruits in here. I confess when I come inside, it feels as if time stands still. My aunt is frequently forced to send a footman to fetch me for meals."

She nodded at Jacob, one of the undergardeners, before looking up at Mr. Chanderly. "Would you like to see our pineapples, sir? I am rather proud of them."

"I would. I assume you use tan pits?"

She led him across to the south side of the greenhouse. "Yes, we do." She glanced up at him. "You are familiar then with the process of growing pineapples?"

"I have greenhouses at my principal residence."

"Ah. So you are a horticulturist as well."

"It has always been more my mother's domain than mine. As

a result, I have spent very little time in my hothouses over the years, though I plan to join the Horticultural Society of London soon to extend my knowledge of the subject."

Alexandra's lips curved into a smile. "It is an excellent Society. My father was a member." She drew to a sudden halt in front of a row of young pineapple plants planted in pots. "Here we are."

"These are beautiful specimens," he said gravely, studying the plants for a few moments. He glanced across at her. "However, I am gaining the distinct impression that you are attempting to distract me from the purpose of my visit, Miss Grantham."

"You did say that you wished to have a tour of the grounds." Her voice was defensive.

"As an excuse to converse with you. Will you take me somewhere we can have a private discussion? There are far too many gardeners in this building."

Alexandra sighed and turned around to lead him out of the greenhouse. She guided him toward a quiet alcove, which overlooked a pretty pond. An ornamental iron garden seat, set upon a pedestal to avoid the damp ground, faced the body of water, and Mr. Chanderly waited for Alexandra to be seated before he took his place next to her.

She felt his gaze on her averted face. "I await your explanation, Miss Grantham."

"I fear I cannot explain well enough to make you understand."

"I am waiting."

She looked at him warily and released her breath in a long sigh. "Very well then."

She stared at the pleasant vista before her but barely noticed the sloping lawns surrounding the pond or the gardeners tending them. What was the best way to try to untangle her actions for this man? Finally, taking a deep breath, she raised her eyes to his. "I am not sure if you are aware of it, Mr. Chanderly, but several landowners in this district mistreat their laborers grievously. Many of these poor people live a hand-to-mouth existence in utter penury and can barely feed their children. It is a terrible way to live, sir, and I determined to do something about it when I discovered the extent of their ill-treatment." She pleated the skirt of her gown as she paused for a moment. "Unfortunately, my money is tied up in a trust fund until I either marry or attain my majority, which means I am unable to help the poor from my own purse yet, but they are in need now. So... so I decided to obtain the money they needed but weren't receiving from the proper source—the local landowners who were failing in their duties to care for them in the first place."

"Poetic justice thereby being served." His tone was dry.

Alexandra studied her feet, not wanting to look at him, fearing the condemnation she would see in his face. Finally, she said in a small voice, "I thought so."

Mr. Chanderly was silent for a moment. Then he touched her arm. "Your actions, my dear, although well-intentioned, are decidedly foolish. You must see that."

Alexandra's heart fluttered. His touch brought to the fore the disturbing memory of his kiss that morning, something she had decided it would be in her best interests to forget. So, wriggling away from him, she moved to the opposite end of the garden seat. "I do not consider it foolish to help the poor, Mr. Chanderly."

"No. But it is decidedly foolish to risk your life." He watched her calmly. "I do not intend to kiss you again, Miss Grantham, as I am confident I have your full attention, so you can stop looking at me like a startled hare."

"A startled hare?" Her voice rose to a squeaky pitch.

His lips twitched. "Hmm. Perhaps you are correct. You look more like a wide-eyed fawn, intent on escaping from a ruthless predator."

She sniffed. "Thank you, sir. A fawn is a far more acceptable animal to be compared to."

He laughed, but after a moment, his expression sobered. "I want you to give me your word that you will immediately cease your highway activities. You were fortunate that it was me this morning and not someone else."

"I—I know. I am in your debt." She eyed him uncertainly. "How did you guess it was me?"

"Your voice had a cultured intonation, although you tried to disguise it. So, initially, I assumed you were a young gentleman out for a lark."

"What made you change your mind?"

"At Mrs. Hadley's party, when mention was made of the Bow Street Runners, you appeared frightened and paled considerably. And when you looked across at me, with your bright blue eyes, I suddenly realized why you had seemed so familiar that first day I met you on my estate. That mask you wore only served to emphasize your most distinctive feature."

She grimaced. "And I believed my disguise to be perfect. I am most grateful to you, sir—truly—for coming to my rescue this morning."

"I could not very well leave you to the mercy of the Runners, although you undoubtedly deserve it for terrorizing the region in this manner," he said sternly.

She hung her head. "It was all for a good cause."

"A foolish cause. You have yet to give me your word, Miss Grantham, that you will cease your activities."

"But if I do not help the poor in our neighborhood, they will be in a very bad way. I cannot leave them to such a harsh fate."

"There are other methods of helping them that do not involve stealing for them."

She studied him doubtfully. "What kinds of methods? The local landowners seem to have little inclination to institute reforms."

"They may be open to persuasion. I know of many landlords in the country, the Duke of Bedford and the Earl of Egremont being of their number, who have devoted themselves to bettering the conditions of their tenants by teaching them the agricultural methods that can bring them prosperity."

"What did they do?" At his hesitation, she drew in a sharp breath. "Before you tell me that a lady should not worry her pretty little head about farming, may I inform you that I am well acquainted with the matters that pertain to managing an estate as my father taught them to me."

Mr. Chanderly raised his brows. "I was not about to say anything of the sort. You are prickly."

She flushed. "Usually, the gentlemen of my acquaintance fail to take my opinions or knowledge seriously. It vexes me considerably."

"I can see that. However, the reason for my hesitation was not the one you assumed. Unfortunately, I have another appointment this afternoon and therefore do not have time to discuss this matter with you further. But I shall endeavor to do so at a later date. In the meantime, I would like your reassurance that you will cease your activities forthwith."

"I give you my word, Mr. Chanderly."

"Good."

He rose to his feet, and, taking her hands, he drew her up from the seat. "Who was your accomplice, Miss Grantham?"

"My coachman, Ben. He refused to aid me in my attack today, though, saying that with the Runners due to arrive, it was too dangerous."

"He was correct. I thought you would have had more sense than to attempt another robbery when you knew the Runners were in the district."

"I thought they were only due to arrive at the end of the week."

"You should never rely on hearsay, Miss Grantham. You will learn that soon enough, no doubt, when you arrive in the capital. Rumors run rife there, and it is never wise to take them too seriously."

Alexandra withdrew her hands from his. "Of course."

They made their way back to the manor together then. After Mr. Chanderly took his leave, Alexandra walked into the drawing room, where her aunt still sat. The older lady stretched out her hand eagerly. "My dear child, do be seated so that we can discuss this latest turn of events. I am of the decided opinion that Mr. Chanderly has averted his attentions from Jane Hadley to you!"

Alexandra blinked as she sank onto the chaise longue. "I think, Aunt, that you are mistaken."

"Indeed, child, I am not. Remember, I am far wiser in the ways of the world than you are. When a gentleman starts calling on a lady, you can be sure that he is developing an interest in her."

Alexandra studied a point somewhere above her aunt's head. "Mr. Chanderly merely wished to see the grounds of Grantham Place, Aunt Eliza. He has a keen interest in gardens."

"That was what he *said*, Alexandra, but you can be sure that that was not the principal reason he called on you. Oh, I am quite delighted for you! Mr. Chanderly is such a distinguished-looking gentleman, and he is also possessed of a handsome fortune, I dare say." Her lips curved into a complacent smile. "Mrs. Hadley will not be pleased with this turn of events, but I was always doubtful of Jane's chances of winning a proposal from Mr. Chanderly. She is so very *plain*-looking."

Alexandra gazed at her aunt helplessly. It would be pointless to try to convince her that she was mistaken in her supposition. Nevertheless, she said firmly, "Even if Mr. Chanderly does wish to make me the object of his attentions, Aunt Eliza, I have no desire to enter the married state."

Her aunt looked horrified. "My child, do not say such things. It is unnatural—wicked, in fact—to speak thus. Imagine if someone were to hear you!"

"Someone were to hear what?" John asked, coming into the room.

Mrs. Grantham threw her hands up in the air. "Dear John, perhaps you can reason with your sister. She has just informed me that she has no desire to find a husband!"

An amused expression crossed John's face as he sat on the

sofa. "Well this is hardly the first time she has said so. And Alexandra has always known her own mind, Aunt. Nothing I say will make her change it."

"But my dear! For her to talk thus when she is about to go to London for the Season! It is improper. Most improper." Her voice wavered.

"I am sorry, Aunt Eliza, but I simply cannot see the purpose in getting married. I enjoy my freedom and independence far too much to give them up willingly."

"But, dearest, what if you were to fall in love?"

"I have every intention of avoiding that particular trap." Alexandra's voice was firm. "If I marry and have children, I will have very little time to devote to my horticultural interests, and you know how important they are to me. Besides, I couldn't bear to be tied to a man who treats me as if I have no intelligence. So many men think women should not pursue scholarly interests at all. What kind of life would that be?"

"My dear, dear child, you sadden me. Indeed you do." Aunt Eliza shook her head mournfully. "You are sure to have a most wretched Season, holding such odd views. I merely hope that the gentlemen will not ostracize you."

John smiled. "Somehow, I doubt that will happen. Alexandra's lack of interest in the gentlemen of our circle has not prevented them from paying court to her."

Aunt Eliza's face brightened a little. "That is true. Not many young girls can boast that they have turned down three offers of marriage before their first London Season!"

Alexandra wrinkled her nose. "Those boys only offered for me because they want my dowry. They have no real interest in me as a person. If I had a small portion, they would never have pursued me."

"It is the way of the world, my love." Aunt Eliza waggled her chin sagely. "But you and your sisters are very fortunate that Lord Longmore secured you and your sisters' financial future by settling such large dowries on you when your mama died."

"And fortunate that the trust Father set up ensures your money is protected." John studied his sister with a wry smile. "I know you wish you had access to the money now, Alex, but perhaps Father had a canny inkling that you would have given all the money away if it weren't in a trust."

Alexandra wrinkled her nose again but said nothing. Her brother knew her too well.

Fifteen minutes later, she left the drawing room and walked slowly upstairs to her bedchamber. The tensions of the day had tired her out, and she was in need of some solitude. Walking over to the window, she gazed out at the grounds, her eyes going involuntarily to the garden seat where she and Mr. Chanderly had sat.

Her brow creased in puzzlement. Mr. Chanderly's anger over her actions seemed to have miraculously faded, and he had been more understanding toward her than she would ever have expected. She hoped, for the sake of the people she was no longer able to help as she wished, that their neighbors would be open to persuasion regarding the implementation of reforms.

But, knowing the man, he would probably be successful in changing their minds. He had something about him, a certain authority, that people seemed to respond to without question. If anyone could get his own way over something, it was Robert Chanderly.

Chapter Eight

A FEW DAYS later, when Alexandra arrived back at Grantham Place after delivering a food basket to Mrs. Smith, she learned from Higgins that her grandmother, Lady Longmore, had arrived half an hour earlier and was resting in the Pink Bedchamber.

Startled at this news, Alexandra hurried up the stairs to visit her esteemed relative. She knocked on the door, and upon hearing her grandmother's voice bid her enter, she opened it and walked in to greet her. A fire had been lit in the grate, and its dancing flames added to the sense of comfort of the room, with its rose chintz curtains and Aubusson carpet featuring pink cabbage roses in a grand central medallion. "Grandmama! How lovely it is to see you!"

Her grandmother, a distinguished-looking woman of about sixty years, reclined on the curtained bed with a pile of pillows behind her back. She smiled and said in her low, deep voice, "You grow prettier every time I see you, Alexandra. Come over here and give me a kiss. It has been an age since I saw you last."

"So it has, Grandmama," Alexandra agreed as she embraced her. "And you have taken us quite by surprise."

"Yes. I grew concerned that if I left you any more time to think of a reason for not coming to London for the Season, that you might actually succeed in finding one. And I could not risk that at all. So I thought it would be best to carry you off to Town without further ado."

Alexandra laughed. "I am becoming quite reconciled to going to London. In fact, I am beginning to look forward to it."

"What has brought about this change in your frame of mind, my dear?" The older lady's voice held a note of surprise. "In the last letter you wrote to me, you stated that you did not wish to leave Grantham Place. I did not think you were so capricious."

Alexandra pressed her lips together. The previous day, one of the Bow Street men had called at Grantham Place as part of his duties to inquire whether they were missing any horses. She had recognized the man in an instant and stayed as distant from him as possible during his call, terrified he would recognize her "most distinctive feature," as Mr. Chanderly had. She had immediately begun to see the benefit of departing the county for a time. It would probably be best, however, to give her grandmother a lesser part of the reason for her change of heart. "I was concerned that if I went to London, John would be very lonely here. But he has assured me this will not be the case, and, consequently, I feel far happier about the scheme."

"Oh, so that was the reason." Her bright blue eyes narrowed. "I was afraid that you had fallen in love with a provincial nobody, or someone equally horrific, and, obstinate creature that you are, you would refuse to come to London. Needless to say, I am delighted that is not the case."

"I can assure you I have not fixed my affections on any man. I am perfectly content to remain unwed for the rest of my days."

Her grandmother slowly sat up. "Oh are you? Then why do you wish to come to London?"

"I think I will enjoy exploring a new city. And I wish to see the fruit and vegetables for sale in the Covent Garden market. According to Papa, there is a vast quantity of produce grown in London to feed the large population. I believe it is now over one million?"

"I suppose it must be. And your father was always eager to

visit the market gardens which encircle London. Your mama used to accompany him at every opportunity when they came to Town."

"I am not surprised. Mama always loved gardening." Alexandra sat on a nearby chair and folded her hands in her lap. "I believe most of the market gardens are situated near the Thames as it is cheaper to transport produce up and down the river by boat?"

"I would not know." Her grandmother's voice was faint. "And I cannot give my permission for you to traipse around London looking at kitchen gardens. It wouldn't be safe."

"Oh. Well, in that case, Papa told me there are some well-cultivated gardens near Regent's Park, which is a more genteel part of town, is it not? I would like to see the rows of lettuces and beds of cucumbers that are grown there."

"Lettuces and cucumbers?" Her grandmother's eyes boggled at her.

"They are of an excellent standard due to the quality of the soil and the large amounts of manure available in London."

"*Manure?*"

"Yes." She tilted her head innocently to one side. "It contributes to the fertility of the soil, you know."

"Yes. I know." Her grandmother cleared her throat as she settled back against her pillows. She studied her granddaughter in silence for a long moment. "I do hope you are as enthusiastic about the various balls and parties you will be attending as you are about the capital's produce."

"Yes, of course, Grandmama." Alexandra's tone was polite. She did enjoy teasing her grandmother but decided she had probably suffered enough for now.

Her grandmother sighed. "I wish to rest a while before luncheon, my love. However, this afternoon we must be sure to enjoy a comfortable coze. I have so much to tell you about the upcoming Season."

"I shall look forward to our tête-à-tête, Grandmama." Alexandra rose from her chair. Then, walking out of the room, she quietly closed the door behind her and hurried back downstairs.

After a light luncheon with John and Aunt Eliza, Alexandra and her brother were in the drawing room when Higgins informed them that Mr. Chanderly had called. After telling the butler to show him in, John said, with a surprised note in his voice, "I wonder why he has come again so soon after his previous visit."

Before Alexandra could enlighten John as to the probable reason, Mr. Chanderly entered the room. After he greeted them and refused Alexandra's offer of refreshment, he sat down in the chair she indicated. "I am happy to find you both at home, as I have something of a particular nature I wish to discuss with you."

John raised his brows but said nothing, waiting for the older man to continue.

Mr. Chanderly glanced at Alexandra before returning his attention to her brother. "I am not sure if you are aware of this, Sir John, but your sister and I recently discussed the problems many of the laborers face trying to make a decent living. She informed me that the local landowners are reluctant to institute reforms."

John nodded gravely. "That is true. In the past, I have tried to persuade them to make changes, but I suppose they have never taken my suggestions seriously because of my youth. Though they never paid much heed to our father's suggestions, either."

"Well, after discussing the matter with your sister, I realized that it would be in our best interests to arrange a meeting of the landowners in the district. Even small changes can make big differences to the quality of life of the poor, and, as I shall point out to our neighbors, it would be foolish to allow conditions to deteriorate to the extent that these unfortunates are tempted to riot."

Alexandra frowned a little. "But will our neighbors be open to your suggestions, Mr. Chanderly? As you know, they have resisted implementing any reforms up until now."

"I am sure once I have presented the benefits of my plans to them, they will see the sense in my reasoning."

The door opened at this moment, and their grandmother walked into the room. She paused in the doorway, transfixed as she stared across at those present. As John and Mr. Chanderly both rose to their feet, she said in a surprised voice, "So this is where you have been hiding yourself, Stanford! All of London has been speculating about your whereabouts."

Alexandra opened her eyes wide. "You—you are acquainted with Mr. Chanderly, Grandmama?"

She frowned. "Mr. Chanderly? What are you saying, child? His Grace is the Duke of Stanford and Earl of Chanderly. And I have 'been acquainted' with him since he was a babe in arms, as his mother is one of my dearest friends."

Alexandra gazed at her grandmother first in disbelief, then in dawning horror, as she realized her adversary of the past few weeks was none other than Robert, the ninth Duke of Stanford, recognized leader of the *ton*. Even here in her patch of countryside, so far removed from London, news of this man had reached her ears. He was the spoilt darling of Polite Society, known breaker of hearts, and object of conquest for every young unmarried lady in the land.

"I see you have heard of me, ma'am," he murmured.

"Your reputation goes before you, sir." Alexandra's voice was haughty.

The duke's green eyes gleamed, but before he could respond, her grandmother said in a puzzled voice, "Why have you concealed your identity, Stanford? And what brings you here?"

"I inherited Durbridge Hall some months ago, and I am here to set the estate in order. Not wishing to draw undue attention to myself, I thought it would be prudent to dispose of my titles for a few weeks."

"Thereby deflecting the schemes of any matchmaking mamas?"

"Precisely, ma'am." He bowed. "You know me too well."

"Well, your secret is safe with me—and with John and Alexandra, I'm sure."

"Thank you, Lady Longmore. In any case, I won't be here for much longer."

"You will no doubt be returning to London for the Season?"

"As soon as my affairs are in order."

They conversed for a few minutes more before the duke took his leave. When he left the room, her grandmother said in a brisk voice, "What a surprise to find Stanford here!"

Alexandra folded her arms. "A surprise, indeed."

John left shortly afterward to meet with his bailiff. When he departed, her grandmother cleared her throat. "Dearest, have you been seeing much of Stanford? I hope you haven't developed an interest in him. Because if you have, you will be doomed to disappointment. Many young ladies have had romantic dreams of ensnaring him, but they have come to naught. He is a confirmed bachelor, you see. Although he knows it is his duty to marry, he is in no hurry as his younger brother has already sired twin boys, and there is very little chance of the title passing out of the family. So do not let him charm you, my love! You will only be disappointed."

"Rest assured, Grandmama, that I am in no danger of succumbing to his charms. In fact, I would rather marry a viper than that mendacious man!"

Her grandmother blinked. "A viper, child?"

She nodded. "I am sure such a creature would be a far more pleasant companion than the Duke of Stanford."

"Well, I am grateful that you appear to be in no danger of yielding to his charm."

"I cannot understand why any woman would be so foolish as to lose her heart to that—that deceiver! And now, Grandmama, if you will excuse me, I have some letters I need to write."

Alexandra walked out of the room and closed the door behind her with a decided click. She leaned against the wooden panels for a moment and then ran up the stairs to her bedchamber. She desperately needed some time alone to regain her composure. Mr. Chanderly—no, the Duke of Stanford—had seen her in her worst possible light and knew her deepest secret. How could she trust him, though, with it when he had been concealing his own identity all along? She believed she had been getting to know an ordinary country gentleman, but now he seemed an utter stranger. And if he let slip about her escapades to anyone in the upper echelons of Society, his word would carry so much weight that the news would spread all over London in a trice. She could be arrested just as easily in Town as in the country.

How horrid to be entirely at his mercy.

Chapter Nine

THE NEXT DAY, the duke called again at Grantham Place. After Higgins announced him, this time with his proper title, he entered the drawing room where Alexandra sat on the window seat, looking absently out of the window. She turned in surprise at his arrival and murmured a more formal greeting than she'd yet given him.

He bowed and inquired after her health before strolling across the room to her. "I wish to speak to you, Miss Grantham, regarding a certain matter. Would you care to walk with me in the gardens?"

Alexandra remained seated. "I cannot see what a noble personage such as yourself could possibly have to say to me, *My Lord Duke.*"

"I see that rankles."

"I do not enjoy being deceived, Your Grace."

He chuckled. "Coming from you, Miss Grantham, that is rich indeed."

"But at least my deception was for a good cause."

"I can assure you mine was as well." The duke's voice was dry.

"Your conceit amazes me, sir! I cannot believe you are so pursued."

"You would be surprised at the lengths some women will go

to in order to secure an offer of marriage from a duke."

"I am sure I would."

Closing the distance between them, the duke said in a calm voice, "You must strive to cultivate a civil tongue in that head of yours if you are to become the rage, Miss Grantham."

She frowned up at him. "What do you mean?"

He flicked some dust off the sleeve of his coat. "I mean precisely what I said. I have decided to bring you into fashion when you arrive in the capital." He paused for a moment. "You see, if you are to successfully 'take' in London, you will need my endorsement. You are far too eccentric in your outlook on life for the Polite World to welcome you with open arms."

Alexandra sniffed. "I refuse to behave like a milk-and-water miss in order to please Society."

"Precisely. Which is why I have decided to make you the toast of the town."

Alexandra knit her brows together. "But why should you? What possible interest can you have in launching an insignificant country girl into London Society?"

The Duke looked down at Alexandra with a decided glint in his green eyes. "It will be most entertaining to make the high sticklers of the *ton* accept an unconventional creature such as yourself."

"I am happy to be such a source of amusement for you." Her voice was tart.

"A never-ending source, I can assure you." He paused for a moment, studying her thoughtfully. "I appreciate unconventional people who care for more than just fashion and appearance. I do not want to see you ostracized for being different."

Alexandra, somewhat unnerved by his scrutiny, rose swiftly to her feet. "If you would wait here, I will fetch my hat."

She hurried from the room, and when she returned a few minutes later, they left the house together.

Wrapped up in her thoughts, Alexandra made no effort at conversation as they walked across the lawns of Grantham Place.

The duke remained silent as well, for which she was supremely grateful as her mind buzzed with a hundred different considerations, very much like a swarm of bees flying through her head. She had never desired social success, preferring to retreat to her garden and her scientific work and avoid conversing about superficial topics with strangers. The idea of becoming the toast of the town filled her with a greater measure of dread than joy. She was unlikely to fit in with the more fashionable set, and how tiresome it would be to always be on display to people like some sort of decorative trophy.

Yet, she had to go to London and participate in the Season. If she were able to attain a measure of influence in the *ton* while she was there, perhaps she could use it to help the poor in some way and bring attention to their plight. It could give the duke's strange scheme some purposeful meaning. And, if he were intent on making her a success, he would, of course, guard her secret carefully, which was an enormously reassuring thought after her panic of the night before.

When they eventually returned to the house, Alexandra came out of her brown study, and turned to the duke, "I think, sir, that you are faced with a very difficult task if you intend to bring me into fashion."

"I know I am faced with a difficult task. But a challenge never deterred me. All I demand from you is a basic respect for the conventions that govern our society. For instance, you cannot go about unattended in London."

Alexandra sighed. "Such rules are so irksome, Your Grace."

"Nevertheless, you shall respect them."

Alexandra remained silent, annoyed at his highhandedness. He seemed to think he had the right to order her about as if she were a puppet and he held all the strings. Well, if he believed he could have the ordering of her life, then he was in for a nasty surprise. She was not eager to give up on her resolution that she would never allow a man to control her. Not even this one who purportedly had her best interests at heart.

Higgins opened the front door as the duke stood looking down at her, a contemplative expression on his face.

"Would you care for some refreshment, Your Grace?" she asked, a trifle self-consciously.

His eyes creased at the corners as he smiled. "Your company was all the refreshment I needed this morning. Farewell, Miss Grantham."

He turned and walked down the steps, and Alexandra was only recalled to the present when Higgins murmured, "Lady Longmore wishes to see you, Miss Grantham."

Alexandra was about to hasten up the stairs to her relative's bedchamber when her aunt came out of the drawing room and said in a faltering voice, "May I talk to you, dearest?"

Alexandra suppressed a sigh. The last person she felt like speaking to was her aunt, but she followed her dutifully into the drawing room and sat beside her on the striped-silk sofa.

Aunt Eliza raised a trembling hand to her face. "Dearest, Mrs. Hadley has just discovered that the man we thought of as Mr. Chanderly is, in actual fact, the Duke of Stanford! She told me so earlier this morning."

"Yes, he is."

"But he is the leader of Polite Society, and because of what Mrs. Hadley has said to him, he already knows that you are scholarly! My dear child, you are ruined. Quite ruined!"

Alexandra, trying to hide her impatience at her relative's histrionics, placed a calming hand on her arm. "Aunt Eliza. Try not to distress yourself so. No harm has been done."

"Oh, my sweet, ignorant child. You do not know of what you are speaking, so untried in the ways of the world as you are! This means destruction. Complete social destruction!" And upon these words, she sank back against the sofa, shaking uncontrollably.

Alexandra dropped her hand. It was useless trying to reason with her when she was in this state. She rang for Higgins and asked him to send for her aunt's maid. When the servant arrived, Alexandra handed Aunt Eliza over to her tender ministrations and left the room.

Hurrying up the stairs to her grandmother's bedchamber, Alexandra knocked on the door.

"There you are, child." She looked up from her book and smiled, placing her lorgnette to one side. "Pray sit down. We have so much to discuss."

"Before we do, you should know that Aunt Eliza has had one of her turns."

Her grandmother raised her brows. "And why is that?"

Alexandra sat on a chair next to the daybed where her grandmother reclined. "She is in a rare taking because Mrs. Hadley, the squire's wife, described me to the Duke of Stanford as scholarly when he first arrived in the district."

"Did she? But why?"

Alexandra shrugged. "On his arrival here, the duke met Mrs. Hadley and mentioned to her that he had heard I was a lady of considerable beauty or some such nonsense. Mrs. Hadley, who has set her sights on His Grace—or Mr. Chanderly as he was—as a possible suitor for her daughter, Jane, was in all probability not happy to hear this. So, she promptly informed him that I am scholarly, have an interest in horticulture, and that I have no feminine accomplishments whatsoever."

Her brows drew together. "Insolent woman! I always thought that female had a distinct lack of breeding. Shabby-genteel. That's what she is. The squire made a very poor choice when he married her. His first wife was a charming woman. It was such a tragedy when she died in childbirth." She sighed as she raised herself to a seated position. "However, be all that as it may, do you realize that this *could* mean social ruin for you? Why, if Stanford allows it to be known that you are interested in book learning, the gentlemen will not be at all interested in courting you!"

"So Aunt Eliza said." Alexandra lifted her shoulders. "But I am not concerned."

"Not concerned?" Her voice rose. "You do not know what

you are saying! London is a very uncomfortable place for a young lady if she has no suitors. There is not much point going to London if no gentleman wishes even to stand up with you." She shook her head. "I personally admire you for your intellectual leanings, and I am proud of your intelligence. But it is not at all modish for a young lady to appear interested in anything but the latest work of popular poetry. My dear, this could make your London Season unbearable!"

Alexandra pressed the tips of her fingers together. Perhaps it would be best to tell her grandmother at least some of what had transpired between her and the duke. After giving an edited account of her recent meeting with Stanford, she raised her hands, palms up. "And so he told me, Grandmama, that he has decided to make me the rage."

The older lady took a full minute to respond. Finally, coming out of her reverie, she said in a puzzled voice, "I wonder why Stanford has decided to bring you into fashion. Usually, he does not pay any attention to debutantes. He has said on numerous occasions that he considers simpering young ladies to be a dead bore and that they should not be inflicted on the rest of the *ton*."

"To recall his words, he told me that he wanted to make 'the high sticklers of Society accept such an unconventional creature.'" Alexandra lowered her eyes. "You see, Grandmama, I have given him good reason to believe that I am not a—er... simpering young lady."

"Now *that* sounds just like Stanford! He does enjoy stirring up the old tabbies."

"Does the duke really wield so much power, Grandmama?" Alexandra frowned slightly.

"Yes, he does. If he has decided to give you his seal of approval, you will be an immense success. Stanford is acknowledged as an arbiter of fashion and leader of Society. You did very well to tell me about his plans for you. But I must warn you that I totally endorse what he said about respecting conventions. It would be remarkably foolish of you to disregard them in London as thoroughly as you do here. Your aunt should be stricter with you than she is. But knowing you, she probably does not have much say in the matter, does she?" At her grandmother's shrewd look, Alexandra blushed. "Be that as it may, when you are under my aegis, you must have a care to appearances."

"His Grace has told me that, also, Grandmama."

"Yes. Well, I hope you will have the sense to take our advice." She swung her legs off the daybed. "And now, I think I should go and see how your aunt is feeling and try to reassure her."

"Once Aunt Eliza has succumbed to the vapors, she usually takes to her bed for the day."

Her grandmother sighed as she rose to her feet. "I know. But I must at least try to set her mind at rest."

※》》》《《《※

AFTER A LIGHT luncheon of cold meats and fruit, Alexandra and her grandmother, sans Aunt Eliza, who had retired to lie down prostrate in her bedchamber, withdrew to the Yellow Parlor. John excused himself after the meal, laughingly shaking off their invitations to join them with the assurance that he would find looking over his accounts of far more interest than talk of London fashions and Society gossip.

Alexandra worked on her embroidery while her grandmother talked about the latest fashions, threading her needle in and out of the cloth until she suddenly gave a most unladylike howl of pain as her needle pierced the soft flesh of her thumb. She grimaced at the drop of blood that now marred the cloth on her lap.

She laid the embroidery to one side and said ruefully, "I have not managed to master embroidery, Grandmama. I constantly prick my fingers and drip blood all over the cloth. It is most vexing, and I loathe it. I would not embroider if I had the choice, but Aunt Eliza insists that a young lady should have at least one feminine accomplishment to be acceptable even to her family." She released her breath in a long sigh. "It is strange, is it not, that I managed to learn Latin, French, and mathematics with ease, yet all the feminine accomplishments that a young lady should possess have eluded me. I cannot paint with watercolors, embroider, carry a tune, or play the pianoforte. I am a dismal failure at all these things, and I am sure to be a great disappointment in London."

"Nonsense! No matter how much Society prates on about feminine accomplishments, which, in my opinion, are utterly useless in themselves, you have what it takes to be a true success. I can tell you what the *ton*, especially the gentlemen, really value, and you have those qualities in abundance. You have a wonderful face and figure and a sizeable fortune. No matter what anyone else says to the contrary, Alexandra, this is what truly matters in our world," she said rather cynically.

"Well, Grandmama, if that is true, all I need do to obtain overwhelming success is put on a vapid air. I shall simper and defer to the gentlemen at all times, and I am sure to be even more sought after than the legendary Gunning sisters were!"

"Alexandra! Don't even contemplate behaving in such a missish fashion!" Her grandmother's voice was horrified. "Why, if you do as you say, you will become a dead bore, and—." She broke off as Alexandra's lips curved in a mischievous smile. "Oh, you are roasting me, Alexandra. What an infuriating girl you are." Her voice was stern, but a deep chuckle belied her stringent words, and she was smiling as she continued. "On a more serious note, my dear, you must take care what you say in London. Gentlemen do not like the idea of a woman being more knowledgeable than they are. When your poor mama died, I suggested to your father that he send you and your sisters off to a ladies' seminary in Bath, but he was set against the idea. He said the things that such an institution would teach you would be utterly useless to you, and you were all so young. When you girls professed an interest in sharing your brother's lessons, he was overjoyed."

Because John had often been ill as a boy, Papa had decided against sending his son to Eton and hired a succession of capable tutors to educate him at home instead. Thus, Alexandra and her sisters studied alongside their brother from an early age and had excelled at their lessons.

"We were all very eager students."

"I have very clever granddaughters! But it is well to remember that your papa was an eccentric man. Most men would not be pleased to know you are in all probability as well educated or even better educated than they are themselves. A bookish female is looked at askance in Polite Society, so you must take care to keep it to yourself." She wagged a finger. "You were too old to attend that seminary after your papa's death, Alexandra, which is regretful. At least Dorothea and Abigail are there now, gaining a little polish."

Alexandra wrinkled her nose as she contemplated her grandmother's words. She found it irksome when the gentlemen of her acquaintance blindly assumed that she lacked knowledge in traditionally male-dominated fields of learning because she was a woman and hated the thought of giving in to such shortsightedness. Yet she perceived the logic in what her grandmother had said. "I shall be watchful of my conversation, Grandmama, and try not to sound too bookish. In fact, I shall only bring my education to the fore if someone I dislike is plaguing me. I imagine that one or two well-timed comments about the latest crop rotation methods should send the most tiresomely arduous suitor running!"

"My dear, you would not!"

"But, Grandmama, it is a most effective ploy." Alexandra's tone was innocent. "Last year, when Alfred Hadley made a nuisance of himself by constantly showing up on our doorstep and showering me with his bouquets and his even more flowery compliments, I started spouting on about the importance of allowing fields to remain fallow. I have never seen a man turn tail as quickly as he did when I asked him to discuss the merits of this with me. He has not returned to see me since." Alexandra's lips curved reflectively.

"Well, don't play your tricks in London, Alexandra," her grandmother said in a brisk voice. "Assure me you won't."

Realizing the older lady was in earnest, Alexandra meekly promised to guard her mouth. "And I shan't speak about my interest in chemistry or astronomy either, Grandmama."

"Certainly not, my dear. Certainly not." Her eyelids fluttered down, and Alexandra smiled to herself. Her grandmother might look askance at her "tricks" but had never hesitated in employing her own.

Alexandra tipped her head to one side. "Are you quite all right, Grandmama? You have gone quite pale."

Her eyes shot open. "I am surprised I haven't fallen into a decline by now. You are quite outrageous, my girl!"

"I realize that, and I assure you that it is a great trial to me."

Her grandmother made no reply but snorted in a most inelegant fashion. The new underbutler, Meadows, who was bringing in the tea tray at that moment, gazed at her in astonishment as he set the tray on the table. When he retreated to the hall, Alexandra poured out a cup. "Here you are, Grandmama. Mama used to say that tea is very good for settling one's nerves."

"No doubt she needed to drink gallons of the stuff!"

Alexandra suppressed a giggle. "I don't think she drank quite as much as that."

Her grandmother chuckled, but then the laughter faded from her lips. "Funning aside, my love, I must confess to some sleepless nights, as it is not only you that I need to concern myself about. Are your sisters still so focused on their scientific pursuits?" She sat up straighter in her chair. "The last time I visited, I could not drag Dorothea away from that laboratory your father set up for her in the stillroom. And Abigail never stops stargazing. I confess to some qualms about their unusual interests." She pursed her lips. "At least your fascination with gardening is a little more conventional. After all, many great ladies, including the Queen and Princesses Augusta and Elizabeth, take an interest in botany and horticulture. But very few women in Polite Society pursue chemistry and astronomy. All I can say is that I am grateful your sisters are attending that finishing school."

"Yes." Alexandra's brows knit together. "Although it has not been an easy adjustment for them."

"They have complained to you?"

"Not in so many words. It is more what they do not say in their letters to me that makes me suspect they are unhappy."

"It must have been painful for them to leave you and John. But it was necessary for your sisters to go away. I hope you see that." Her gaze was shrewd. "It would most probably have benefited you as well."

Alexandra sighed. "That is what Aunt Eliza keeps saying. But how could I have left John on his own here, with only Aunt for company? He would have had no one of his own age with whom to converse."

"You have been a very good sister to him. But now it is time to think about your future. You have your own life to live, after all."

Alexandra slowly nodded her head. She did indeed. Concern for her family had consumed her for so many years that it was easy to forget that her own life stretched ahead, an unpainted canvas. Hopefully, she would be able to color it with some splendid new adventures soon.

A sense of sadness flooded through her, however, as she contemplated the upcoming Season. It would be wonderful to have her mother by her side as other young ladies did. She adored her grandmother, but Mama had simply understood and loved Alexandra as no one else ever could. Now she would have one more wandering path to traverse without her.

After tea, she excused herself and hastened upstairs to retrieve a book from her bedchamber before making her way out to her favorite spot in the garden, a shady arbor among trees and perennial shrubs situated above a clear, translucent spring that murmured through the valley. The spire of the village church was visible through the foliage, and Alexandra gazed at the beautiful vista for a long while before picking up the volume of poetry she'd brought with her and paging through the book until she came upon the familiar verses by Lord Lyttleton:

> *"Sweet babes, who, like the little playful fawns,*
> *Were wont to trip along those verdant lawns*
>   *By your delighted mother's side,*
>   *Who now your infant steps shall guide?*
> *Ah! where is now the hand whose tender care*
> *To ev'ry Virtue would have form'd your Youth,*
> *Add strew'd with flow'rs the thorny ways of Truth?*
>   *O loss beyond repair!*
>   *O wretched father left alone*
> *To weep their dire misfortune, and thy own!*
> *How shall thy weaken'd mind, oppress'd with woe,*
>   *And drooping o'er thy Lucy's grave,*
> *Perform the duties, that you doubly owe,*
>   *Now she, alas, is gone,*
> *From folly, and from vice, their helpless age to save?"*

Chapter Ten

A WEEK LATER, Alexandra and her grandmother bid goodbye to John and Aunt Eliza and made an early morning start for London.

Her grandmother settled back against the luxurious squabs of the carriage with an air of satisfaction. "I must say, much as I have enjoyed my stay at Grantham Place, I am pleased to leave. A sennight in the country, and I am already pining for the city. I am so looking forward to the Season. Bringing you out is going to prove most enjoyable." Darting a quick look at her granddaughter, she continued, "I am especially looking forward to seeing you in some decently fashionable clothes."

Alexandra blinked. "Truly, Grandmama, I am very happy to wear the gowns I have."

The older lady shook her head. "Your wardrobe is woefully inadequate for a London Season. Some of your gowns, I grant you, are pretty enough, but it is all too easy to detect the hand of a country dressmaker in them. Rusticity is not at all in vogue."

"If that is the case, I place myself totally in your hands. I remember when I was a little girl Mama saying that you have exquisite taste in fashion and a remarkable eye for color."

A shadow of pain crossed her grandmother's face at the mention of her beloved daughter. "Your mama was quite right. And you will be a joy to clothe. Your lovely figure and striking coloring will present a challenge any modiste worth her while will be eager to take up."

"I have always felt it is rather a pity my coloring makes me so dissimilar to others." Alexandra's tone was brooding. "My red hair draws far too much attention."

"Yes, my love, but in a most excellent way." Grandmama pressed the tips of her fingers together. "I think I shall entrust you to Madame Bouchet. Although she is the most expensive modiste in London, she is also by far the most talented. She can be relied upon to turn you out in style, especially for your first appearance at Almack's. You must make a good impression then."

"Emily Hadley told me that if one fails to receive vouchers for Almack's, that one is socially damned. Can that be so?"

"Oh, yes. A young lady who fails to be approved of by the Lady Patronesses of Almack's might as well pack up and return home for all the good staying in London will do her. Fortunately, it will not be difficult for you to obtain vouchers. Lady Sefton is a close friend of mine and has already, on condition of first meeting you, of course, promised to send them." She studied Alexandra thoughtfully. "Speaking of Almack's, my dear, do you know how to waltz?"

"No, I don't. I am familiar with the country dances, the quadrille, the cotillion, and the minuet, but Aunt Eliza nearly had hysterics when I suggested that I learn the waltz. She described it as 'extremely fast.'"

"It certainly is. But since Countess Lieven introduced it into Almack's, it has become accepted everywhere. Consequently, it is vastly important that you become familiar with it. Immediately we arrive in London, I shall engage a dancing master to give you some lessons and teach you the steps. Then, once you have gained permission to waltz from one of the patronesses, you will be ready."

"With all these rules and regulations, I am afraid I may forget one and make a hopeless social blunder."

"Nonsense, you will manage perfectly." Her grandmother's

brow creased. "Nevertheless, I know London Society well enough to realize the futility of tossing you into the *ton* by having you make your first London appearance at Almack's Assembly Rooms. Therefore, you must attend some of the smaller parties given at the beginning of the Season. And when your horse arrives in London, you will be able to ride in the Park, which is a less formal way to become accustomed to Society. I am sure you will also welcome the exercise."

"Yes, indeed, Grandmama. I shall be delighted to have Starlight with me. I only hope this disagreeable weather improves, so that she can be brought to London soon. Her wonderfully familiar presence will be very comforting since I doubt I'll know anyone who is in London for the Season—besides the Hadleys, that is. And the duke."

Her grandmother patted her arm. "I know it sounds quite overwhelming, but you will manage perfectly. We must commission Madame Bouchet to design one of her particularly dazzling creations for your presentation at Almack's. An ivory gown with azure blue satin trim would look enchanting on you. With your mother's sapphires—sapphires are not too overwhelming for a young girl to wear—you will be captivating."

"Grandmama, when is my coming-out ball to be held?"

"I think two months or so after the Season starts. That will be just before the peak of the Season so that we can be assured of a full house."

Alexandra turned to look out of the carriage window at the passing scenery. The unseasonably warm weather of the last few weeks had turned suddenly, giving place to cooler temperatures, and a drizzle now fell from a grey overcast sky.

The countryside appeared bleak in the cold morning light. Yet neither the inclement weather nor the dreary outlook could lower Alexandra's spirits. John had told her yesterday that the duke had persuaded their neighbors to implement some reforms. And although the situation in her neighborhood would not change overnight, it was a start.

And in the meanwhile, the vicar's wife had agreed to deliver Alexandra's food baskets to the poor while she was away. Mrs. Simpson had smiled gently when Alexandra approached her outside the village church on Sunday with the request. "I should be happy to do so. And I must say that I believe it will be a good thing for you to have a change in scene." She hesitated a moment. "Your diligent work to help the poor in our neighborhood is much appreciated. However, I have gained the impression that you have been burdened of late as if you bear a great weight."

The older lady's brows were raised in faint question, and Alexandra lowered her eyes and studied her clenched fingers. Eventually, she released a sigh. "So many people go hungry if I fail to deliver the baskets. I carry that knowledge with me every day."

"It is not your burden to bear alone, my dear." Mrs. Simpson's smile was gentle. "Let not your heart be troubled."

Alexandra inclined her head gravely as she took her leave of the clergyman's wife. The older woman had become something of a mother figure to her over the past few years as the devout lady worked tirelessly to lighten the load of their indigent neighbors in the district. Frequently when Alexandra arrived at a cottage with food, cordials, clothing, and money, Mrs. Simpson was already there, offering the gifts of her kindness and attention to those in distress.

Alexandra knew the vicar's wife would be faithful to deliver the food baskets and take care of the impoverished cottagers, freeing her to consider her own future for the first time. Tendrils of excitement began to unfurl in the pit of her stomach as she anticipated her time in London, where she would be free to broaden her horizons and see something more of the world.

The only city Alexandra had visited previously was Bath. She had traveled to the hot spring resort a few years before to visit an elderly aunt who resided there. The bustle of town life was fascinating. Although Alexandra had been too young to attend any of the assemblies, she had enjoyed herself immensely visiting the libraries, attending the theatre, and shopping in Milsom Street.

The amusements of the Metropolis promised to be even more entertaining. Yet she was determined, no matter how unfashionable it might be, to view something more of London than the average young lady would. Her thorough education made it inconceivable that she should visit London without viewing the wonders of the British Museum. She was also interested in visiting Shakespeare's memorial at Westminster Abbey and the Royal Botanic Gardens at Kew, about which her father had told her so much.

Alexandra's thoughts revolved around and around in excited circles as she envisaged all the wonders in store for her. Hopefully, her visit to London would prove to be not only entertaining but educative as well.

※※※

ALEXANDRA'S GRANDMOTHER DISLIKED traveling fast and instructed Biddle, the coachman, not to spring the horses but to take the journey in easy stages. The party, which included her grandmother's lady's maid, Jarvis, and Alexandra's maid, Hobbes, traveled through Devizes that day and carried on to Marlborough, where they put up for the night at The Castle Inn. They retired early, and Alexandra, unfamiliar with the rigors of traveling, slept like one dead. Not even exciting thoughts about London could keep her heavy eyelids from closing the second her head touched the soft down pillows.

The following day their party set off early again. They traveled past the Forest of Savernake, on to Hungerford, and then to Newbury, where they stopped for the night before proceeding on the final stage of their journey to London.

Alexandra looked around her in wonder later that afternoon as the carriage wheels eventually struck the cobbled streets of the

Metropolis. The noise was overwhelming, and she moved closer to the carriage window to better take in the sights.

Flower sellers, carrying fresh blooms in baskets and carts, and hawkers of fine herbs such as rosemary, sage, and lavender, called out their wares as they walked along. Their voices mingled with the cries of men selling herrings, mackerel, pies, and tarts, all bustling along in their eagerness to attract customers.

Biddle steered the horses expertly through the complicated network of streets, and the din abated somewhat as they left the city center and entered the more fashionable part of town. Alexandra's grandmother informed her that they would dine early and spend a quiet evening *à deux* before retiring to bed in preparation for the busy days ahead. "Because you will need to be refreshed to enjoy the social whirl to the full. And traveling, as I well know, is an exhausting business which can sap the strength of even the hardiest person."

Notwithstanding her interest in her new surroundings, Alexandra was more than pleased when the coachman eventually drew up before her grandmother's imposing townhouse in Berkeley Square. She left the constricting confines of the carriage and stretched her cramped limbs, thankful that the seemingly interminable journey had ended.

Leighton, Longmore House's stately butler, formally welcomed his mistress and Alexandra before relieving them of their cloaks and instructing one of the footmen to conduct Miss Grantham to her bedchamber.

Alexandra released a happy sigh when she crossed the threshold of the charming room, rendered snug and welcoming by a large fire roaring in the grate and fresh flowers artistically arranged on the mantelpiece.

The bed with its soft, blue counterpane looked most welcoming, and Alexandra lay down thankfully, leaving Hobbes to unpack her trunks. She drifted off to sleep and awoke only a short while before dinner. Startled that she had slept for so long, Alexandra hastily changed her crumpled gown and left her bedchamber to make her way to the drawing room where her grandmother awaited her.

"We shall dine lightly tonight, Alexandra. I cannot abide a heavy meal after a long journey." She contemplated her granddaughter. "I hope you will sleep well later as I plan to take you to Madame Bouchet in the morning. Being fitted for new gowns can be an exhausting business, particularly if you aren't used to being pinned and prodded and measured." She narrowed her eyes. "And you must have your hair cut into a fashionable style. It is far too long, you know."

Alexandra pressed her lips together. "Shorter styles are far more difficult to manage, Grandmama. When Hobbes puts my hair up in the morning, it is out of my face and eyes, which makes it much easier for me when I'm working in the garden."

"I am afraid you will simply need to suffer the inconvenience of having more hair around your face now. It is the fashion, after all. And you won't be working in a garden while you are in London."

"May I not work in yours, Grandmama?" She struggled to keep the dismay out of her voice.

"I don't believe you will have the time. We will be quite busy!"

"But I am an early riser. Perhaps I could work in the garden while you are still asleep?"

Her grandmother tapped a finger on the side of the sofa. "I suppose you could. I never wake early as we keep such late hours here in London, and I need my sleep! But you are so young and energetic—if you rise before me, you may spend some time outdoors. But do wear your hat, my love! I don't want you to develop any freckles."

"Very well, Grandmama." Alexandra pressed her hands tightly together. "I assure you I'll never take my hat off if you will allow me to work outside."

Her grandmother chuckled. "What an odd girl you are, to be sure. We arrive in the Metropolis, and the first thing you want to do is dig around in the dirt." She paused for a moment, her expression more sober. "I do hope you won't find the adjustment to living in Town too difficult."

Alexandra lifted her shoulders in a half-shrug. "If I work in the garden every morning, I will be more than content to spend the rest of my day experiencing all that London has to offer. It is about time that I broadened my horizons."

After sampling the culinary delights of her grandmother's French chef, Alexandra retired to bed at the unfashionably early hour of nine o'clock. She slept soundly, her slumber undisturbed by her new surroundings. However, she was somewhat annoyed when she awoke in the morning and recalled how a pair of glinting green eyes had persistently invaded her dreams.

True to her word, her grandmother whisked Alexandra off to Madame Bouchet's elegant establishment in Bruton Street the next morning. The two ladies were ushered into a showroom carpeted with an Aubusson and furnished with the carved, gilt armchairs that were all the fashion in London.

Madame Bouchet, a slim, elegant woman of indeterminate age, moved forward to greet Lady Longmore, curtseying respectfully. She listened to Alexandra's grandmother's request that she design an entire wardrobe for her granddaughter with an anxious expression on her face, and said in regretful tones, "Madame, usually I would welcome such an order, but I fear that with the Season almost upon us—."

Madame Bouchet turned to look apologetically at Alexandra as she said this, but her expression changed as her sharp eyes looked over Alexandra's person. "But, Madame, you bring me a goddess to clothe! I shall, of a certainty, undertake to fashion Mademoiselle's wardrobe. The limited time we have—it will be difficult, *bien sûr*, but I shall contrive!" She scrutinized Alexandra's face. "Your coloring, Mademoiselle—it demands that you do not dress in the colors that are too pale. They will not do you justice. We must look elsewhere *pour l'inspiration!*"

Madame Bouchet hastened away and returned with silks and

satins in various shades and seemingly endless rolls of muslin and cambric. She immediately fell into a discussion with Grandmama about styles and fabrics while Alexandra stood mutely by.

She was amazed at the number of dresses her grandparent was intent on ordering for her. Hopefully, she did not become confused and wear a morning gown in the evening. Hobbes would need to help her there. Such a faux pas would not be overlooked by the fastidious members of beau monde, with their set rules for every occasion.

When Madame Bouchet showed Alexandra some of her finest muslin material, she frowned. "Surely this material is too flimsy, Madame? The weather has turned quite cold."

Madame Bouchet gave her a reproving look. "If you desire to be modish, Mademoiselle, you must be obliged to make the sacrifices that are necessary. Many, many fashionable ladies wear these gowns even when the weather is cold."

Alexandra tilted her head. "Very well. It is a good thing then that I brought my mother's Cashmere shawl to London. It should keep me warm."

"Indeed, Mademoiselle. Cashmere shawls are the perfect accompaniment to these thin muslin gowns! And they are of such superb quality that they last for many years."

Her grandmother gave a faint sigh. "Elizabeth loved that shawl, Alexandra. I am glad you brought it with you."

Alexandra's lips trembled slightly. She had packed the garment not for fashion purposes, as she had not been aware that her shawl could still be modish, but rather because she felt wrapped in her mother's love whenever she wore it—a tangible reminder of all her devotion and care.

Two hours later, they left Madame Bouchet's rooms and proceeded on to Miss Walker's milliner's shop in Conduit Street. The proprietor was all attention and urged Alexandra to try on a hat of lustre straw, turned up in the front. The elegant creation was decorated with a flower and trimmed with a blue ribbon, which Alexandra tied under her chin. "It frames your face exquisitely, Miss Grantham!" the lady declared in a rapturous voice.

Her grandmother agreed that it suited her very well, and Alexandra did not protest when Miss Walker smilingly placed the bonnet in a bandbox to be delivered to Longmore House later that day.

Alexandra then tried on a hat of white satin trimmed with beads and a couple of ostrich feathers, but she put it aside in favor of a simple fur bonnet decorated with a curled plume. "At least my ears will be warm, Grandmama!" Her voice was placating as she caught a glimpse of her grandmother's doubtful expression in the mirror.

Grandmama purchased Alexandra's choices and four more stylish bonnets from a delighted Miss Walker. The two ladies then left the milliner's exclusive establishment and climbed into the Longmore barouche, which awaited them outside. Biddle then drove to Bond Street, where her grandmother explained that they would be able to purchase the various items of fashion without which a lady's wardrobe was incomplete.

Half-boots, slippers, lace handkerchiefs, silk stockings, fans, gloves, colorful ribbons: to Alexandra, the list of essential items seemed endless. Eventually, her grandmother declared they could return home. Settling back against the squabs of the barouche as it moved forward, she sighed in satisfaction. "We have done very well today! There are a few trifling purchases yet to make, but I am quite dead on my feet, so they can wait. The important thing is that you are well on the way to becoming one of the most fashionable young ladies in London."

"I hope I shan't disappoint you, Grandmama." She knit her brows. "I fear very much that it will take more than an elegant wardrobe to make a modish lady of me."

"You have natural grace and style," her grandmother reassured her. "You will be surprised at how quickly you adjust to being a lady of fashion."

Monsieur Dupont, an acclaimed Society hairdresser, descended on Berkeley Square the next day to style Alexandra's copper tresses. When he set eyes on her hair, the dapper little Frenchman's eyes sparkled in gleeful anticipation. *"Mademoiselle, vos cheveux sont très magnifiques!"* He rested his chin on his hand. "Such an unusual shade of red. And so very long!"

"I am not sure I wish to cut it, monsieur."

He tilted his head to one side. "I understand that. It is like losing an old friend when one is obliged to cut one's hair, is it not? But you are in good hands, mademoiselle, I can assure you of that."

Alexandra doubted she would be happy with a shorter style. However, at the end of the morning, she had to admit that the Frenchman had not exaggerated his talents. He had arranged her hair in a mass of curls which framed her face in the front, while her hair at the back was tied into a loose, elegant bun. The new look emphasized her high cheekbones and brought out her blue eyes, and when her grandmother walked into the room to see the result, she said in an awed voice, "My child, you look exquisite!"

Alexandra laughingly brushed the compliment aside. But she could not fail to notice the difference the new hairstyle made to her appearance. It lent her an air of refined elegance, which was quite at odds with how she had always viewed herself.

But, although filled with a sense of expectation for the future, a feeling of melancholy that was hard to shake off suddenly settled upon her. Her new appearance seemed to emphasize how nothing ever stayed the same. Life was always in a state of flux or change, and one never knew if those changes would ultimately be for the better or not. It was a sobering thought. She had been content with her country existence. Would she be as happy with her city life?

Even if she had wanted to, Alexandra had little time to dwell on such thoughts during the next few days. These were busy, filled with dancing lessons every morning, shopping expeditions, and frequent outings to the Park where she attracted no little notice.

Nattily attired dandies and daring bucks alike ogled her, and she received even more attention from turbaned matrons driving along with their daughters. Many of these ladies' stares were more hostile than admiring, to the extent that Alexandra began to wonder whether she had unwittingly offended them by making some sort of social blunder. Her grandmother set her mind at rest on this score with a derisive snort. "My dear girl, the only 'social blunder' you have made is to cast the rest of Society's damsels into the shade—something not easily forgiven, I'm afraid."

One afternoon, Alexandra was driving along with her grandmother at the hour of the Grand Strut in Hyde Park when she set eyes on a young exquisite dressed in canary yellow pantaloons and a striped waistcoat. The dandy's shirt points were so highly starched that he could barely move his head. Alexandra was wondering with some amusement what would occur if he happened to sneeze when her grandmother instructed Biddle to stop the barouche alongside a landau drawn up on the carriageway.

In response to Alexandra's inquiring look, she whispered, "Lady Jersey, and with her is Lady Sefton," before turning to greet the two Lady Patronesses of Almack's.

Alexandra viewed the two ladies about whom she had heard so much with some interest. Lady Jersey was an elegant woman dressed in the height of fashion, but she had a rather sharp look about her. It did not seem as if she would suffer fools gladly.

Lady Sefton, on the other hand, seemed of a placid and kind disposition, as was apparent in the generous welcome she accorded her friend's granddaughter. "Welcome to the Capital, my dear. Your grandmother told me you were lovely, and I can see she did not exaggerate. You are certain to take the town by storm. Do you not agree, Sally?" She turned to look at Lady Jersey.

"Yes, indeed. Your granddaughter will liven up the London scene considerably, Anne," Lady Jersey said. "I shall look forward to seeing you at Almack's. Your vouchers will be forthcoming, of course," she continued with a brief smile and nod in Alexandra's direction before turning back to the older lady.

Alexandra rapidly lost interest in the ensuing conversation, as the people of whom the older women spoke were as yet mostly unknown to her. She turned her attention instead to a group of fashionably dressed ladies and gentlemen standing nearby. She was admiring a particularly fetching bonnet worn by one of the ladies when her attention was quickly reclaimed and held by something Lady Jersey was saying to her grandmother.

"I hear that Stanford is to return to London within the sennight. I am sure that once he is in occupation of that enormous house of his opposite you, life will become more interesting."

"Stanford does add a certain spark to the London scene."

"More than a spark. A veritable fire, I would say." Lady Jersey's lips curved into a wry smile. "I wonder how many hearts he will break this year. You know, I sometimes doubt that he will ever be caught by parson's mousetrap."

"He is bound to enter the state of matrimony one day, even if it is only to ensure that a son succeeds him," Lady Sefton remarked comfortably. "Speaking of successions, did you hear that old Pemberbrook has finally died? His nephew has inherited the estate, but along with it came a mountain of debts, poor man!"

Alexandra sat frozen in her seat, barely listening to the rest of Lady Sefton's conversation as she assimilated the fact that the Duke of Stanford would be residing directly opposite her for the next few months. She welcomed the idea with very little enthusiasm because, for all her avowals of dislike and her genuine determination to remain unwed, she was also well aware of the dangerous attraction he possessed. Although the duke could be domineering at times, he was also charming, articulate, and far too handsome for his own good. And he had a devastatingly attractive smile. And those green eyes.

Alexandra resolutely drew herself up at this point. She would not allow herself to fall foolishly into the trap of thinking about him more than she should.

CHAPTER ELEVEN

WITH HER GRANDMOTHER acting as chaperone, Alexandra spent nearly every evening of her first week in London attending some party or other. These affairs, organized by a group of society matrons, were given so that these ladies' daughters could begin to make the acquaintance of other young people their age before the official engagements began. Alexandra was duly invited to all of these ensembles and invariably found herself regularly waylaid by gentlemen eager to be introduced to her.

Far from being pleased or flattered by their attentions, she found the conversation of the young dandies who seemed most abundant as excruciatingly dull as she had feared. They struck soulful poses while regarding her from under lowered brows and made speeches that were more silly than anything else. Alexandra considered them quite ridiculous and, by the end of her first week in London, heartily wished that they would transfer their tiresome attentions to someone else.

On Tuesday evening at Lady Derringer's rout, Alexandra found herself suffering the attentions of a particularly ardent young suitor who had been reciting lines of Lord Byron's latest poem to her. Unable to endure her persistent admirer's blandishments any longer, Alexandra requested that he obtain a glass of lemonade for her. When he left to execute her request, she hastily escaped to the balcony.

She let out a sigh, welcoming the solitude the evening invited, though, when her eyes adjusted to the darkness, she became aware that she was not, as she had initially thought, the sole occupant of the balcony. A couple stood close together at the far end in what appeared to be a particularly earnest conversation.

The gentleman said something in a low, urgent voice. The young girl to whom he spoke shook her head. Finally, the man clasped the girl's hands before walking down the steps, leaving his companion staring after him, her shoulders drooping disconsolately.

Rather uncomfortable at having witnessed such an intimate scene, Alexandra was about to slip quietly back inside when the young girl turned and saw her standing there, illuminated by the bright light streaming through the windows. "Oh! You startled me. I thought you were Amelia." When Alexandra raised her brows, she continued, "She's my chaperone—my cousin, you understand—and she would be extremely angry to discover me out here unattended. She would be sure to tell my brother about it, and he would be even angrier."

"Brothers tend to be protective of their sisters," Alexandra murmured.

"Yes, but Robert is not just protective. He's quite puritanical when it comes to the female members of his family. Hence Cousin Amelia." She peered behind Alexandra in search of her unwelcome duenna.

Alexandra studied the other girl more closely, noting her familiar dark hair and green eyes. She had distinctive features which definitely bore a resemblance to those of a certain man Alexandra had recently encountered, although they were cast in a far more delicate mold. Consequently, in a determinedly careless voice, she asked, "Are you by any chance related to the Duke of Stanford?"

The girl rolled her eyes. "I am his sister, Letitia. Ever since I arrived in London, people have been informing me that I have a likeness of Robert. And I do not view it as a compliment either! Robert has a square jaw, for heaven's sake. And the most forbidding-looking eyebrows. It is a great trial to me that people consider that we look alike. I, for one, cannot see the resemblance."

Alexandra laughed. "I assure you, Lady Letitia, that you do not have a square jaw nor forbidding eyebrows, for that matter."

"That may well be, but it does not help the fact that I am known wherever I go—and singled out. It means I must always exercise considerable discretion in whatever I do, especially when meeting—" she broke off and gazed anxiously at Alexandra.

"The gentleman you were with a moment ago?"

"Yes. Oh, but please assure me that you won't inform anyone, Miss—. Forgive me, but I do not know your name?"

"I am Alexandra Grantham, Lady Letitia. And no, I would never inform anyone of your clandestine meeting. I am no tale monger, I assure you."

"I did not mean to imply that you were, Miss Grantham." Her hands fluttered. "Are . . . are you, by any chance, acquainted with my brother?"

Alexandra was about to dodge this question by making some vague response when a deep voice came from behind her. "Miss Grantham is indeed acquainted with him."

Alexandra's breath caught in her chest upon hearing the disturbingly familiar voice. She spun around and uttered one pithy word to the dark-haired man leaning nonchalantly against the balcony doors: "You!"

A pair of forbidding eyebrows rose at this, and he said urbanely, "I, Miss Grantham. And I am delighted to see you too."

Alexandra flushed at how rude she must have sounded and then sank into a deep curtsey befitting the duke's rank. Upon rising, she said politely, "Your Grace. What a . . . er . . . pleasant surprise to meet you again."

He straightened from his lounging position. "You may be surprised to see me, Miss Grantham, but you are certainly in no way pleased."

She lifted her chin. "Sir, you presume too much! I am wholly unaffected by your presence. One could even say indifferent."

"I see your tongue has not lost its sharpness. Are you normally so caustic, or do you save your particular brand of set-downs just for me?"

"Set-downs, Your Grace?" Her voice was bland. "I was not aware that to be unaffected by someone was to insult them. Pray accept my heartfelt apologies."

His eyes acknowledged the hit, but Alexandra had the uneasy feeling that she was taking on more than she could manage by engaging the duke in verbal swordplay. If she was not mistaken, he was a master at that particular game and would be a formidable adversary once challenged.

He did not respond to her audacious comment. Instead, he turned his attention to his errant sister. "And may I inquire, Letty, as to what you are doing out here—alone?"

Sending a desperate look in Alexandra's direction, Lady Letitia said, "But I am not alone, Robert. I am accompanied by Miss Grantham."

Unable to resist the expression of pleading on Lady Letitia's face, Alexandra came to her rescue. "Yes, Your Grace. It was so stifling indoors that Lady Letitia and I decided to come outside for a breath of fresh air."

The duke raised one eyebrow this time. "As a respectable companion for my sister, you would be the last person I would choose, Miss Grantham. If I accurately recall, when I last encountered you, it was precisely because you were unaccompanied that I took you to task."

Alexandra was about to make an extremely unwise retort to this when the balcony doors opened again, and her grandmother appeared. She looked around and, spotting Alexandra, said in an exasperated voice, "Oh, there you are, child! I have been searching all over for you. There is someone in particular to whom I wish to introduce you." Upon seeing the duke and his sister standing nearby, she continued, "Good evening, Stanford, Letitia. I trust that you are well?" Not waiting for a reply, she carried on, "I am surprised to see you at a gathering of this sort, Your Grace. I supposed coming-out parties were not quite your style."

"You supposed correctly, madam. I am on my way to White's and only stopped here to see whether Gerard wishes to join me."

Letitia's lips twisted into a sympathetic smile. "He will be most thankful that you have come to his rescue, Robert. Gerard was extremely put out when Cousin Amelia insisted that he accompany us here. He said he had no wish to 'do the pretty to a bunch of females,' but Cousin Amelia said it was his fraternal duty to escort us here. So he agreed—albeit very ungraciously. I think you will find him in the card room."

"He has more than likely escaped into the garden to blow a cloud. Somehow, I can't imagine Gerard playing whist for sixpenny points."

The duke then answered Alexandra's grandmother's queries about the state of his mother's health before excusing himself and escorting his sister back inside.

"So you have made the acquaintance of Letitia Beaumont," her grandmother said after they had gone. "She is a charming girl but far too headstrong. Stanford keeps a close eye on her for she is apt to fall into the most unfortunate scrapes."

"If that is so, Grandmama, I suppose the duke's attention may be diverted away from bringing me into fashion." Her voice was thoughtful.

The older lady snorted. "Don't count on it. Once Stanford has made up his mind to do something, he invariably does it. And he has promised to make you the talk of the town."

"I am not at all sure I want that to happen, Grandmama, if it means that at every party I attend, I must endure the attentions of a set of veritable mooncalves. That is why I escaped out here."

"You should not have come out here unattended, Alexandra. I was looking all over for you and could not find you."

"Forgive me, Grandmama. I did not realize."

"Never mind. I can quite see why you are frustrated with having to endure the conversation of a set of callow youths only a few years your senior. That is why I wish to introduce you to my godson, Sir Charles Fotherby. He is all that a gentleman should be. I am sure you will get along famously with him." On this optimistic note, her grandmother shepherded Alexandra back inside, locating Sir Charles on the other side of the room, near the drawing-room door.

"Your servant, Miss Grantham!" he said upon being presented to her. "I hope you have settled into Town? I believe this is your first visit to London."

"It is, Sir Charles. I am finding it all very interesting, although I haven't seen much of London yet. There are so many places I would like to visit."

Her grandmother's smile was warm. "I have been thinking of your desire to explore the gardens of the Metropolis, my love. Thus far, you have only seen the inside of shops and drawing rooms!" She turned to her godson. "Would you be so kind as to escort us to Kew one day this week, Charles? Alexandra is a keen gardener and would enjoy visiting the Royal Botanic Gardens."

A smile lit up his pleasant features. "I should be delighted to escort you, ma'am. The gardens are always worth visiting."

Alexandra beamed in sudden anticipation at both her grandmother and Sir Charles. "Oh, thank you! Papa told me the Gardens include a variety of exotic trees. I particularly wish to see the pomegranates, the myrtles, and the bay trees."

"The Orangery is also worth seeing, Miss Grantham. It is quite splendid."

"My father described it to me in great detail, so I am quite looking forward to visiting it myself."

He bent his head. "I am pleased to be able to accompany you there, ma'am."

After the plan for visiting Kew Gardens was firmly settled, Alexandra had spent some few minutes conversing with the engaging baronet on a range of topics, from her love of horses, which he shared, to the intricacies involved in successful fly-fishing. He was kind, solicitous, and agreeable company. Unlike a certain other man who was nothing of the sort.

Later that evening, Alexandra smothered a yawn as Hobbes helped her undress. Then, climbing thankfully into bed, she reflected on the remainder of the gathering, which had been far more enjoyable than the first part, primarily because Sir Charles Fotherby had turned out to be as charming as her grandmother had suggested he would be.

But Alexandra couldn't hold at bay the memory of her other notable conversation that evening, and she glowered into the darkness. The Duke of Stanford was far too sure of himself and part of her longed to be able to put him properly in his place. She was pleasurably conjuring up wonderful situations where the duke, for some obscure and utterly improbable reason, was under her power and begging her for mercy when tiredness overtook her and her heavy eyelids closed in sleep.

CHAPTER TWELVE

AFTER BREAKFAST THE following day, Sir Charles Fotherby was admitted to the morning parlor. After Alexandra responded to his pleasant greeting, he said, "I trust that you feel as refreshed after a good night's rest as you look, Miss Grantham? I have called with the hope of inviting you for a drive in the Park. My curricle awaits me outside."

"Then we must not keep your horses standing, Sir Charles. If you will grant me a few minutes, I shall join you directly."

Alexandra smiled inquiringly at her grandmother, who nodded in approval, before hastening upstairs to put on one of her fashionable new bonnets, a charming primrose yellow affair with an upstanding poke and high crown. No curled plumes adorned this artful confection, but the matching yellow satin ribbons, tied in a bow under one ear, set the hat above the ordinary.

Alexandra met Sir Charles in the hall, and the baronet walked her to his curricle and handed her into the vehicle. With a nod in his groom's direction, he set the restless horses in motion.

Alexandra looked admiringly at the pair of perfectly matched chestnuts harnessed to the curricle. She sat quietly as Sir Charles maneuvered his conveyance into the busy London traffic. The chestnuts were spirited animals, and Sir Charles needed all his attention to keep them in check.

When they turned into the gates of Hyde Park, she said appreciatively, "I must compliment you on your splendid horses, Sir Charles. They are fine-steppers, indeed."

"They are prime bits of blood and bone. I have received numerous offers for them from hopeful buyers, but I will never part with them." He paused briefly, then continued with a sheepish look, "I fear I may sound odiously sentimental, Miss Grantham, but to me my horses are like old friends."

"It is the same for me," Alexandra said with a smile. "I am embarrassed to say that I miss my faithful mare, Starlight, far more than I do my aunt, both of whom remain at Grantham Place. A shameful state of affairs!"

"Do you intend to ride when you are in London?"

"Grandmama has arranged for Starlight to be brought here. I am fairly aching to exercise my limbs. The sedentary life of a town-dweller is not for me."

"Feeling a little cramped?" His smile was sympathetic.

"Quite so. At home, I had the advantage of enjoying far more freedom than a young lady in London is allowed. The majority of gentlemen I have been introduced to here treat me as though I were a piece of porcelain. I believe they fear I may break, so solicitous are they in their attentions."

"You cannot entirely blame them, ma'am. You have a marked air of daintiness about you."

"Well, it is deceptive," she said tartly. "I am as strong as an ox and dislike being thought of as a helpless creature, unable to take care of herself. The very idea is nonsensical."

He chuckled. "If you flash your eyes like that at your numerous suitors, they will very soon come to realize it, Miss Grantham."

A matron waved imperiously at them, and Sir Charles drew the curricle up on the side of the carriageway. Alexandra suppressed a sigh. It was none other than Mrs. Hadley, out for a morning stroll and accompanied by her daughter Jane and another lady of middle years. Alexandra forced a smile to her lips, but her expression brightened into genuine warmth when she spotted Emily, Mrs. Hadley's stepdaughter, tucked in behind them.

The squire's wife stopped beside the open carriage. "My dear Miss Grantham. How delightful it is to see you again! I hope that you are well? May I present my sister Mrs. Morecombe to you? We are staying with her while we are in Town. Miss Alexandra Grantham is a neighbor from home and a dear friend of my daughters," she added to her sister.

Mrs. Morecombe smiled thinly. "Miss Grantham."

"I am pleased to make your acquaintance, ma'am." Alexandra acknowledged Jane and Emily before returning her attention to Mrs. Hadley. "I trust that you had a good journey to London?"

"We did. You left earlier than planned, did you not?" Her eyes narrowed into slits.

"Yes, Grandmama arrived earlier than we expected her, and before I knew what she was about, she whisked me off to London." Alexandra glanced at Sir Charles. "You must all allow me to present my companion to you—Sir Charles Fotherby, my grandmother's godson."

Sir Charles bowed politely. "Delighted to make your acquaintance, ladies. Mrs. Morecombe and I are acquainted." He directed a formal nod in Mrs. Morecombe's direction.

"It is quite like my dear sister to be acquainted with all the most charming people in London, Sir Charles." Mrs. Hadley's voice was complacent. "You, of course, will know that she cuts quite a figure in polite circles. With her vast acquaintance, we're sure to be busy every evening." She cleared her throat. "We're also quite looking forward to seeing the Duke of Stanford, who is another kind friend, now that we are all in Town. Are you on terms with the duke, Sir Charles?"

Her companion shifted uncomfortably. No doubt he found the woman's obvious tuft hunting as distasteful as Alexandra did. "I am acquainted with His Grace but stand on more familiar terms with his younger brother, Lord Stephen, who is closer to my age."

"Of course, of course. You seem to be quite a young man." Mrs. Hadley looked archly up at Alexandra. "I do hope you haven't been regaling Sir Charles with strange facts about trees and vegetables."

Sir Charles lifted an eyebrow. "As a matter of fact, I share Miss Grantham's interest in gardening. We plan to drive to the Royal Botanic Gardens in Kew tomorrow. It is well worth visiting if you are looking for an outdoor excursion. Ladies." He bowed again and then prepared to set the horses in motion, leaving Alexandra to make her somewhat stilted farewells.

She pressed her lips together as Sir Charles drove on. She could not believe the spite of the other woman. Mrs. Hadley's disingenuousness was vastly annoying, but hopefully their paths would not cross too frequently. However, she must contrive to see more of Emily. Her poor friend had looked like a shadow of herself, standing half-hidden behind her stepmother. How miserable she must be trapped in a house with Jane and Mrs. Hadley and that sour-looking Mrs. Morecombe. Alexandra gazed unseeingly at the passing scenery as she considered the problem. She would simply need to find a way to meet Emily on her own. Perhaps she could invite her to go walking in the Park one day, or something of that nature.

When Sir Charles drove out of the Park, he glanced down at her with a frown marring his smooth brow and finally broke the thoughtful silence. "I would advise you to be wary of Mrs. Morecombe. She is mean-spirited gossip who would be overlooked by Society were it not for the fact that her brother-in-law is Sir Jason Morecombe, a man of standing though even more of a mischief-maker. It is best to avoid them both."

Alexandra had fully intended to follow Sir Charles's advice, but the very next evening, after enjoying a wonderful excursion to Kew Gardens, she was unfortunate enough to encounter Sir Jason himself. She and her grandmother were attending another gathering at the home of one of her many friends when he approached them and begged an introduction.

One of Grandmama's acquaintances hailed her shortly afterward, and she moved a short distance away, leaving Alexandra alone with the baronet. He raised his quizzing glass to his eye to study her more closely, and she flushed. Sir Jason reminded her strongly of a lizard she had once seen basking in the sun, with his hooded pale blue eyes and sandy-colored hair. His skin had a sallow tinge, and his thin lips were twisted in a grimace as he surveyed her through the eyepiece.

Disliking the insolent nature of his silent appraisal, Alexandra haughtily raised her brows. When Sir Jason eventually lowered the quizzing glass, she said in a cold voice, "I trust I meet with your approval, sir?"

Sir Jason's lids dropped even lower over his eyes. "I am unaccustomed, Miss Grantham, to a young woman of your tender years speaking to me in such a tone. I would advise you to put a guard on your tongue if you do not wish to be perceived as a forward young miss."

Alexandra frowned. She knew she ought to be cautious, but this man was entirely galling. "I object to being looked over like a piece of prime horseflesh, Sir Jason."

"I would think that you were . . . ah . . . used to such appraisals, Miss Grantham."

"I think you mistake me for a woman of a somewhat different class."

Again, he raised his quizzing glass to his eye. His lips twisted in a cruel smile, and he said softly, "Oh, I think not, Miss Grantham. From what I have heard of you, you are a young woman of—let us say—somewhat flexible morals. I have heard rumors—very interesting rumors—about the methods you employ to aid the poor. I would surmise that you are accustomed to associating with men of a certain class."

Alexandra drew in a sharp breath. "Sir! You insult me! I— I. . . . Who has been spreading such falsehoods?"

"Are they falsehoods, though? My information is from a most reliable source." Sir Jason paused in his speech to withdraw a snuffbox from the pocket of his coat. He opened the enameled *objet de luxe*, and after taking a pinch of snuff and delicately inhaling it, he looked at Alexandra again. "Have you nothing to say, Miss Grantham?"

Alexandra's fingers clenched tightly around the fan she held in her hands. Still, the agitation she labored under was not betrayed in her voice as she replied, "I shall not dignify your insinuations with a response, Sir Jason. Now, if you would excuse me."

Her mind a jumble of confusing thoughts, Alexandra made her way over to her grandmother, who stood in conversation with Lady Armstrong. Her relative took one look at Alexandra's face and brought the conversation to a swift close, shepherding her out of the crush and into an antechamber.

Fortunately, no one was in the room as her grandmother chafed Alexandra's icy hands. "What is it, my love? You look unwell. Did Sir Jason say something to distress you? Drat the man! I know he has an acid tongue, but you must not let him upset you so!"

Alexandra drew in a shuddering breath. "Oh, Grandmama, he implied that I am a—a woman of loose morals."

Her grandmother's brows snapped together. "What? My dear child, that is ridiculous. Quite ridiculous. But I don't understand—" her eyes narrowed suddenly. "Ah, it begins to make sense. In the letter I received from your aunt the other day, she mentioned that Sir Jason had stayed with the Hadleys on his way to Town. Mrs. Hadley must have put false rumors in his ear to attempt to tarnish your name."

Alexandra's forehead creased. "But why would Mrs. Hadley discuss me with Sir Jason?"

"It has been plain that Mrs. Hadley has always viewed you with a jealous eye because you outshine that plain daughter of hers. No doubt she gossips about you all the time. But to spread such rumors about you! It is wickedness beyond belief."

Alexandra chewed on her bottom lip, tasting blood. "Does

this mean I must return home in disgrace?"

Her grandmother stiffened. "Good heavens, no! I have a certain amount of consequence in polite circles, and no one would dare to snub my granddaughter with no more evidence than that man's insinuations. All the same, I shall speak to the Patronesses of Almack's and inform them of the true state of affairs. Lady Sefton and Lady Jersey will, I am certain, oblige me by championing you when they know that Hadley woman has been spreading tales. They have expressed their approval of you, you know. So do not fret, my love!"

"Very well," Alexandra whispered.

Her grandmother patted her on the arm. "Besides, Stanford has promised to launch you into fashion. In the Polite World, he has far more influence than Sir Jason Morecombe. Of that I can assure you!"

However, when Alexandra returned home later that evening, the sick feeling in her stomach would not go away. Though it was likely Sir Jason had insulted her in exactly the way she reported to her grandmother, she was concerned that, instead of referring to loose morals, he might somehow have discovered her highway activities. But how? No one except Ben and the duke knew her dangerous secret.

She drew in a shaking breath. She must remain calm and logical. There was not one shred of evidence that she was a highwayman. If there had been, the Bow Street Runners would have come knocking on her door long before now.

Besides, even if Sir Jason did hint at it to various members of the *ton*, it was doubtful anyone would give any credence to such a far-fetched tale. They were far more likely to think her guilty of some other indiscretion, something less illegal. But the problem still weighed on Alexandra's mind, and it was a very long time before she fell asleep that night.

Chapter Thirteen

Alexandra rose early the following day. Donning an old gown, she made her way out to her grandmother's walled garden. It was a beautiful space with a paved gravel path winding its way between geometric beds containing various shrubs and flowers. Potted plants and urns adorned the pathway, while rose trellises and wall climbers drew the eye up from the ground, adding a touch of enchantment.

Concealed behind a high hedge at the far end of the enclosure was a small kitchen garden, where herbs and produce were grown. Alexandra headed there now. She passed a topiary and a sundial and then disappeared behind the tall border.

Working in the kitchen garden had become the most treasured part of Alexandra's day. The gardener, Gibbs, was suspicious at first when she offered her services, but after observing her for a day or two, he left her to her own devices, remarking in a gruff voice, "Well, you appear to know what you are about, miss."

As it was still quite chilly, Gibbs made judicious use of hotbeds, bell-shaped glass covers, and pots to protect the garden produce from the cold, thereby extending their growing season. Alexandra lifted one of the cloches now and inspected a beautifully-formed cauliflower before moving on to the two hot-beds, constructed with frames of wooden planks that had been raised above the ground.

Alexandra had already prepared the first hot-bed. She had laid down a mixture of straw and horse manure in the wooden structure before adding a layer of soil, which would support the tender root systems of the seedlings once they were planted. The heat generated in the beds from the manure breaking down would sustain her grandmother's fruit and vegetable crop in the critical transition period between winter and spring when the plants needed careful nurturing. Then, after the seedlings had been started, Gibbs would transplant them into the open kitchen garden.

A three-foot layer of straw and manure was required to provide sufficient heat for the bed. The stable-boy had left a pile of horse manure nearby, but it did not look adequate for Alexandra's purposes. Picking up a wheelbarrow, she maneuvered it toward a small gate in the high wall, which led out to a cobbled courtyard. She made her way to the stables where a groom obligingly filled her barrow for her. But when he offered to take the manure back to the garden, Alexandra politely declined. Her grandmother's servants must think her an oddity to perform such lowly tasks, but she enjoyed all aspects of gardening, not just the gentler activities traditionally favored by ladies.

When Alexandra returned to the kitchen garden, she picked up a spade and began to fill the hot-bed. She was so engrossed in her work that she nearly jumped out of her skin when a deep voice came from behind her: "Miss Grantham?"

She stood stock-still for a moment before setting the shovel down and turning around. The Duke of Stanford stood at the entrance to the enclosed space. A flush of mortification spread up her cheeks as she brushed away a few strands of her hair. "Your Grace."

"I see you are engaged in your favorite occupation."

"Yes. Grandmama permitted me to work here as I am an early riser and have many hours to fill until she leaves her bedchamber. It is so dull to sit in the drawing room all morning, you see, and I have read nearly every book in Grandmama's library." She caught her breath. Why was she gabbling so?

Stanford's green eyes were alight with amusement, and her cheeks heated even more. "I am sure Grandmama will emerge soon," she added desperately. The smell of fresh horse manure assailed her nostrils. It was so pungent. And he was so very well-dressed.

"I have not come to see your grandmother, ma'am. I came to invite you to drive in with me in the Park this afternoon."

Alexandra's eyes widened. "Oh. Yes. That would be delightful, Your Grace. I will go and change my gown."

"I will return later so that we can appear during the fashionable hour. To begin the process of making you the rage."

She forced a smile. "Thank you, Sir. I shall see you later." She took a step back and then paused. "Your Grace... I think I should tell you that Sir Jason Morecombe approached me last night. He—well, he threatened me, saying that he had heard rumors about the methods I use to aid the poor."

His brows shot up. "He actually said that?"

"Yes. I have been wretched with anxiety ever since."

The duke frowned. "Perhaps he has merely heard about your visits to the poor, Miss Grantham? Did you always take a footman with you?"

Alexandra slowly shook her head. "No. No, I didn't."

"Sir Jason likes to play games, and he will use any hint of impropriety to unsettle his targets." A smile tugged at his lips. "I would not be too concerned, my dear. When one has a guilty conscience, it is easy to assume the worst."

"Yes. Yes, that must be it." A sense of relief permeated her body as she sank onto a nearby bench. She respected the duke's opinion, and it was vastly reassuring to have him mitigate her worst fears.

He studied her for a long moment. "Before you come out with me, Miss Grantham, I suggest you... ah... spend some time in front of your mirror." He gave her a glinting smile as he turned on his heel and left.

Her mirror? A frown descended on her brow. What did he mean—was she in greater disarray than she thought? She had not allowed Hobbes to arrange her hair this morning due to her eagerness to escape outside, but she was wearing an old straw bonnet, so she must appear vaguely presentable.

She gathered her tools—and her thoughts—together and swiftly returned to the house. When she entered her bedchamber, her mouth dropped open in horror as she gazed into the mahogany mirror on the wall. A clump of horse manure hung in her hair. No wonder the duke had studied her in that quizzical fashion.

She groaned. Was there no end to the humiliations she seemed doomed to suffer in his noble presence?

⸻

ROBERT CALLED ON Miss Grantham earlier than he would usually do when taking a lady driving in the Park. But he wished to engage her in private conversation before the fashionable throng descended on Rotten Row.

He exchanged observations about the Season thus far with Lady Longmore for a few pleasant minutes before Miss Grantham entered the drawing-room. She was attired in a spotless white jaconet muslin gown, edged with embroidered flowers, and a straw bonnet adorned with white roses was perched on top of her head.

He bid farewell to her ladyship before escorting Miss Grantham out of the door.

"A hint of the garden is still present in your appearance, I see," he said with a pointed glance at her bonnet.

Her gaze flew to meet his. "I ensured all other traces of it were thoroughly washed away."

He laughed as he helped her up into his curricle. "Who taught you to garden?"

"My father. He had a keen interest in all matters horticultural."

Robert took the reins from his tiger, Jimmy, who jumped up onto his perch behind them. "He must have been an excellent teacher to have encouraged you to embrace all aspects of it as you do."

"Papa did not believe in half-measures. He told me that if you wish to learn anything in a garden, you need to soil your hands."

"Your hair too, it seems?"

She caught her lip between her teeth. "That was . . . regrettable." She twisted in her seat. "How did you even know I was in the garden?"

"Your grandmother's butler informed me that you were taking a stroll outside and that he would send a footman to find you. As the morning room leads directly onto the garden, I forestalled him and went looking for you myself."

"Ah. I sense Leighton doesn't entirely approve of my gardening activities. He probably wishes I would confine myself to taking strolls outside, poor man."

Robert directed his horses out of Berkeley Square, and they drove the short distance to Hyde Park in silence. When they entered the gates, he glanced down at her again. "Are you enjoying your time in London, or are you pining for the countryside?"

She hesitated. "I am not pining precisely. London is a fascinating city, and I was fortunate enough to visit the Botanic Gardens in Kew yesterday, which has been a years-long dream. And there are so many other places I am longing to explore."

"However?"

"Yes." She released a sigh. "I cannot help but be concerned about the poor families I left behind."

"You believe they are your sole responsibility?" A quick frown descended upon his brow.

"I suppose I do."

He remained silent as he directed his vehicle around a barouche that had drawn up on the verge. When he passed it, he said, "That is a vast weight for one person to bear. I understand your urge to help the poor, Miss Grantham. What I don't understand is why you have taken it to the extreme and have risked your life to do so."

She turned her head away to collect her thoughts. "It is surely our duty to help our fellow man, Your Grace."

"I am not disputing that."

When she looked up at him again, her cheeks had whitened, and her eyes bore a haunted expression that made him catch his breath. "I—" she inhaled deeply. "Could... you please tell me about your plans to implement reforms in the district, Your Grace?"

He searched her face. What had she been about to say? He turned his attention back to his horses. "Very well. What would you like to know?"

"I understand the need for the enclosure of land as my father explained the laws to me. What I don't understand is why the large estate owners in our district have such an all-or-nothing approach. So many country people whose forebears traditionally worked the land have had to seek employment elsewhere. I just wish that there were other ways the remaining laborers could supplement their wages."

"Some land has been allocated to compensate for the loss of common rights, I believe."

"The allotted land is of poor quality, and it's barely enough space for a cottager to keep a goose, let alone a cow! It is shameful and indefensible to have stripped the poor of their independence in this manner."

He drew his curricle to a gradual halt. "Unfortunately, temporary harm to a community is sometimes necessary to effect enduring gains. A more scientific approach to farming is necessary to prevent future food shortages for the entire population of the country, which is growing at a rapid rate. Besides, a resident landlord with improving ideas can affect a great deal of good."

"While a neglectful landlord can do a great deal of harm." Her voice was low and impassioned.

He studied her averted profile. "In my meetings with the local landowners, I discussed the discontent and the need to improve wages. I think that's a start, Miss Grantham. But I believe in taking one step at a time."

"Very well."

"I fear I have disappointed you."

"No. It is just that as a duke, I hoped your influence would be greater, swifter."

Robert felt his conscience prick. Although he ensured his laborers were well paid, he had not given much thought to the loss of dignity the poor had suffered due to being forced to give up their traditional rights to graze their livestock on common land. Instead, he had viewed it as a necessary evil to accomplish a greater good. But Miss Grantham saw beyond the improving policies to the suffering of the people. Something stirred within him, but he did not care to examine it too closely. After a protracted moment, he gave his horses the office to start again. "I shall see what I can do, Miss Grantham."

"Thank you, Your Grace. That is all I ask."

Lady Jersey hailed them at that moment, and there was no time for further discussion as Robert stopped to speak to the influential patroness as well as a number of other acquaintances sure to help Miss Grantham climb the first few rungs on the ladder to social success. Reminded of the reason he had taken Miss Grantham out in the first place, he smiled wryly. Amazing the ability she had to distract him!

When he drove her home later, she spoke about inconsequential matters. But as he drew up before Longmore House and helped her to alight from the coach, she gazed up at him and said in a quiet voice, "Thank you for engaging in conversation with me on our earlier topic, Your Grace. Not many gentlemen of my acquaintance would."

He bowed and escorted her up the shallow stairs, murmuring

a farewell. After Leighton shut the door behind her, Robert climbed into his curricle and stared straight ahead. Only the restive movement of his horses alerted him to his surroundings a few minutes later, and he drove off, unsettled.

Miss Grantham was an unusual young lady.

Chapter Fourteen

The Season began in earnest the following week with the first of the Almack's subscription balls. On this most important occasion, Alexandra's grandmother told her it was vital she make a good impression. "For, no matter how beautiful you are, my love, it is so easy to get lost in the crowd of young ladies making their first appearance in London."

Madame Bouchet had created a celestial blue silk gown trimmed with silver filigree work for Alexandra to wear on her formal introduction to the beau monde. The high-waisted style of the dress suited her willowy figure, and the color of the material contrasted strikingly with her pale skin. On the night of the ball, Alexandra studied her reflection in the glass with a pensive air before turning abruptly away. How different she appeared from the girl who used to wander around the grounds of Grantham Place in the worn-out gowns she'd favored for gardening.

As Alexandra descended the stairs, she smiled as she met her grandmother's warm gaze. Upon reaching the bottom of the stairs, she impulsively embraced her. "Thank you for making this all possible, Grandmama."

"Nonsense, child. It is my pleasure," she said in a gruff voice. "Bringing you out has brought back all the excitement of your mother's first Season and has given me a renewed zest for life." She indicated to Leighton that they were ready to take their cloaks. "Now let us depart—the doors of Almack's close strictly at eleven, and nothing will induce the Patronesses to allow anyone in after that set time. Sometimes the traffic can be so snarled up that it takes an age to arrive."

Fortunately, the traffic was not as heavy as Grandmama had feared, and they arrived in good time. Alexandra gazed around in surprise, however, upon entering Almack's rather unassuming rooms. The *ton* made such a great fuss about the place that she had imagined something grander, more impressive than the somewhat plain, sparsely furnished ballroom with which she was confronted.

When she mentioned this to her grandmother, that lady shook her head. "Do not let the Patronesses hear you make any disparaging comments about these hallowed portals, my dear," she warned in a low voice. "The appearance of these rooms does not matter. It is the exclusivity of Almack's that counts."

And so saying, she turned aside to greet an old friend who had hailed her as she entered the room.

Standing dutifully at her grandmother's side as she conversed with her friend, Alexandra looked around and noticed two of her youthful admirers were present. Upon catching sight of her, these gentlemen approached and engaged her for a couple of dances.

First partnered by a shy young cavalier, Alexandra twirled down the room in a country dance a short while later, feigning an interest in his somewhat stilted attempts at conversation. Halfway through the dance, she became aware of a stir at the entrance to the ballroom, and her spine straightened when she saw the reason for the disturbance. Standing nonchalantly in conversation with Lady Jersey was the Duke of Stanford.

Alexandra had not expected to see him this evening. Jerking her gaze away, she stared fixedly in front of her. Would he approach her? She was puzzled as to why Stanford had decided to grace Almack's with his distinguished presence. Her grandmother had informed her that he rarely visited the exclusive rooms. Becoming aware that her dancing partner was speaking,

Alexandra returned her attention to him.

"I say! It is surprising to see Stanford attending an Almack's Assembly." The mystified expression disappeared from his face. "Oh, Lady Letitia is beside him. He must be escorting his sister to her first ball."

Of course the duke would escort his sister to her first Almack's Assembly! He would probably take himself off to White's within a few minutes and not seek out Alexandra at all. Not quite sure why she felt a tinge something like disappointment at the thought, Alexandra chatted with determined animation to her young swain and then smiled and laughed again with her next dancing partner before finally returning to her grandmother's side when the time for the first of the waltzes arrived.

※

ROBERT HAD IMMEDIATELY noticed Alexandra as he stepped into the well-lit ballroom. After Letitia and Amelia Beaumont greeted Lady Jersey and moved away in search of amusement, he exchanged a few pleasantries with his old friend before saying directly, "Sally, what do you think of Alexandra Grantham?"

"She seems a charming girl. Full of spirit and wit. And what a face and figure!" Her eyes narrowed. "Usually, I would predict that someone like her would become the success of the Season."

"What is there to prevent her from being exactly that?"

Lady Jersey gave a tiny shrug. "Alexandra Grantham has managed to upstage every other young lady in the short time she has been in Town. Any girl with her looks and her fortune would be bound to attract males in droves. But she has another quality— one that is not much appreciated in a woman in our world." She paused and looked steadily at Miss Grantham as she went down the line of a country dance. "That girl has intelligence, and she doesn't bother to hide the fact. That, and her spirited nature, causes her to be the antithesis of the typical, vapid young Society miss."

"And will provide all those jealous mamas with a perfect reason to discredit her," he finished smoothly.

"Precisely so." Lady Jersey nodded. "As it is, a few piqued mothers have been putting it about, ever so subtly, that it is obvious that poor Miss Grantham, brought up in the country as she was, is unaccustomed to the refined and cultured ways of the *ton*, because she has actually dared to state an opinion of her own!"

"What precisely did she say?" An amused smile tugged at his lips.

"Oh, at Lady Becksworth's rout Lord Hardman was giving an account to an enthralled audience about the flora and fauna in India. And Miss Grantham actually dared to correct him on some of his so-called facts when he was explaining which plants were used as a source of medicine. She seemed to recollect herself afterward and reverted to the usual manners of a debutante, but the damage had been done, as you can imagine. Certain ladies have begun delighting in saying that Miss Grantham is a little too forward, perhaps even a little brash, and—worst of all—bookish! All said in the kindest possible way, of course."

Lady Jersey gave Robert a look that spoke volumes. Everyone in Polite Society knew how damaging it could be for a young lady to appear to be putting herself forward in any way. And to disagree with the opinions of an educated gentleman—and in public! That was a social solecism, beyond a doubt.

Lady Jersey glanced across at Miss Grantham again before turning back to Robert, frowning slightly. "Also, Lady Longmore informed me that Sir Jason Morecombe has been spreading malicious rumors about her granddaughter, whispered in his ear, no doubt, by that dreadful Morecombe woman. I have heard from other sources, as well, that she is gossiping about Miss Grantham. They are scandalous untruths, obviously, but could do irreparable damage to Miss Grantham's reputation. And, although not all of her suitors have fallen away from her skirts, I know some of the Dowagers view her with a censorious eye although they are careful not to say anything within Lady Longmore's hearing." Lady Jersey raised her shoulders again. "Obviously, their disapproval will damage her chances of being an unqualified success."

Robert studied Miss Grantham, whose partner had just led her back to Lady Longmore's side. "I have met Alexandra Grantham, Sally, and find her to be a refreshingly different kind of girl, which is why I have decided to launch her into high fashion and effectively silence the old tabbies." He raised his quizzing glass to his eye, surveying the crowded ballroom through it. His gaze eventually came to rest on Sir Jason, who stood in conversation with Lord Sheldon at the other end of the room.

He lowered the eyepiece and returned his gaze to Lady Jersey. "The *ton* will follow my lead, I believe. But, in order to launch Miss Grantham successfully, Sally, I need a little help from you."

Lady Jersey raised her brows. "My dear Stanford. You are an acknowledged leader of the *ton*. How could I, a mere Lady Patroness of Almack's, aid you in any way?"

"You are much too modest. You know very well that only a Patroness of Almack's can give a young lady permission to dance the waltz."

"And you wish me to present you as a desirable partner to Miss Grantham, I suppose?"

"Of all your remarkable traits, Sally, the one I admire most is your astuteness. That is precisely what I wish. How ever did you realize that?"

"Wretch!" Lady Jersey laughed up at him. "Very well, Your Grace. I shall do as you wish. I have a feeling that Miss Alexandra Grantham, once successfully launched, will brighten up the London scene considerably."

"Yes, she certainly seems to possess that particular knack," he said dryly.

Miss Grantham was conversing with her grandmother when

Robert and Lady Jersey approached. After greeting Lady Longmore, the Patroness turned toward Miss Grantham. "My dear, I wish to present to you the Duke of Stanford as a most desirable partner for the upcoming waltz." She darted a roguish look up at Robert as she said these words. "This means, naturally, that you now have permission to dance the waltz here at Almack's."

Miss Grantham curtsied and thanked Lady Jersey before taking Robert's proffered arm as the first strains of the waltz sounded. Then, she stepped into his embrace and began the dance in silence.

His eyes met hers. "You enjoy waltzing, Miss Grantham?"

"I do. It is quite exhilarating. But perhaps I shouldn't admit to that."

"Why ever not?"

"Well, you must know that it is only rustics who admit to enjoyment of any kind. It is *de rigueur* to appear totally uninterested in everything."

"Ah, but in your present position, ma'am, you can set the fashion rather than just follow it."

"Indeed?" She tilted her head to one side. "Because you have, most obligingly, officially launched me into fashion by dancing with me?"

"Precisely" he smiled down at her.

Miss Grantham knit her brows together. "Odd expression that—being launched into fashion. It always makes me think of a ship about to set sail."

He laughed. "In order to be sure that you do not, shall we say, go off course, and also for Society to realize that you have my firm seal of approval, I think it would be best for me to take you for another drive in the Park tomorrow."

"I shall look forward to that with great pleasure, Your Grace."

"I had expected you to raise some sort of objection, Miss Grantham, in the face of the fact that you view me with such marked . . . what was it you said at Lady Derringer's rout? Ah, yes—indifference."

Her lips curved upwards. "But Your Grace, I could never live with myself if I passed up the opportunity of driving behind your pair of matched greys again. You must be aware they are almost as well-known as you are!"

"You disappoint me, ma'am. I had thought it was my humble self that you were so looking forward to seeing."

"Oh, and that too, of course," she said politely.

"Putting me properly in my place, Miss Grantham? Just below the horses?"

"Not at all." She smiled up at him. "How ever did you receive that impression?"

The decidedly impish twinkle in her eyes did not escape Robert's notice, and it was with an amused chuckle that he brought their dance to a halt at the edge of the ballroom as the music died away.

When he returned Miss Grantham to her grandmother's side, she smiled at him warmly. "Thank you, Duke. I hope your dance with Alexandra will put a stop to those rumors Sir Jason is spreading about. We are most grateful for your support."

He looked across the room at the baronet, who now stood alone. "I believe it should scotch the tales." He returned his attention to the older lady. "My mother wrote to me the other day to ask me to keep an eye on Miss Grantham as you expressed concern over the fact that she has no male relatives in London to protect her. Please call on me if the need arises."

Lady Longmore nodded. "Thank you, Stanford. That is most kind of you."

"I should not wish to impose on your goodwill in such a manner, Your Grace," Miss Grantham murmured.

He smiled. "Rest assured, my dear. It is no imposition at all. I am very well accustomed to taking care of my younger sisters in London."

After a few more minutes of conversation with the two ladies, Robert took his leave of them. He departed the rooms a short while later, having accomplished what he had set out to do, and sure in the knowledge that Miss Alexandra Grantham was about to become the most sought-after young lady in London.

CHAPTER FIFTEEN

THE NEWS THAT the Duke of Stanford had set his firm seal of approval on Alexandra appeared to spread like wildfire throughout the *ton*. Before the ball at Almack's, her most attentive suitors had been indigent younger sons on the lookout for a well-dowered bride. Now, all sorts of gentlemen flocked to pay court to her, vying amongst one another for her favor. Invitations to various routs, balls, and musical evenings began to roll into Longmore House in ever-increasing numbers. She had become, as her grandmother phrased it later that week, "an official success."

With the advent of this increased popularity, Alexandra found herself the object of the attentions of gentlemen of a distinctly different caliber. Perhaps noting the Duke of Stanford's interest in her, these older men of the town followed his lead and paid court to her. Their company was far more stimulating than that of her previous swains. At the same time, she recognized them for what they were—rakish Corinthians, wise in the world's ways, and *not* safe company for an inexperienced girl fresh from the country.

As her resolve to remain unencumbered had not wavered, she had no intention of accepting a proposal from any of them, so she determined not to give any the slightest bit of encouragement and kept all at arm's length. However, one man, a Mr. Thomas Kendle, perhaps too credulous of the Morecombes' salacious rumors, clearly had the misconception that she would willingly indulge in the kind of loose behavior only practiced by members of the daringly fast set. His behavior became increasingly familiar, and Alexandra began to suspect that he held very little claim to the title of "gentleman."

He pursued her with the tenacity of a terrier, frequently appearing at her side at balls and routs to press his unwelcome suit on her to the extent that Alexandra began to dread attending parties in the evening. Instead of being deflated by her cool manner toward him, he seemed to view it as marked encouragement of his attentions, and Alexandra began to feel like a hunted animal, cornered by a ruthless predator.

A fortnight after he had first been introduced to her, he approached her as she looked for her grandmother at a musical evening hosted by Lady Airington. Under the cover of music and with an unctuous smile he said, "I have heard that, unlike other prudish young ladies, you are quite open to dalliance, Miss Grantham." He lowered his voice further. "I wanted to advise you that I would be happy to oblige you, my sweet."

The breath caught in Alexandra's chest, and she took a hasty step back. "You insult me, sir. Pray do not speak to me ever again. I have no desire to further my acquaintance with you."

"Oh, oh, oh!" he said, not one whit abashed. "I do love the chase."

Although Alexandra was usually at her grandmother's side when she wasn't dancing, she could not always be with her chaperone, and the odious man continued to hound her at every opportunity.

Later that same week at Lady Bradshaw's soirée, Alexandra was delighted to see Emily Hadley in attendance and ignored all the young men in favor of speaking with her friend. Emily had been present at very few of the Season's social events thus far, and Alexandra hoped to persuade Emily to join her and Lady Letitia in an informal outing to the Green Park one morning to watch the guards parading on the Queen's Walk. However,

Emily told her in a quiet aside that she spent a large portion of each day at home, as her stepmother gave her very little freedom, and it seemed unlikely Mrs. Hadley would give her permission to go.

Alexandra was about to question Emily further when she spotted Mr. Kendle threading his way toward her. Panic-stricken, she mumbled an excuse to her friends and began scanning the room for her grandmother, hoping she would agree to leave the party.

"Is anything the matter, Alex?" Emily asked in her soft voice.

Not wishing to burden her friend with her troubles, Alexandra shook her head as she continued to search for her chaperone.

"Are you certain?" Letitia said. "You've gone quite pale, you know."

Alexandra looked from one concerned face to the other and pressed her lips together. "It's Mr. Kendle. He's quite awful, and he won't leave me alone."

"I met him the other day." Emily gave a delicate shudder. "Stepmama wants me to consider his suit, but I don't like him at all."

"Nor I. He makes my skin crawl." Alexandra eventually caught sight of her grandmother across the room, but her relief was short-lived when she noticed her in conversation with Lady Jersey. She had no intention of laying herself open to the prying questions of that sharp-eyed lady should she descend breathlessly upon them, asking Lady Longmore to leave.

Alexandra chewed on her bottom lip as she looked around the room again. Her heart pounded as her gaze alighted on a pair of French doors, partially hidden by heavy rose-pink silk curtains. She twisted her head back to look at her friends. "Letitia, do you think you could quickly persuade your cousin Amelia to chaperone us outside? And Emily, could you tell Grandmama that I'm looking for her and then join us on the balcony?" She failed to keep the anxiety out of her voice. "If we are all outside together for a breath of fresh air, he will hopefully give up looking for me."

At Letitia's quick nod, Alexandra hastened toward the doors and stepped outside to await her friends. The cool night air came as a welcome respite from the closeness of the room, and she drew in a deep breath to calm herself after her narrow escape.

A frown marred her brow when she considered her lecherous suitor. She must think of some way to discourage him from pursuing her. Dashing out onto conveniently situated balconies with her friends was surely not the ideal solution.

Hearing a sound behind her, Alexandra spun around, relieved. But instead of Emily and Letitia coming through the doors, Mr. Kendle appeared, closing them behind him. Her stomach lurched as she stared at him. Perhaps she could try to run past him and return to safety? No, he was completely blocking the way.

She shrank back as he sauntered over and snatched her hands up in his. She tried to pull them away, but his grip only tightened. Finally, glaring up at him, she said as forcefully as she could muster, "Kindly unhand me, sir!"

He only leered at her. "I see, my clever Miss Grantham, that you were of the same mind as I. A romantic assignation in the moonlight—how utterly delightful."

Before she could utter another word of protest, he drew her closer. Alexandra froze for a moment, then she began to struggle, but the man who held her so insolently was far stronger than she. Tears of rage burned her eyes as she renewed her efforts to free herself from her tormentor. She was about to kick him sharply in the shins when a cold voice ordered: "Unhand Miss Grantham at once!"

Mr. Kendle slackened his grip on Alexandra's arms, and she jerked away from him, hastening to Stanford's side, who seemed to have appeared out of nowhere. She had never been more relieved in her life.

The duke glanced down at her, a frown in his eyes. "Did he hurt you, my dear?"

When she shook her head, he turned back to Mr. Kendle. "I

shall not call you out for this night's work as I wish no blemish to mar Miss Grantham's reputation. But I advise you to keep your distance from her in the future, or you will live to regret the consequences. You understand my meaning?" The threat in his voice was unmistakable.

Mr. Kendle swallowed convulsively and nodded. Then, sketching a bow in Alexandra's direction, he hastily apologized before scurrying back inside.

"I intercepted my sister and Miss Hadley on their way out to you. An acquaintance had waylaid them, but Letty whispered in my ear that you'd left the room to escape Kendle. How long has he been plaguing you?"

Alexandra licked her dry lips. "I met him about two weeks ago, and although I made my lack of interest in him clear, he has refused to accept it. When I saw him this evening, all I could think about was how to escape him."

The duke frowned. "Why did you not inform me of his behavior? A word in my ear and I would have made certain he never bothered you again."

Alexandra looked at him in surprise. "But, Your Grace, I am not a member of your family, and I am therefore in no way under your protection. Although you have condescended to bring me into fashion, I cannot make such claims upon you."

He studied her for a long moment. "As I told your grandmother when we were all together at Almack's, you are free to call upon me should you need assistance of any kind while you are in Town. Please do so in future."

Alexandra inclined her head. "I will remember that. Thank you."

He offered her his arm. "I shall escort you back to your grandmother now."

She placed her hand on his arm. "I am much obliged to you—for everything."

His lips twisted into a wry smile. "I know you are an uncommonly independent young lady, Miss Grantham, but surely you must realize that it shows strength, not weakness, to admit you need a helping hand sometimes?"

She swallowed. "I am beginning to realize that, Your Grace." And, as she looked up into his handsome face, she knew it would be all too easy to grow accustomed to accepting this man's help. His solid dependability was so reassuring, and when she was with him, she felt no harm could come to her.

However, becoming too dependent on the Duke of Stanford would not do. Accepting an occasional helping hand from him was all very well, but that noble hand was sought in matrimony by countless young ladies across the kingdom. As she was not one of them, it would be foolish to come to rely on his support. She needed to be careful not to veer over that line of familiarity with the duke, no matter how tempting it might be at times to venture over it.

Chapter Sixteen

Once Thomas Kendle was no longer bothering her, Alexandra, with a great weight lifted from her shoulders, was able to begin enjoying her time in London again. She saw a great deal of Sir Charles Fotherby over the next few weeks. He escorted his godmother and Alexandra to various balls and parties and often called at Longmore House to invite Alexandra to drive in his curricle.

Once her mare, Starlight, was finally brought to London, Alexandra and Sir Charles rode together daily in the Park. They tended to favor the early mornings for their equestrian excursions rather than the fashionable hour of the Grand Strut because there were fewer people in Hyde Park, and they could give the horses their heads.

Sir Charles was a delightful companion. Alexandra quickly came to view him in a brotherly light, and their teasing friendship and occasional disagreements emphasized for her the fraternal nature of their relationship.

Lady Letitia Beaumont sometimes accompanied Alexandra and Sir Charles on these expeditions. She and Alexandra had struck up a friendship since the evening of Lady Derringer's evening party when Alexandra had rescued her from incurring the duke's wrath. As Alexandra had not attended one of England's select ladies' seminaries in her schoolgirl years, she had few female friends of her age in London. And, as she could not see as much of Emily as she wished, Alexandra was delighted to have found another friend with whom she could share confidences.

Letitia was also acquainted with Sir Charles. He was a lifelong friend of her brother, Lord Stephen Beaumont, and had frequently visited Stanford Court during his Harrow and Cambridge days. Letitia treated the baronet with a casual familiarity that her strict chaperone abhorred, and she refused to pay any attention to her cousin's lectures on the correct manners a young lady should employ when speaking to a gentleman since, as she informed Alexandra, she had known Sir Charles since she was in the nursery. "I see no reason why I should suddenly stand on ceremony with him, just because I am in London for the Season," she declared.

Sir Charles was an affable escort, but Alexandra noticed that he kept a keen eye on Letitia when they rode together in the Park. The younger girl was a bruising rider, and she had no fear at all when she was in the saddle. The baronet shook his head dolefully when Letitia galloped back to them one morning. "For such a dainty pair of ladies, you are both remarkably brave on the back of a horse. I believe I shall be growing my first grey hairs before long."

Her friend rolled her eyes. "Oh pah, Charles! When did you become so stuffy? This is the only freedom a young lady is allowed in London. I intend to make the most of it."

But then a few mornings passed in which Letitia did not join them. Alexandra was beginning to wonder if all was well, when Letitia called at Longmore House. After taking one look at her friend's stormy face, Alexandra insisted she sit down and tell her what had happened at once.

Letitia sank onto the sofa and sniffed. "Oh, Alexandra, I am so angry I could cry! Charles has been the veriest beast! He—oh!" Letitia stopped abruptly and scowled at the absent Sir Charles.

Alexandra, who was by now used to Letitia's tempestuous mode of speech, said sympathetically, "What has he done to upset you?"

"What has he done?" she wailed. "What has he done? I'll tell you what he's done! The horrid, reprehensible, despicable beast!" Letitia sat bolt upright in her chair. "He has taken away my freedom! The only reason that I am able to visit you today is that you live across the Square from us, and my maid is seated in the hall, guarding me with her life."

"What happened? It sounds very serious."

"It is! It is quite dreadful." She leaned back against her chair and stared straight ahead before focusing her gaze again on Alexandra. "Yesterday morning, I informed Cousin Amelia that I had arranged to go on a shopping expedition with you. She believed me, of course, because we are so often together. But instead I made arrangements to meet the ... the gentleman you saw me with at Lady Derringer's party—Vernon Winters—in the Green Park. I had not seen him in weeks, and—Oh, Alex! I have missed him so! We met in a secluded area of the park, and I thought we would be perfectly safe from discovery when Charles came into view. Vernon and I hid behind a few bushes, and I thought Charles hadn't seen us.

"However, this morning he called and, in the most odiously highhanded manner you can imagine, informed me he was taking me for a drive to Richmond Park. Cousin Amelia, as you can imagine, was delighted. She deems Charles to be a most eligible catch—although I cannot begin to think why! Charles lectured me in the most horrid manner all the way there and informed me that it was beyond the bounds of propriety for me to meet a gentleman clandestinely. He then told me the most wicked lies about Vernon. He said he was a gazetted fortune hunter and that I was a fool to imagine myself in love with him."

Letitia paused for breath, her green eyes sparkling militantly. With a grim little smile, she continued, "I informed Charles that not every gentleman I have met in London treats me as though I were a child. I told him that he was a dead bore and that there was nothing wrong with me falling in love with a perfectly respectable gentleman. I also said," Letitia carried on, warming further to her theme, "that he was too dull to know the meaning of the word 'love' and that he wouldn't know love if it hit him on the head! He then told me that I was a foolish child. A foolish child, Alexandra!"

"Perhaps it was only out of concern for you that he took you to task, Letty," Alexandra suggested. "I have noticed Sir Charles appears to be very fond of you."

"Fond of me! Fond of me?" Letitia's voice rose even higher in indignation. "You have not heard the worst of it yet. Charles actually had the audacity to inform Cousin Amelia and Robert about my meeting with Vernon. He did so after we returned home this afternoon, and Cousin Amelia invited him to partake of luncheon with us." Letitia's brows snapped together in a frown. "Cousin Amelia lectured me endlessly on the impropriety of my behavior. And Robert! Robert informed me that if I continued to 'behave foolishly,' he would send me home forthwith to Stanford Court, and I would only be able to come back to London next year. Next year! Why next year I'll be an old maid. On the shelf. A veritable spinster!"

Alexandra carefully refrained from pointing out to Letitia that, according to her calculations, she herself, being a year older than her friend, was already "a veritable spinster." Instead, she said in a calm voice, "I agree, Letty, that it was unsporting of Sir Charles to reveal your rendezvous with Mr. Winters. But is there any chance that Sir Charles may be correct in assuming he is courting you only for your fortune's sake? In the brief time I have known him, I have found Sir Charles to have an uncommonly level head on his shoulders."

"Oh, Alex! You're as bad as they are," Letitia said crossly. "Just because a man is *poor* does not necessarily mean that he is a fortune hunter. Vernon has told me all about his worthy ambitions to increase his fortune. He has dealings in the City or some such thing. It's very complicated, but he's explained it perfectly well. But even if Vernon never becomes any wealthier, I shall always love him."

"My apologies, Letty. I am sure Mr. Winters is everything a gentleman should be."

"Oh, he is, he is." Letitia's voice was earnest. "Vernon is considerate, kind, handsome—in every way a perfect suitor." She sniffed and, withdrawing a scrap of lace that passed for a handkerchief from her reticule, blew her pretty nose. "But now, Alexandra, I am to be cut off from my One True Love! I am cast in the role of Juliet, and my Romeo is cruelly separated from me. I shall probably sink into a decline and die of a broken heart." Letitia paused to admire this heart-rending speech. The picture she had painted of herself as a tragic Shakespearean heroine was ruined, however, when she continued with a smug little smile, "That should teach them! Robert, Charles, and Cousin Amelia will be extremely sorry when they attend me on my deathbed and realize that my death is on their consciences."

Alexandra valiantly controlled her twitching lip. "I am sure they will be overcome with remorse when they realize they have driven you to an early grave."

"You are not making light of my predicament, are you, Alexandra?" Letitia eyed her suspiciously.

"Of course not, Letty. If I can aid you in any way, I shall."

She smiled tremulously. "Thank you, Alex. I knew I could rely on you. Best of all my friends!"

After Letitia left, Alexandra wondered whether she ought to say a few words in her friend's defense to Stanford when he came to take her driving in Hyde Park this afternoon. She had not seen him in a while as he had paid a flying visit to one of his estates the week before. But he was back in London now and had sent a message via her grandmother that he wished to see her this afternoon. Although she hated to admit it to herself, Alexandra could not prevent a flutter of excitement in her stomach at the prospect of seeing him again.

As she sat beside Stanford in his curricle later that day, Alexandra stole a glance up at his profile. The duke's mouth was set in an uncompromisingly stern line, and he did not appear to be in the best of humors. He would be unlikely to welcome any interference on her part. And, by stirring up coals, she could, perhaps, land Letitia in even deeper trouble.

When they passed through the gates of Hyde Park, he spoke abruptly: "Miss Grantham, am I correct in assuming that you have eaten your words about the undesirability of the wedded state and that you intend to marry soon?"

Alexandra choked on her surprise. "I am not sure I understand you, Your Grace."

His lip curled. "Don't you? Sir Charles Fotherby appears to have been courting you in earnest, and you, it seems, are not averse to his attentions. The members of the *ton* have begun to link your name and Fotherby's together." He frowned. "I spoke with your grandmother before you came downstairs, and she informed me that she entertains great hopes that you and Sir Charles will become betrothed before the end of the Season."

"Grandmama said that?" Alexandra's voice rose in dismay.

"She did. Now, will you answer my question, Miss Grantham? Are the banns soon to be read?"

Unsettled by the unexpected course their conversation had taken, Alexandra did not feel forthcoming. She saw no reason why she should enlighten the duke about her relationship with Sir Charles and said vaguely, "He hasn't asked me to marry him."

"And when he does?"

"I shall make sure that you are the first to know," she responded lightly.

The duke's eyes narrowed. "I would advise you, Miss Grantham, *not* to play games with me."

"Play games with you, Your Grace?" She opened her eyes wide. "What ever do you mean?"

"You know precisely what I mean. I have asked you a direct question, and I expect a direct answer. Do you intend to marry Sir Charles?"

Alexandra eyed him, taken aback at his interest in this matter.

She wanted very much to put him in his place for subjecting her to such an inquisition. On the other hand, his startling revelation that the *ton* believed nuptials to be in the air for her and Sir Charles had come as something of a shock. It was difficult to believe her grandmother was of the same mind as the rest of *ton* and, without even discussing the matter with Alexandra, had informed the Duke of Stanford of her hopes for a betrothal.

Torn between denying the rumor and giving Stanford the setdown he undoubtedly deserved, Alexandra decided, somewhat reluctantly, to do the former. Speculation about a possible attachment between herself and Sir Charles was embarrassing, not only to herself but also to her good friend.

Therefore, in a rather tart voice, she replied, "Well, if you must know, Your Grace, I do not intend to marry Sir Charles. I have every intention, as I have told you before, of remaining unmarried. I value my independence far too much to relinquish it willingly." After a few moments, she continued in a different, more solemn tone, "I had no idea that the *ton* had begun to link my name with Sir Charles'. He has become a very good friend and is Grandmama's godson, but I see him purely in the light of a brother. I hope he will not be embarrassed by this speculation."

"I doubt he will feel any mortification at all," the duke said urbanely. "No man is embarrassed when his name is linked to that of a beautiful young woman's."

"Oh!" Alexandra was at a loss for words.

"I would advise, if you wish for this speculation to cease, not to be seen so much in Sir Charles's company."

She frowned. "I suppose I shall be obliged to stop riding with him in Hyde Park every morning, then." She released a despondent breath. "I do so enjoy the early morning exercise, and I cannot think of anyone else who would be willing to accompany me. Sometimes Letty does, but so often she sleeps in late. And it is not nearly as enjoyable riding when one has only a groom for company. Besides," Alexandra wrinkled her forehead, "I am not sure whether Grandmama would allow me to go out with only

William for an escort. I think she is concerned I may do something dreadfully improper, like riding down St James's Street and peering in at the windows of all the gentlemen's clubs."

The duke laughed as he maneuvered the curricle between a landaulet drawn up on the verge of the carriageway and a barouche passing on the other side. "Why does that not seem entirely implausible to me?" His eyes were alight with amusement as he glanced down at her before allowing his horses to pick up some speed again as they left the Park. "I am perfectly willing to accompany you on your morning rides," he said after a moment.

"But Your Grace, won't the *ton* then begin to link our names together?"

His smile was enigmatic. "You must be aware that it will do your image a world of good if Society believes you to have captured my attention. Remember, my continued endorsement is necessary for your social success. Sir Jason Morecombe's malicious rumors have been ignored because you have my seal of approval. But if the *haut monde* believes my interest in you has waned, they will, in all probability, listen to Morecombe's sayings—they are, after all, added grist to the rumor mill. It is necessary, therefore, for you to be seen as often as possible in my company."

"You won't mind being the subject of idle speculation?" Her tone was doubtful.

He smiled again. "As I said before, Miss Grantham—no man is embarrassed when his name is linked to that of a beautiful young woman's."

Alexandra blushed and decided to change the subject. She found it far easier to spar with Stanford than accept his compliments. She began rattling on about what a crush Lady Jersey's ball had been the previous evening. When her disjointed monologue eventually came to an end, the duke introduced another subject of a general, non-inflammatory nature before delivering her safely back to Longmore House.

After she bid him a formal goodbye, Alexandra hastened upstairs to her grandmother's bedchamber. The older lady enjoyed a nap in the afternoons, and Alexandra found her there now, reclining on a daybed. After apologizing for disturbing her in her hour of rest, she said, "Grandmama, the Duke of Stanford has just informed me that you entertain hopes that I will become betrothed to Sir Charles before the end of the Season. I cannot understand why you said such a thing to him. His Grace quizzed me about it when I went driving with him."

Her grandparent yawned sleepily. "Did he, my dear? That is a charming bonnet you are wearing, Alexandra." She regarded Alexandra admiringly. "Even though the price we paid for it was extortionate, I am of the considered opinion that it was well worth the expenditure. Blue suits your coloring. And that afternoon dress you are wearing is quite lovely. Even though I say it myself, my taste in clothes is never far off. You present a very pretty picture."

"Thank you." Alexandra tried to hide her impatience at her grandmother's obvious avoidance of the subject. "Are you hopeful of seeing me married to Sir Charles, Grandmama? Because I am sorry to inform you that I do not regard him as a suitor. He is merely a very good friend."

She settled herself more comfortably on the daybed. "Well then, there is nothing more to be said on the matter, is there?" Then, yawning again, she said, "Would you be so kind as to pass me that book on my bedside table? It is such an improving volume that it is sure to make me fall asleep. When we visit Hookham's next, I wish to borrow *Pride and Prejudice*. It is reputed to be a very witty piece of work. Thank you, my love." She smiled as Alexandra handed her the book.

Alexandra was taken aback by her grandmother's disinclination to engage on the topic but decided not to press her and risk an argument. Perhaps she had allowed it to grow too large in her own head.

"I received a letter from John this morning, Grandmama. He

mentions that he obtained a copy of *Pride and Prejudice* from a bookshop in Bath and that he enjoyed it very much. I must read it after you."

"Yes, of course. And how is my grandson?"

"John says he is in excellent health and that he plans to visit us later in the Season. He hasn't given me a date yet, though." She frowned. "He must be quite lonely at Grantham Place, although he never complains. But he seems in good spirits in his letters. He says that Stanford has sent an army of workers to improve the Durbridge estate."

"A relief to you, no doubt."

"Yes. So many of my food baskets were distributed to the duke's tenants. It is quite reassuring to know they are now being taken care of. A weight off my mind."

"Your aunt wrote to me this morning, and she is in good spirits as well, which I was pleased to hear." She opened her book. "Now you run along and rest awhile in your bedchamber. We have a busy evening ahead of us."

Alexandra's brow furrowed as she withdrew from her grandmother's bedchamber. She was bewildered by her unusual behavior. But it would be futile to ask her to elaborate on the mystifying nature of her remark to the Duke of Stanford. Because although Grandmama liked to declare that Alexandra was far too stubborn for her own good, this characteristic was just as evident in her nature as in her granddaughter's. And Alexandra knew of old that once she made up her mind about something, she rarely, if ever, departed from the stance she had taken up.

CHAPTER SEVENTEEN

LATER THAT DAY, at a musical evening given by Lady Selby, Alexandra informed Sir Charles about the gossip linking their names together.

"But, Miss Grantham," he said with a quick frown. "Is the gossip so rampant that we must not be seen together at all?"

Alexandra inclined her head. "Unfortunately, yes. The Duke of Stanford told me this afternoon that many people expect a betrothal before the end of the Season." Alexandra refrained from mentioning that his own godmother had been one of their number until recently. She released a sigh. "I am sorry to say that our morning rides will need to cease. It is most vexing, but in order to put an end to such comment, it is necessary." Her lips curved into a wry smile. "The duke has offered to accompany me instead. It is ironic, is it not, that when you accompanied me on my rides, the *ton* immediately assumed greater intentions. When the Duke of Stanford does so, all they will say is that I am his latest flirtation!"

Sir Charles searched her face. "Are you aware . . . that is, will Lady Letitia still accompany you on your rides on occasion?"

"I don't see why not. Although her brother exasperates her sometimes, she is very fond of him. She is sure to join us in the Park some mornings."

He smiled. "Well then, Miss Grantham, the tongues of the

gossip mongers cannot wag if I meet you there—quite by chance, of course—some mornings as well. A foursome, I suspect, will give rise to less talk than a party consisting of only three riders." He laughed suddenly. "Either that or gossip will arise linking Letty and me together!"

Alexandra shook her head. "In this world, indulging in speculation about other people's lives seems more natural to some people than breathing. I should not be surprised if such gossip did arise, Sir Charles."

"I wonder what Letty would say?" His voice was thoughtful.

"She would believe such rumors groundless, as I am sure they would be."

"Yes, indeed." He frowned a little. Recollecting himself, he smiled at Alexandra. "Well, may I say that I shall miss our morning expeditions together? You are a young woman of remarkable sense, you know. Not many ladies of my acquaintance are as well educated as you are."

Alexandra put a finger to her lips. "You must promise not to let it become known that I am a bluestocking. My continued social success rests entirely in your hands."

He grinned. "Never fear, Miss Grantham. Your secret is safe with me."

Alexandra curtseyed. "Thank you, kind sir. I am most obliged to you!"

Catching sight of Letitia across the room, Alexandra bade Sir Charles a cordial goodbye before making her way over to where her friend sat.

"Alexandra! Pray sit down. Cousin Amelia has just this moment gone to speak to your grandmother, so we can enjoy a comfortable coze together before she returns."

Alexandra lowered herself onto the chair beside her. "How are you, Letty? Are you in better spirits than when I saw you last?"

She shrugged pettishly. "I am still angry with Charles. He had no right to take me to task as he did. But let us speak of more pleasant subjects. That is a lovely evening dress you are wearing. Is it new?"

Alexandra glanced down at her person. She wore a white crepe tunic, trimmed with lace and fastened in front with a wreath of yellow roses, over a white satin slip. "Yes. Madame Bouchet made it up for me."

"Cousin Amelia thinks Madame Bouchet is the best modiste in town. I am inclined to agree with her. Certainly, you look very well in her creations. I think—" Letitia broke off and scowled terribly at something over Alexandra's shoulder.

"What is the matter?"

"*She* is back in Town! I might have guessed that she would return and try and get her clutches into Robert! She is the vilest, most contemptible, grasping creature alive."

"Who is, Letty?"

Letitia continued to frown. "Lavinia Furlough! Her father is the Earl of Cadden. I like the earl and his wife, but Lavinia is quite awful."

Responding to Alexandra's inquiring look, she explained in scandalized tones, "At one time, it was clear for all to see that Lavinia hoped to marry Robert. I was still in the schoolroom, but my elder sister, Serena, told me how she made a positive spectacle of herself trying to entrap him. When she realized Robert had no intention of marrying her, she accepted an offer from the Marquess of Ballington, an elderly man with an enormous fortune. Well, he died a year or so ago, and when Mama and I visited Lavinia at her parents' home to offer her our condolences, she showed no signs of unhappiness. She merely said that her husband had been very old and that it was better that he had died a sudden death instead of lingering on, being a nuisance to everybody. She spoke thus of her own husband, Alex!"

"How very callous!"

"Yes. She is a revolting female. So condescending and full of all manner of airs and graces. Oh no!" Her face was a picture of dismay. "She is making her way over here." She looked frantically about her. "Where can I hide? Quickly! I have no desire to exchange meaningless civilities with that woman."

But it was too late. A moment later, Lady Ballington was upon them.

"Letitia, how lovely it is to see you again. You *have* grown up since I last saw you!"

Letitia raised her nose in the air, becoming suddenly every inch a duke's daughter. "Lady Ballington." She nodded coolly. "I hope that you are well. May I present my good friend, Alexandra Grantham, to you? Alexandra, Lady Ballington."

Alexandra greeted the woman politely. The marchioness appeared to be in her middle twenties. Taller than average, she was also very slender, with an erect carriage. She smiled now at Alexandra. "Miss Grantham. I have heard so much about you. You are the child that Stanford launched into fashion, are you not?"

Alexandra stiffened. "I would not describe myself as a 'child,' precisely, Lady Ballington. I am nineteen years old."

Lady Ballington laughed. "As I said, a child and far too young to be playing games with the Duke of Stanford! My advice to you, my dear, is to guard your heart against him. He is far too charming for his own good." She said these last words lightly, but Alexandra detected a note of bitterness in the cool voice.

"I am perfectly able to take care of myself, thank you. I may be young, but I am in no way stupid."

"Well, I certainly hope that is the case. The hearts that His Grace has broken in the past do not bear counting." Her eyes glittered as she sat beside Letitia in an upright chair. "Now, Letty, pray tell me how you are enjoying your first Season. Is everything as you expected it to be?"

Alexandra thoughtfully regarded Lady Ballington as Letitia answered the older woman's question. The marchioness awakened no warm feelings in her breast. She seemed both objectionable and insincere, and her condescending manner was intolerable.

Alexandra spotted her grandmother waving at her across the room and gratefully seized on this as an excuse for her and Letitia to leave. Lady Ballington gave her a nod and a thin smile as she walked away. When Alexandra looked back over her shoulder a short while later, Sir Jason Morecombe had engaged the marchioness in conversation. Alexandra's heart sank to her slippers as they both glanced at her for a long, unnerving moment before falling back into intimate conversation. Hopefully, the baronet wasn't spewing poison into her ear. A shiver ran down her spine.

London suddenly felt like a rather dangerous place.

※※※

True to his word, the duke started accompanying Alexandra on her daily rides. She had been a trifle wary of his escort when he arrived promptly the morning after Lady Selby's concert, but as soon as James, the footman, scratched on her door and informed her he had called, she pulled on her gloves and made her way downstairs.

She wore one of the new riding habits her grandmother had ordered for her upon her arrival in Town. It was a dark indigo blue, and her eyes widened a little as she caught a glimpse of herself in the mirror on the landing as she walked by. This habit was a far cry from the ones she had been accustomed to wearing at home. A hat adorned with gold tassels was perched on top of her head and black half-boots, laced and fringed with gold, completed the elegant ensemble. She suddenly felt like a stranger, unknown to herself.

"You look very charming, Miss Grantham," Stanford murmured when she reached the bottom of the stairs. She smiled her thanks as she placed her hand on his arm and allowed him to escort her outside.

At first, she feared that, unlike Sir Charles, he might frown on her practice of giving Starlight her head on Rotten Row when no other riders were in sight. However, Stanford proved to be an excellent riding companion, as he made no attempt to curb her, and it was not many mornings before Alexandra began to look forward to their excursions.

They often encountered Sir Charles, who favored solitary morning exercise in the Park to shake the fidgets out of his horse's legs. When Letitia accompanied her brother and Alexandra, Sir Charles invariably joined their party. At first, Letitia treated the baronet with distinct coolness, the memory of his perfidy fresh in her mind. But she was not one for long grudges and, before long, she and Sir Charles were on easy terms again, and their foursome was one of perfect amity.

One morning, early in this new arrangement, Sir Charles and Letitia engaged in debating the merits of Sir Charles's latest equestrian acquisition. "Your mount lacks constitution, Charles," she declared. "It is merely a showy animal. And I thought you to be a good judge of horseflesh!"

Sir Charles grinned. "Letty, once you have gained membership to the Four Horse Club, as I have, then I shall listen to your criticisms. Not before!"

Letitia gasped in indignation. "Charles! How unfair. You know perfectly well that only gentlemen are allowed to be members of your silly club."

"It is not silly, and our members are generally reputed to be excellent judges of horseflesh. So, no more impertinence from you, Letty. I shan't countenance it."

Letitia merely laughed before making a light rejoinder and cantering off, leaving Sir Charles to catch up with her.

The duke regarded their swiftly disappearing backs with an arrested expression in his eyes. A short while later, he slowed his mount to a walk and indicated to Alexandra that he wished to speak to her. "Miss Grantham, you are Letty's friend. Has she spoken to you about Sir Charles?"

Seeing which way the wind was blowing, Alexandra replied slowly, "I believe Letty views Sir Charles as a brother, Your Grace. You are sadly mistaken if you believe her to have developed a *tendre* for him."

"That is a pity, then. Charles would make my feckless young sister an excellent husband."

Alexandra kept silent. The duke must believe Letitia to have recovered from her attachment to Vernon Winters, and she had no intention of enlightening him to the contrary. Letitia had spoken to her in confidence about her forbidden love, and Alexandra would never betray her trust. She couldn't help agreeing with His Grace, though, that it was a pity Letitia did not favor Sir Charles's suit. It had become clear to her, recently, in which direction Sir Charles's affections lay. How sad for him that Letitia did not return his love.

Alexandra frowned as she stared between her horse's ears. The game of love was so very complicated. Like the duke, she was persuaded that Sir Charles would make Letitia a wonderful husband. However, the heart was fickle, and one could not love to order.

Alexandra glanced up to see Lady Ballington and Sir Jason Morecombe approaching them on horseback. She suppressed a sigh—her two least favorite people in London. Lady Ballington wasted no time bringing her horse up beside Stanford's stallion. After greeting Alexandra coolly, she engaged the duke exclusively in conversation, leaving Alexandra to ride beside Sir Jason. She kept silent, the memory of her most recent encounter with him fresh in her mind.

Sir Jason subjected Alexandra to a leisurely appraisal before saying in a low voice, "What a cozy picture you and Stanford present, riding together in the Park every morning. I do hope that you haven't set your heart on marrying him, Miss Grantham. Lady Ballington, a more mature woman, is far more to His Grace's taste than a schoolroom miss such as yourself and has known him all her life."

"Indeed?" Alexandra's voice was cold.

"Yes. And she is determined to have him."

She straightened her back. "Well, I wish her good luck in her endeavors. I am surprised that you even mention Lady Ballington's wishes. As far as I can see, they have nothing to do with me."

"Come, come, Miss Grantham." His laugh was scornful. "You are laying it on much too rare and thick. I wasn't born yesterday, and I am of the decided opinion that Lady Ballington's desires have everything to do with you."

"My previous comment, Sir Jason, was meant as a polite rebuff. I have no intention of discussing my private affairs with a perfect, or should I say—imperfect—stranger!"

"Careful, Miss Grantham. Do not make an enemy of me."

"Make an enemy of you?" She swallowed hard. "As far as I am aware, you already are my enemy."

The baronet's lip curled. "I would advise you not to try your hand at cards. You lack the necessary finesse to outwit your partner. Do you always make it a practice to lay your cards on the table in such a fashion?"

"I believe in honest dealing if that is what you mean."

"A rather foolhardy practice when you are dealing with an opponent like myself who does not believe in such a, er . . . noble practice."

At that moment, Lady Ballington turned to Sir Jason and stated her desire to ride on, sparing Alexandra the necessity of replying to him. Instead, she bade Sir Jason a formal goodbye before riding on in silence beside Stanford.

She had never before encountered a man such as Sir Jason. His clear animosity toward her left her feeling vulnerable and exposed. If he had the opportunity to harm her in any way in the future, no doubt he would. And unfortunately, she lacked the necessary armor to ward off his poisonous arrows. She hoped he would soon tire of the game of baiting her, though, and leave her alone.

The duke spoke quietly, "Did Morecombe say anything to upset you, my dear? You appear a trifle out of sorts."

She forced a smile to her lips. "Oh, he spoke to me in his usual barbed fashion, all insinuations and insults. But let us speak of something more interesting. I am looking forward to Letty's coming-out ball next week. She is very excited about it."

"You do not need to inform me of that fact," he said dryly. "All I have heard from my sister over the last few days is talk of her upcoming ball. She speaks about it morning, noon, and night."

Alexandra smiled. "Then I shall not add to your agony by discussing it with you now."

She knew from experience that most men disliked talking about balls and gowns, and she would not have brought up the subject of Letitia's ball now had she not been looking for a quick way to change the subject. When she had attempted to speak to her brother about matters of purely feminine interest in the past, his eyes assumed a peculiarly glazed look, and he always turned the subject. She was, therefore, very familiar with the signs exhibited by an indifferent male. Letitia had apparently not yet learned to recognize them or, just as likely, chose to ignore them.

Her friend and Sir Charles rejoined them then, and they rode on in silence together. As they reached the entrance gates, Letitia turned to her. "Oh, I nearly forgot, Alex. I mentioned to Robert that you would like to visit the Covent Garden Market but that Lady Longmore won't allow you to go without a male escort. He has offered to accompany us one morning as I also would dearly like to see the flowers."

"Oh, that would be wonderful." Alexandra turned to the duke, her smile radiant. "Thank you, Your Grace. I have been longing to go."

"Should we meet tomorrow morning?" he asked. "I suggest we leave quite early before the market is depleted. It is quite a sight to see, but nearly all the produce is sold by midday."

Alexandra nodded. "I am an early riser, so any time would

suit me."

"May I join the party?" Sir Charles's voice was diffident.

"Please do," Alexandra said warmly. "Grandmama will surely have no objections now that I have two male escorts!"

Chapter Eighteen

Early the following morning, the duke's coach stopped outside Longmore House to collect Alexandra, and they drove the short distance to Covent Garden. When they entered the busy market, Alexandra gazed around in amazement, breathing in the sweet, heady smells. The quantity of fruit and vegetables on display was astounding. But the market did not only accommodate sellers of garden produce. Haberdashers, cooks, bakers, and butchers also exhibited their goods, while vendors of glass, earthenware, ironmongery, and other merchandise had their products on sale as well.

A hawker came up to Alexandra, offering her a cake, while other informal sellers raised their voices, advertising combs, pocketbooks, and even knives.

They passed a coffee house, and when Sir Charles stopped to buy Letitia a bun, the duke offered Alexandra his arm.

"It is a wholesale market today, Miss Grantham, so the market has been flooded by growers and gardeners."

Alexandra stopped in front of a stall where a man was selling cauliflowers. She could hear a grower making a delivery at the back of the booth, talking about the potato crop he was expecting later that year. "This sort of potato has been propagated for too long, I fear. It's lost some of its goodness. It was once a fine variety, but now—" he shook his head.

"Are you fearful it won't produce at all this year?" the vendor said.

"Aye. The only method of propagating them is by dividing the roots, and the quality's not the same."

"I know of an excellent method to propagate early varieties of potatoes," Alexandra said in a clear voice.

When the vegetable seller and the grower only stared at her, she continued, "If you see that you have a good variety, you should obtain seeds from the potato in its early stages to take advantage of that goodness. Unfortunately, the duration of any variety is limited to only about fourteen years, and by then, it's too late to obtain good seeds."

The grower shook his head again. "Begging your pardon, miss, but you've been misinformed. Seeds can only be obtained from the late kinds, and they are but rare."

Alexandra opened her hands wide. "I assure you I am informed by my own research and the potatoes I've produced. I promise, if you use the same method, you will be able to obtain seeds from the earliest and best varieties of potatoes."

The grower folded his arms. "I cannot credit it, miss."

"Early potatoes fail to produce seeds only due to the early formation of tuberous roots which draw off sap for its support, instead of supporting blossoms and seeds."

The grower frowned as he glanced at the duke before fixing his gaze on Alexandra once again. "So what do you do, miss? I've tried it in the past with naught success."

"To prevent tuberous roots from forming, one must allow blossoms to grow. First, fix some sturdy stakes in the ground. Then raise the soil in a heap around their bases and plant the potatoes on their south sides. When the sprouts are about four inches high, secure them to the stakes with shreds and nails and wash away the soil with water from the bases of the stems so that only the little fibrous roots enter the soil." She spread out her hands. "As the runners spring only from the stems that are now out of the soil, tuberous roots are easily seen and prevented.

Whenever this is done, blossoms will appear, and nearly all of them will give seeds."

His eyes widened as he listened to her, following closely as she spoke. "Thank you, miss. I believe I shall try that."

Alexandra nodded and smiled at the men before stepping away. She placed her hand on the duke's proffered arm once again. When they moved off together, he said, "Miss Grantham, I think you astounded those good men. Where did you learn about that method of obtaining seeds from potatoes?"

"Thomas Andrew Knight wrote a paper explaining his method in *The Transactions of The Horticultural Society of London*. It works very well, you know."

"I am certain it does." His shoulders shook slightly. "I must say, you were quite magnificent. How did you obtain a copy of this paper?"

"From my father's library. He was a member of the Society."

His expression was thoughtful. "One of my estate managers requested my opinion on a particular variety of yellow potato. He says that they can be forced early, so they are commonly cultivated in the London markets. Do you know anything about this?"

Alexandra tilted her head in thought. "Oh, yes. Your manager must be referring to Fox's Seedling. It's true that this variety can be forced early and yields adequate produce, but it is deficient in virtually every other way. Unfortunately, market gardeners have not yet found a good potato for forcing. I would advise your manager to keep looking for a better variety for your estate."

"You are a fount of knowledge, Miss Grantham. I must contrive to obtain a copy of that paper you mentioned to educate myself about potatoes further. Your knowledge of horticulture puts me to shame. I have an understanding of the general principles of managing agricultural estates but not of the finer details. I am becoming acutely aware of the gaps in my horticultural knowledge." His voice was wry.

"I have the article, Your Grace. I brought that particular copy of *The Transactions of The Horticultural Society of London* to Town, amongst other books. You are welcome to read it."

"Thank you, ma'am. I would be delighted to do so. May I call on you tomorrow?"

She smiled up at him. "Yes, of course."

They stopped at a stall to examine some delicious-looking grapes, and the duke bought her a bunch.

"Thank you." Alexandra popped the succulent fruit in her mouth and closed her eyes at its sweetness. Heaven. "I am so grateful to see this market. My father told me all about it, but it is difficult to imagine the sheer scale of this place." She glanced around. "I am afraid we have lost Letty and Sir Charles."

"I told Charles to meet us at the entrance in an hour."

"Oh." She glanced up at him. "How very kind of you to sacrifice your morning for us in this way."

"It is no sacrifice." They started walking again. "How old were you when you developed this interest in horticulture from your father?"

"It was actually my mother who inspired my initial interest. She loved gardening, and when I was a little girl of six, I would trail after her, picking up the petals from the roses she pruned."

"You must miss her."

She bowed her head. "Yes. I was thirteen when she died."

He pressed her hand but did not say anything, and Alexandra exhaled slowly. "She . . . she perished in a carriage accident on her way to deliver food baskets to some of our poorer tenants. I begged to go with her that day, but Mama refused. She only wanted me to start accompanying her when I was a little older, you see."

She swallowed past the restriction in her throat as he drew her to a halt and gently turned her to face him. "So you have followed in your mother's footsteps."

"I have tried to. I do my best for the poorer families on our estate and have tried to take care of John and my sisters. But—but I wasn't Mama."

He frowned. "When did your aunt come to live with you?"

"A few months after my mother died. Aunt Eliza was somewhat out of her depth, though, with four children to look after, and my father had fallen all to pieces. They were very much in love, you see, my mother and father, and Papa took it very hard. And John was so ill at the time." She drew in a shuddering breath. "I am not sure why I am telling you all this. Forgive me."

He covered her hand with his again, and they walked on in silence. But somehow, for the first time in a long while, the burdens she carried felt shared. It was a seductive sensation. But strictly forbidden. She must not forget that.

Alexandra and the duke returned an hour later to join Letty and Sir Charles at the entrance. As they followed the other couple to the carriage, a young woman dressed in dirty rags walked past them, stopping just before the entrance to the market. She waited there, perhaps hoping to obtain some scraps of food when the stalls closed up business for the day. She held the hand of a painfully thin little girl of perhaps four or five. The small child's cheeks had none of the plumpness of youth, and her dark eyes were huge in her pinched face. Alexandra's heart contracted. "Could you procure a couple of buns for me, Your Grace?" she asked, tilting her head in the direction of a nearby seller of baked items.

The duke's gaze came to rest on the mother and child, and with a nod, he stepped away to buy the bread. When he returned, Alexandra took the buns from his hands and walked toward the young woman. "Here, please take these for you and your daughter."

"Thank you," she whispered, accepting them.

Alexandra's lips curved into a smile. "What is your name?"

"Martha, miss."

"And your daughter's?"

"Sarah." The woman crouched down to hand the bread to her daughter.

"May I help you in any way, Martha? May we take you

home?"

The woman jerked her head up. "We lost our room when my husband died."

Alexandra's gaze rested on the little girl. She was devouring the bun, her full attention focused on the source of nourishment. How long had it been since the poor child last had a proper meal?

Alexandra looked back at the mother. "You have no family to support you?"

Martha shook her head. "Came to London five years ago from Newbury to find work, we did. I washed dishes in a coaching inn before Sarah came along."

"When did your husband die?"

"Just last month."

"And since then, you have been wandering the streets?"

The woman nodded her head jerkily. "I want to go home to Newbury—to my ma, but—." Tears welled up in her eyes.

Alexandra nodded in sympathy. "Please wait here a moment."

Alexandra walked the short distance to where the duke waited for her. "Is there any way in which we can help Martha and her daughter, Your Grace?" she asked in a low voice. "When her husband died last month, she lost her room and has no way to support her daughter. She wants to return to Newbury to her mother, but she has no money for the stage."

A frown descended on Stanford's brow as he glanced at the woman and child, and then he looked across the road at his carriage, where Letitia and Sir Charles awaited them. "Let me have a word with my driver." He crossed the street to speak to the coachman before returning with Sir Charles and Letitia in tow.

"I have told Jim to go home. It is only a mile or so to Berkeley Square. We can walk back together and discuss the matter with the woman once we are there."

Martha appeared startled when Alexandra asked her to accompany them, but she clutched her daughter's hand and walked silently behind them.

When their party entered Berkeley Square, they crossed to Stanford House, where the duke led the way into the hall. He murmured some instructions to the butler, hovering near the front door, before approaching a green baize door hidden by a painted oriental screen. His gaze encompassed Martha, Sarah, and Alexandra. "Please come downstairs." He turned his head to speak to Sir Charles. "If you would remain upstairs with Letty, Charles, we shall join you in a moment."

With an encouraging nod, Alexandra indicated that Martha and Sarah should go before her. She followed them down some narrow stairs, which ended in a corridor leading to a kitchen.

A plump, cozy-looking woman was conversing with a cook who was peeling vegetables at the large wooden table in the center of the spacious room.

Stanford spoke quietly to her. "Ah, Mrs. Reynolds. Just the person we need." He glanced at Alexandra as she ushered Martha and Sarah inside. "Miss Grantham, this is my housekeeper, Mrs. Reynolds, and Molly, the assistant cook."

He turned back to the housekeeper, who rose from the curtsey she had sunk into upon their entrance. "This young woman's name is Martha, Mrs. Reynolds. She is recently widowed, and she and her young daughter require a room in the servants' quarters tonight. Then, tomorrow morning, I want you to arrange for two tickets to be purchased for the stagecoach to Newbury." Stanford studied Martha. "Is your mother in a position to take care of you and your daughter once you return home?"

The young woman shook her head, her expression scared. "No, sir. She's but a poor widow herself."

"But she is able to look after your daughter so that you can seek work?"

"Yessir. That's my dearest hope. If I only I can return home."

"I happen to have an estate about fifteen miles from Newbury. I shall furnish you with a letter of introduction to my housekeeper there, where you can apply for work once you return home if you wish."

Martha's mouth dropped open, and she simply stared at the duke until Mrs. Reynolds cleared her throat reprovingly. The young woman glanced at the housekeeper then and snapped her lips together before opening them again to say in a rush: "Thank you kindly, sir."

"If you would come with me, Martha, I will settle you in," the housekeeper said in a comfortable voice.

Martha turned to follow Mrs. Reynolds out of the room. But then she paused and, releasing her daughter's hand abruptly, hurried to the doorway of the kitchen where Alexandra still stood. "Thank you ever so much, miss," she whispered before leaving with Sarah.

The duke walked over to Alexandra and, with an encouraging nod, led the way out of the kitchen. He must have noticed she was in something of a daze. She followed mutely behind him, quite unable to take in his unexpected generosity.

Even though she had hoped Stanford's plan to make her the rage would enable her to share her concerns about the plight of the poor with other members of the *ton*, it had been very difficult to broach the topic in the circles in which she now moved. When she had attempted to introduce the problem of poverty in the countryside into general conversation on a couple of occasions, she had received either blank stares or slightly incredulous looks.

The members of the beau monde were far too concerned with keeping up appearances to care about matters they considered beneath their notice. And the gentlemen, in particular, were disinclined to listen to her views on serious subjects, just as most of the men of her acquaintance had dismissed her opinions in the past.

But, for reasons she couldn't quite fathom, she seemed to have influence on this man climbing the stairs in front of her. He had just done something extraordinarily charitable simply because she had asked for a small kindness. And she was struck of a sudden that, also unlike most other members of the *ton*, he paid genuine attention to her thoughts and opinions. When she told him about the state of his tenants' lives, he investigated and acted. When she spoke about her passion for horticulture, he asked her questions and advice. It was true that he could be authoritative at times, but she could see now that this behavior had always been rooted in concern for her safety or the safety of someone else he cared for.

He would make someone a fine and trustworthy husband one day.

The wayward thought drew her up short, but as she had now reached the top of the stairs, she dismissed it from her mind and followed Stanford into the drawing room where Letitia awaited them there with Sir Charles and her cousin, Amelia Beaumont. Alexandra murmured a greeting to her friend's chaperone before sinking onto a striped silk sofa.

Letitia looked at her brother inquiringly. "Did you manage to help those poor souls, Robert?"

"They are in Mrs. Reynolds' care now. Tomorrow they will be traveling to Newbury, where I shall arrange some work for the young woman."

"You have done more than I ever imagined or expected, Your Grace," Alexandra said quietly.

"Oh, Robert is good at solving problems." Letitia's smile was cheerful. "Somehow, he is always three steps ahead of the rest of us. It is some sort of talent, I've often thought." Her eyes narrowed. "Or a hindrance when he gets a bee in his bonnet about the proprieties."

The duke raised his brows. "As well I should—with you as my sister."

When Letitia merely released her breath in a sharp huff, Sir Charles chuckled. "Poor Letty. It cannot be easy escaping your brother's eagle eye. Stephen and I could never get away with our tricks at Stanford Court—Stanford always found us out. But, I suppose as the eldest, he had to be the most responsible."

"Indeed—even if I am perceived as highhanded at times." The

duke's gaze rested somewhat quizzically on Alexandra as he said this, and she blushed. It appeared his remarkable powers of perception extended to reading other people's minds as well.

CHAPTER NINETEEN

ALEXANDRA WAS IN the library with her grandmother when Stanford called the following day. Her relative was ensconced near the window, catching up on her correspondence, while Alexandra sat at a table near the door, reading an article about straw, a product of wheat, barley, and oats.

When harvests were abundant, as predicted this year, the extra straw was a boon to the thatching industry. As Alexandra set the article on the table, she marveled at how everything was interconnected. Who would have thought that a good harvest would affect people's roofs?

She smiled at the duke as he advanced into the room. After he greeted her grandmother, who glanced up from her correspondence with an affable nod, Stanford sat opposite Alexandra at the rectangular mahogany table.

A pile of books was on the table in front of Alexandra. She selected the *Transactions of the Horticultural Society* and handed the volume to him. Their fingers brushed as he took it from her, and she snatched her hand away. "You are welcome to take this home, Your Grace, and read it there. It is rather a large tome, I'm afraid."

"I would far prefer to read it here. Then I can discuss it with you should I have any questions."

He settled down with his book while Alexandra resumed her

article and was soon engrossed in thoughts about the stems of beans and peas, called the halm, also used for thatching.

Sensing his gaze on her a few minutes later, she glanced up and met his amused regard and was struck by a sudden fear. *Not again.* She patted her hair self-consciously. She had worked in the garden this morning and had not looked properly in the mirror before entering the library. "Have I something in my hair again, Your Grace?" Her voice was resigned.

His smile broadened. "No, no. I was just thinking how restful you are, Miss Grantham. For someone so active, you exude serenity when you are in repose."

"I suppose when I am reading, I sit very quietly as all my energy floods to my brain."

"Good heavens. That sounds quite fatiguing."

She laughed. "I have immense concentration. When I am absorbed in a subject, I am oblivious to the rest of the world."

"So it is as if I am not here at all? You are completely indifferent to my presence?" He raised an eyebrow.

"Um . . . well, not quite, Your Grace. It is not quite as easy to focus with you here."

The muscles around his mouth twitched slightly. "I am grateful that my presence has some sort of effect on you. I was beginning to wonder."

"Er . . . yes." She hastily looked down at the page again. Finally, after reading the same sentence five times in succession, she glanced up and met his laughing gaze again. "I revise my previous statement, sir. I have immense concentration when I am *alone.*" Her voice was exasperated.

"Would you like me to leave, Miss Grantham?"

"Yes—no . . . as you please." She pressed her lips together and then cleared her throat as she glanced at the book in his hands. "Do you have any questions, Your Grace?"

"Oh, several. But I am not going to ask them now."

"No?"

"The time is not right. But one day, I will."

She met his intent look, and time seemed to stand still as she struggled to drag her gaze away. Eventually, she drew in a deep breath and broke the eye contact first. "Yes, it is probably for the best, Your Grace, if you gather all your questions together for an opportune time."

"I fully intend to do that, Miss Grantham," he said softly.

She let out her breath in a slow puff and looked away.

This was getting out of hand.

⸻

LETITIA'S COMING-OUT BALL the following week turned out to be what Alexandra's grandmother referred to as "the social occasion of the year." When Alexandra entered the magnificent ballroom of Stanford House, she gazed up in wonder at the enormous crystal chandelier that dominated the center of the room. Prisms of light danced off the cut-glass structure and were reflected in the mirrors that lined the walls, creating an effect of a magically lit-up fairyland. Alexandra was brought back to earth with a bump by her grandmother's exasperated voice. "Alexandra! Do attend to me. You seem to be miles away."

"Forgive me, Grandmama. I was admiring that beautiful chandelier. I have never seen anything quite like it."

"Well, don't gawk, my dear. Only provincials show themselves to be impressed by anything. Now, about what I was saying. I forgot to mention to you that the Hadleys will soon be leaving Town and returning home. They did not succeed in obtaining vouchers for Almack's."

"Oh! How terrible for Emily and Jane. They must be so disappointed to be leaving London early." Her brows drew together in a quick frown. "I haven't seen Emily in an age as Mrs. Hadley does not allow her to go out very often. I frequently see Mrs. Hadley and Jane in the Park, but they leave poor Emily at home. I wonder if it is because Emily is so much prettier than Jane and they fear being overshadowed? Mrs. Hadley must be furious at having been refused vouchers."

"I would say so," her grandmother said dryly. "When Mrs. Hadley realized the vouchers would not be forthcoming, she paid a morning call on Lady Jersey and positively harangued her! Lady Jersey was not amused, as you can imagine. She told me all about the unfortunate incident." She broke off. "Oh, good evening, Letitia. Are you enjoying your evening?"

"Oh, yes, Lady Longmore! It is above anything. I am the belle of my very own ball!"

Grandmama smiled indulgently at the young girl and, after engaging her in conversation for a few minutes, turned aside to greet an acquaintance.

Letitia lowered her voice. "Oh, Alex! My evening would have been perfect if only Vernon could have come tonight. It was impossible to invite him, of course. He is not considered a respectable person." She frowned. "And yet, Lady Ballington, whom I despise, was issued an invitation! When I told Cousin Amelia that I had no desire to invite her to my ball, she told me that it would be the height of incivility for us to ignore her in such a fashion because her parents are such close friends of our family. She is a marchioness, as well, and must not be slighted." With a gloomy expression on her face, she continued, "Lady Ballington arrived half an hour ago. Fortunately, so many people are here tonight that it won't be considered strange if I don't speak to her. Oh, here is Robert!" Letitia's face brightened. "I suppose he intends to ask you to dance."

Letitia was correct in her supposition. The duke bowed over Alexandra's hand and led her onto the dance floor. They circled the room a few times in silence before he spoke: "You really are not a kind friend to my sister, Miss Grantham, coming to her ball and outshining her as you have."

Alexandra shook her head. "You do not do your sister justice, Your Grace. Brothers, in my experience, rarely do. Letty looks absolutely lovely tonight. I look merely—well, I managed to leave the garden at home, at least."

"You certainly did. Your dress is quite magnificent. I am generally purported to be an arbiter of fashion, so I do not speak empty words, you know."

When the last strains of the waltz sounded, he escorted her back to her grandmother's side.

"I must inform you, Stanford, that I consider it very unsporting of you to have cut my godson out so completely! You mean to wed him to that sister of yours, do you not?"

He raised his brows. "My dear Lady Longmore, the role of matchmaker is best left to those better equipped to deal with my sister's changeable emotions than I am. And Charles knows his own mind, I am sure. Now, if you would excuse me, ladies, I must attend to my duties." With a smile and a bow, he moved away.

"Scheming young devil." She gazed after his retreating back. "Oh well. Let us sit down somewhere. I am dead on my feet, such a squeeze as this is!"

Alexandra followed her grandmother through the crowded room but lost sight of her when Amelia Beaumont stopped her to ask if she had seen Letitia recently. Alexandra was about to reply in the negative when that lady spotted her charge near the ballroom door and hurried off in that direction.

As Alexandra fought her way through the crush of people, she realized that no one who had received one of the elegantly engraved invitations to the ball at Stanford House must have declined to come. The Beaumonts were far too powerful a family to be ignored by the *ton*, and invitations to any event hosted by the Duke of Stanford were coveted more than gold by anyone aspiring to social heights.

She had just noticed her grandmother in the corner of the room when she felt a tap upon her shoulder.

"There you are, Miss Grantham," Lady Ballington said. "I have been meaning to have a word with you."

"Good evening, Lady Ballington." Alexandra's voice was

wary.

"I am afraid I am the bearer of some bad news, Miss Grantham. I feel it to be my duty, though, one woman to another, to inform you of it."

"Bad news, your ladyship?"

"Unfortunately, yes, my dear. When Sir Jason informed me of the wager, I was shocked. Quite shocked!"

Alexandra stiffened at the mention of her *bête-noire*. "I can't imagine what you might be referring to, your ladyship."

Lady Ballington smiled sympathetically. "Sir Jason has informed me that the Duke of Stanford's pursuit of you is merely the result of a wager that he and Stanford have entered into. A while back, Sir Jason challenged the duke, saying that you were such a high and mighty miss that he doubted whether His Grace could manage to add you to his circle of admirers. So, if you believe his intentions to be serious, I fear you are sadly mistaken, as the duke would never propose marriage to a lady so far below him in station. I thought it would be best to let you know this, so you may avoid further embarrassment."

Alexandra raised her brows. "I was under the impression, Lady Ballington, that the Duke of Stanford and Sir Jason were not on good terms. I find it difficult, therefore, to believe in any such wager."

Lady Ballington lifted her thin shoulders. "My concern is only for you! I would not fabricate such a tale, I assure you. If you doubt my words, by all means, ask Sir Jason to verify them. You will not like his answer, but it will be the truth, nonetheless."

"Better than that, Lady Ballington, I shall challenge His Grace with these accusations." Her tone was cool. "Now, if you will excuse me, ma'am, I must find my grandmother." Nodding, she made to move away.

Lady Ballington put a restraining hand on Alexandra's elbow. "Just a moment, Miss Grantham. I advise you not to question His Grace about what I have said. He will only deny the story, and you will likely anger him, making your own position precarious indeed."

She studied the other woman for a long moment. "I am surprised you say that, your ladyship. I would never have said that the Duke of Stanford was a dishonest man."

"One can never be sure with gentlemen, Miss Grantham. In my experience, men are very rarely honest in their dealings with women."

"And yet you expect me to ask Sir Jason to verify your story of this wager?" Alexandra said gently. "As I have said before, Lady Ballington, I may be young, but I am in no way stupid. Good evening."

Alexandra eventually found Lady Longmore standing adjacent to the dancers at the side of the ballroom. She kept silent, however, about the interview with Lady Ballington. It was too distasteful to speak of. Lady Ballington's malicious stories—and she was certain that they were stories—made her wonder at the nature of the woman.

The marchioness must mistake Alexandra for a fool if she believed she would accept anything as truth from either her or Sir Jason's lips. They had both made it clear that they disliked her and intended to do her harm. From now on, she would watch her way carefully. The London scene held many traps for unwary travelers, and one needed to keep one's eyes wide open to avoid them.

The irony was that if Lady Ballington knew Alexandra had no intention of marrying, she would not have bothered to try to alienate her from the duke, but she had no intention of enlightening the other woman. Let her believe what she wanted.

She turned to speak to her grandmother and then stopped dead in surprise. Lady Ballington had just stepped into the duke's embrace as a new waltz began. He began to whirl her around the ballroom, and Alexandra stared at them, her expression fixed. The marchioness smiled triumphantly at her as she sailed past, and Alexandra attempted to swallow past the giant ball lodged in her throat. She turned hastily away, frowning fiercely at the ground.

This was ridiculous. Utterly ridiculous. She should not be so affected by the sight of the marchioness in the duke's arms. But she was. Undoubtedly, she was.

Somehow, she had grown accustomed to thinking of the duke as *her* particular escort. He danced with her at every ball he attended, after all, and took her on frequent outings to the Park. And sat with her in the library. . . . She drew herself up at this thought. Although Stanford paid such flattering attention to her, she was stepping onto perilous ground by taking him at all seriously.

One thing Lady Ballington had said to her was true. The Duke of Stanford would never propose marriage to the daughter of a baronet.

She needed to remember that.

⋙⋘

THE AFTERNOON AFTER Letitia's ball, Alexandra and Letitia were comfortably ensconced in the morning room of Longmore House, studying the prints of fashion in *La Belle Assemblée*.

Although Alexandra was still happiest in her old gardening gowns, she had grown to appreciate the confidence that being well-dressed brought, especially in London, where clothes were worn as a sort of armor against the world.

"What a lovely jaconet muslin, Alex!" Letitia pointed it out to Alexandra. "Worn with a Norwich shawl, it would look charmingly on you. You must ask your Grandmama to tell Madame Bouchet to make it up for you."

Alexandra's lips curled in a somewhat bemused smile. "You can have no idea, Letty, of the number of gowns I now own. Morning gowns, afternoon dresses, carriage dresses, ball gowns, walking dresses, riding habits—the list is endless. I do not think I am in need of any more."

"Hmm." Letitia leaned back in her chair. "You may well be in need of a wedding gown soon. With your bevy of admirers, you are sure to become betrothed soon."

"I have no intention of becoming betrothed to anyone, Letty."

"But, Alex, you have all of London at your feet! Is there no gentleman for whom you have developed a *tendre*?"

"No. I am perfectly content to remain unwed. I would, more than anything, dislike to lose my freedom."

"Perhaps that is sensible, Alex." She paused and then gave a small sob. "Robert told me this morning that Vernon Winters attempted to elope with an heiress in Bath last year, and before that, he tried to run away with an heiress in Brighton. Robert had heard rumors of this but received written confirmation this morning." She sniffled. "I was so mistaken in Vernon's character. He wanted to elope with me too, you know, but I would never sink so low as to run away with him. I was hoping, instead, that my family would come to realize that they were mistaken about him. I feel like such a fool to have truly believed myself in love with him." Delicate tears rolled down her pale cheeks.

Alexandra pressed her friend's arm. "I am so very sorry to hear that."

"My spirits are utterly cast down. And the worst thing of all was that Robert was right all along!" She glowered into the distance. "Sometimes, I wonder about him, Alex. He has never fallen in love, and he admits it freely. And although I love him dearly, I can't help but hope that when he does eventually meet someone he wishes to marry, he will need to work hard to earn his lady's affection. Everything comes far too easily to Robert!"

Chapter Twenty

ALEXANDRA AND HER maid had just stepped out of Hatchards the next day when the duke himself hailed her and offered to drive her home. Having satisfied her desire for exercise on the way to the bookshop and seeing that the weather was perfect for a drive, she accepted his invitation. After she succeeded in convincing the thoroughly provincial Hobbes that it was perfectly proper for a young lady to drive with a gentleman in London—it was an open carriage after all!—he helped her into the curricle.

"You are driving your bays today, I see." Alexandra looked in admiration at the pair of high-steppers held so expertly under control by the man at her side. Glancing at him sideways, she continued, "I don't suppose you might allow me to handle the ribbons one day?"

"You drive, Miss Grantham?"

"Hmm," she murmured, a reflective smile playing about her mouth. "I plagued my poor father to give me lessons until he finally consented to do so. I'm quite good, you know."

"I shall allow you to try their paces one day then," he promised, ignoring the disgusted snort Jimmy gave upon hearing this assurance.

"Thank you, sir. I was not certain whether you would approve of the fact that I drive."

"I am sure you drive with the same skill that you demonstrate in every activity you undertake."

"I am much obliged to you." She paused for a moment and then cleared her throat. "Will you be attending Lady Rigby's ball?"

"I depart London for Stanford Court the day after her ball, so I may not be able to spare the time to drop in."

"Oh!" Pretending to admire a hideous purple and orange bonnet displayed in a shop window they were passing, she asked nonchalantly, "Will your visit be a protracted one?"

"I shall return within a few days. But there are certain matters in connection with the running of my estates to which I must attend in person." He smiled at her. "You must assure me that while I am away, you will not fall into any scrapes from which I shall, naturally, be unable to extricate you."

"I am not in the habit of falling into scrapes," Alexandra said with dignity. Then, when he merely raised his brows, she revised, with a somewhat rueful laugh, "Well, not many, at any rate."

At this moment, he drew up outside Longmore House. Handing the reins over to his tiger, he descended from the curricle to help her alight. At the front door, he stood looking down at her with an unreadable expression on his face. After a moment, he said quietly, "Do try to behave yourself while I am away." Raising her hand to his lips, he bowed before taking his leave and driving away.

Alexandra sighed as she gazed after the retreating curricle before turning around and entering the house. However, just as she sat down at the writing table in her bedchamber to compose an overdue letter to her aunt, a knock sounded on the door, and a young maid entered and dropped a curtsey. "Begging your pardon, miss, but her ladyship desires your presence in the drawing room."

"Thank you, Gladys."

Alexandra made her way downstairs and entered the well-appointed room to see a familiar red-headed young man conversing with her grandmother.

"John! What a lovely surprise. I thought that you were coming up to London only much later in the Season."

"When I heard that my very own sister had made such an impression in London, how could I stay away?" John grinned. "How do you go on, Alex?"

"Very well, thank you. London is everything and more than I expected it to be. I am courted and flattered at every turn and laid siege to by strategists who rival Boney in their campaigns to conquer that most desirable of prizes—the latest London heiress." Alexandra's smile was wry.

"Well, I hope you will be able to spare some time from beating away your lovelorn swains to accompany me on a tour of the Metropolis. Or have you already visited all the sights?"

"No, as yet, I haven't. To do so with you will be wonderful. Although I promised myself before arriving here that I would take in the aesthetic delights of London, I have simply not found the time. I especially wish to pay a visit to the British Museum."

Their grandmother raised her eyes heavenwards and uttered in a longsuffering voice, "May God spare me from my bookish grandchildren." Then, regarding them with a twinkle in her eyes, she continued, "My dears, do you not realize that it is quite unfashionable to visit fusty old museums?"

Alexandra smiled wickedly. "Grandmama, the Duke of Stanford assures me that in my current position in Society, I have it in my power to set the fashion and have no need to follow its dictates. Therefore, I proclaim that it is now fashionable to visit not only museums but cathedrals, art galleries, churches, and other buildings of historical and architectural interest."

The older lady sighed. "I can see your mind is firmly made up, you obstinate child." At John's chuckle, his grandmother rounded on him and said in a severe tone: "Do not think, young man, that you will be able to merely indulge your passion for cultural pursuits whilst in Town. I insist that you act as our escort to Lady Rigby's ball tomorrow evening."

"But Grandmama! I can think of nothing more dull than an

evening spent trying to remember the steps of all those infernal dances and quadrilles. I had planned to spend the evening with Peter Denville tomorrow night. I'm staying with him in Grosvenor Square."

"I did not know that Peter was in Town, John." Lord Denville owned a large estate bordering Grantham Place, and he and John, having grown up together, were as close as brothers.

"Peter, like me," John looked balefully at his grandmother, "dislikes social gatherings of any sort. I doubt that he has set foot in a London ballroom since his arrival in Town. Grandmama, you cannot expect me to dance attendance on you tomorrow."

"I can, and I do." Her expression softened for a moment. "It would mean a great deal to me, John."

He sighed in resignation. "Well, if you insist, Grandmama, I shall, of course, bow to your wishes. I only hope I won't tread on anyone's feet."

"Poor John," Alexandra said sympathetically. "Life is full of various hardships which one must bear with fortitude." Ignoring his glower, Alexandra linked her arm through his and smiled up at him. "Never mind that. London balls can be vastly entertaining affairs—quite different from those dull country assemblies you dislike so much. If you set your mind to it, you may even find that you begin to enjoy them."

>>><<<

ALEXANDRA LOOKED AROUND Lady Rigby's glittering ballroom and smiled as she caught sight of her brother in earnest conversation with Miss Elizabeth Fenworth. Far from appearing apathetic, John seemed to be thoroughly enjoying her company, no doubt because Miss Fenworth's large brown eyes were focused with unconcealed admiration on his face.

Smothering a yawn, Alexandra waited rather impatiently for Sir Charles Fotherby to return with the glass of lemonade he had left her side to procure for her. All she really wanted to do was return home, climb into bed, and fall fast asleep. The combination of dancing into the early hours of the morning most days while still waking up early enough to work in the garden was starting to catch up with her.

And today had been even busier than usual. She and John had spent three fascinating hours in the British Museum that morning visiting the three Departments of Manuscripts and Medals, Natural and Artificial Products, and Printed Books. However, both of them admitted that this length of time could not do full justice to the Museum and resolved to visit it again.

Their next port of call had been St Paul's Cathedral, but an afternoon shower had forced them to return to Longmore House somewhat earlier than planned. Hopefully, the weather would be better tomorrow, and they could explore Westminster Abbey and the Tower. It was lovely to visit the sights of London with her brother as they shared similar interests, and she intended to make full use of his escort now that he was in Town. Though she must be careful not to do too much in one day as John tended to tire easily, even though he was looking in good health at the moment. Even Alexandra was thinking longingly for the hour when her grandmother would call for their carriage, and they could return home.

Looking around in search of Sir Charles, Alexandra stiffened when she saw Edward Ponsonby approaching her, obviously with the intention of foisting his unwelcome presence on her. The rotund little man had been introduced to Alexandra at a rout the previous week, and she had taken an immediate dislike to him—this largely due to the fact that he combined a conceited and pompous manner with a distinctly roving eye, an unfavorable combination bound to vex any young lady.

Sidling up to her, Mr. Ponsonby said unctuously, "My dear Miss Grantham. How lovely—indeed, how *beautiful* you are looking this evening. Your creamy skin, your strawberry lips, and the peaches of your cheeks overwhelm my senses." His avid gaze dipped to her cleavage.

She glared at him. "Sir, you must be extraordinarily hungry to liken my face to a fruit platter. If I am not mistaken, the buffet is next door, not in here."

Mr. Ponsonby's jowly face became a dull brick red, and, with an apprehensive glance over her shoulder, he scuttled away.

A quiet, amused voice said in Alexandra's ear, "You *are* developing the art of delivering a good set-down. You will soon rival me in depressing the pretensions of toad-eating mushrooms."

Alexandra turned and smiled up at the duke. "I do not think anyone could quite do that, Your Grace. I quell with words. All you need do is raise a lordly brow, and your assailant cowers in fear before you."

"Baggage!" He chuckled. "You make me seem a veritable ogre."

"Oh, not an ogre, Your Grace." Alexandra eyed him consideringly. "Merely an imperious nobleman far too used to getting his own way."

Smiling lazily, he murmured, "You would do well to remember that in your dealings with me, my dear."

She shook her head, laughing. "Touché, Your Grace. I must concede the point."

"Now that is a first, Miss Grantham. I must say that I am delighted to progress beyond 'En garde.'"

The look in the duke's eyes was so intent that the laughter hovering on her lips vanished as she gazed up at him. It was only when Sir Charles appeared with her promised drink, handing it over to her with a smile and a bow, that she managed to drag her gaze away from Stanford's.

She took a hasty sip of the refreshing drink as Sir Charles, looking from one to the other, said with mock severity, "I do hope you are not allowing Stanford to turn your head with his compliments, Miss Grantham. His devastating effect on impressionable young ladies is legendary."

Alexandra, hoping to regain lost ground, raised her brows. "His compliments, Sir Charles? His Grace is well aware that there is no point wasting them on me. Thank you for the warning, though."

Sir Charles crowed with laughter. "Miss Grantham, I congratulate you. That comment is bound to render our noted Corinthian here speechless with shock."

"Hardly speechless, Charles. Merely a trifle put down," he said mildly, although with an unreadable expression in his eyes that made Alexandra wonder about the prudence of her provocative remark. The Duke of Stanford was not a man to take a challenge of that nature lying down. Before she could wisely temper her comment, an acquaintance of Stanford's hailed him, and with a glinting smile and a bow, he moved away.

"Cool devil, ain't he?" Sir Charles looked at his retreating back.

"Hmm," she said distractedly. She was becoming more and more confused about her feelings for this enigmatic man and how she should treat him. At one moment, she could swear that the duke was flirting with her; the next, he played the role of a dictatorial older brother. What she did know, and resolved to remember on all occasions, was that it would be to her peril to take Stanford at all seriously. If she ever started to do so, she was sure she would be like a drowning woman grasping at straws, and Alexandra, more than anything, desired to stay afloat.

Sir Charles's expression sobered. "I hope that Ponsonby fellow hasn't been plaguing you, Miss Grantham. His estates are encumbered, and it is well known that he is desperately seeking a wealthy bride."

She grimaced. "He is vastly annoying, but I have made it clear that I will not welcome his advances. I trust he will leave me alone in the future."

Letitia and her cousin joined them then as Letitia was eager to discuss a play she had attended the previous night at Drury Lane, which Alexandra had yet to see. The conversation then became a more general discussion of their favorite Shakespearean actors. Letitia and Sir Charles were quite heated in their debate about Edmund Kean's ability to portray tragic emotions. They barely seemed to notice when Alexandra murmured an excuse and moved away to speak to her brother, who now stood alone.

"I wish to escape this crush," he said in a low voice as she approached. "It is far too warm in here."

"Are you feeling faint?" She studied his pale countenance in concern. He shook his head, but Alexandra, noticing the beads of sweat on his forehead, said in a brisk voice, "It *is* rather crowded. Let us see if we can find Lord Rigby's library. I believe it is quite splendid."

They left the room, and Alexandra tried a door on the opposite end of the hall, but it opened into a parlor. She was about to shut the door and try the one next door when she heard a muffled sound near the window.

"Emily!" Alexandra advanced into the room. "I didn't know you were here this evening. How lovely to see you." When she saw her friend's red-rimmed eyes and pale cheeks, she frowned. "Are you unwell, my dear?"

Emily gave a tiny sniff as she stared down at her hands.

"May we help you in any way, Miss Hadley?" John asked diffidently.

Emily shook her head. "No. I . . . I just wanted to be alone. I shall leave."

"You cannot return to the ball looking like you do, Miss Hadley, if you don't wish to draw attention to yourself." John frowned. "Would you like me to call your stepmother for you?"

She looked at him in horror. "Oh no! Please don't do that, Sir John. She . . . she . . . I . . ." Emily trailed off into tears.

Alexandra gently took her arm and led her to a sofa situated near the window. "What is the matter, dearest? Please tell me."

Emily sat down, and when Alexandra took the seat beside her, she murmured. "This is to be my last ball, and next week I am returning home with Stepmama and Jane."

Alexandra clasped her friend's hands. "I heard from my grandmother that you had failed to obtain vouchers for Almack's, Emily. You must be so disappointed."

Emily shook her head. "But that isn't so, Alexandra. It is true that Lady Jersey refused to grant me vouchers initially, but when Lady Sefton heard of Lady Jersey's decision, she asked her to change her mind. You see, Lady Sefton and my mama were bosom-friends as young girls, and I believe Lady Sefton feels some sort of responsibility toward me. So she and Lady Jersey have agreed to grant me vouchers after all."

"How wonderful!" Alexandra smiled, but after a moment, her brow creased. "But why are you leaving London then?"

Emily sighed. "Lady Jersey dislikes Stepmama intensely, and she is adamant in her refusal to grant vouchers to her and Jane. Stepmama is so angry and . . . and I am afraid to return home with her and Jane. They feel as if they have been doubly slighted, and I am the target of their wrath. And I cannot return to Bath just yet as my godmother is unwell."

Alexandra's eyes widened. It was true that Mrs. Hadley had always treated Emily poorly, accepting the squire's first child in her household only on sufferance. Alexandra could well believe that her fury would be incited by the knowledge that her stepdaughter had been admitted to the highest circles of Society while she and her daughter had not. Alexandra placed an arm around her friend's shoulders and said gently, "You cannot return home with them, Emily. They will make your life intolerable. Is there no one else here in London—a cousin or an aunt perhaps—with whom you could stay?"

She shook her head. "I have no family in London—except my uncle, and he is unmarried."

Looking across at John, who all the while had been standing in the doorway, Alexandra said quietly, "Do you think Grandmama would agree to have Emily stay with us?"

"You could certainly ask her, Alex."

Emily gasped. "But I could not impose on your grandmother

in that way!"

"Hush, Emily. And try not to be anxious about this. I shall speak to my grandmother after the ball."

"You are a dear friend, Alexandra." She appeared slightly bemused. "Thank you for trying to help me. But rest assured that I shall perfectly understand if your grandmother does not extend an invitation for me to stay with her."

"I will see what can be done. I think, though, that we should return to the ballroom now before Grandmama comes looking for me."

She nodded. "Do I look presentable?"

Alexandra smiled as she stood up. "Your nose and eyes are just a little red but noticeable only if one looks very closely indeed."

Emily also rose to her feet and said in a shaky voice, "Well, I hope that no one looks too closely then."

They walked toward the door, and John offered them each an arm. "May I escort you ladies back to the ballroom?" he asked gravely, a smile lurking smile in his eyes. Emily accepted his arm shyly, and Alexandra, seeing that her friend was looking a little better, moved away from them when they returned to the ballroom. She glanced around the room and spotted the other Hadleys engrossed in conversation with Mrs. Morecombe. Mrs. Hadley did not appear to be searching for her charge, and Alexandra hoped Emily would continue to go unnoticed by them for the remainder of the ball.

John devoted the rest of his evening to Emily without interference from her relations. He danced with her twice that night and looked after her carefully until it was time to leave, even though he seemed exhausted by the end of the party.

When they returned to Longmore House, Alexandra asked her grandmother if she and John could speak to her privately.

"Certainly, my dears," she said. "We can speak in the drawing room."

When they were all comfortably settled, Alexandra explained

Emily's problems. "She is desperately unhappy, Grandmama, and I am convinced that if she returns home with Mrs. Hadley and Jane, they will make her life unbearable. Could you not speak to Mrs. Hadley and offer to have Emily stay with us?"

"Naturally, I would like to help her, but you must be aware that your suggestion is rather irregular." She frowned a little. "We have no social connection to Miss Hadley, and it is quite an undertaking for me to chaperone another young lady. Although I believe Miss Hadley has been out for a few years in Bath, this is her first visit to London, and she should have a coming-out ball like all the other young ladies."

"Emily has been my own close friend for many years, Grandmama, and she will be no trouble to you at all. She is two years older than I am and therefore very mature, and unlike me, she is very sweet and biddable!"

Her grandmother smiled, but she still looked doubtful. "I am not sure." She looked across at her grandson. "What do you think, John?"

"I agree with Alexandra," he said slowly. "Miss Hadley has always appeared to be a gentle soul. I don't think she has the necessary armor to withstand Mrs. Hadley's cruel treatment of her."

Their grandmother sighed. "You children have made it difficult for me to refuse—my conscience will not allow it. The curse of a soft heart! We shall call on Mrs. Hadley tomorrow."

"Oh, thank you, Grandmama!" Alexandra said in relief.

"It is possible she may not allow me to take Emily into my care. She is a spiteful woman and may not want to give Emily the chance of having a London Season."

However, when Alexandra and her grandmother called on Mrs. Hadley the next day, the squire's wife was eager to release her stepdaughter.

"Take Emily into your home, Lady Longmore?" she said after the suggestion had been put to her. "I would be happy for you to do so if you think you can stand it. I do not wish to see the little minx ever again."

Grandmama raised her brows. "Indeed?"

Mrs. Hadley's eyes narrowed. "That child is full of airs and graces. She has always looked down her nose at me because *her* mother was the granddaughter of an earl, and for years I have had to have That Woman's child living in my home. The sight of her sickens me, and it's so hard on my poor, sweet Jane."

"I only hope Emily finds an eligible husband in view of what you say."

"Oh, you must force her to accept any offer she receives, Lady Longmore. I do not wish to have her under my roof again. She is parading around with the smuggest expression on her face at this time because she has received those wretched vouchers and we have not. It is unjust. Terribly unjust. I cannot abide it." Her fists clenched tightly in her lap until her knuckles whitened. But, after a moment, she seemed to collect herself, and she rang for her butler.

When the man entered the room, she said, "Send Miss Hadley to me, Forbes."

The butler bowed and withdrew, and a few minutes later, Emily crept into the room.

"You wish to see me, Stepmama?" she asked.

"Yes. Be seated."

Mrs. Hadley nodded in Lady Longmore's direction. "Her ladyship has been so kind as to offer to take you into her home. You will leave here as soon as possible and take up residence for the remainder of the Season with her."

Emily stared wordlessly at her benefactress for a few moments. Finally, she took a deep breath and murmured, "Thank you, Lady Longmore. I am most grateful. I shall try not to be a burden to you."

"It will be my pleasure to have you stay with me, Miss Hadley."

"I have told her ladyship that it is imperative that you find a husband, Emily." Mrs. Hadley frowned at her stepdaughter. "You are virtually on the shelf and must not turn up your nose at any offer of marriage you may receive. I trust I make myself clear?"

"Yes, Stepmama."

"Very good. We shall be quitting this house within the next day or so. Will you be able to receive Emily into your home tomorrow, your ladyship?

"Certainly, Mrs. Hadley. The sooner your stepdaughter arrives, the better." Her task accomplished, Grandmama rose from her seat and nodded coolly. "Good morning, Mrs. Hadley. I trust that your journey home will be a safe one."

"I hope so, as well." Their hostess stood. "Thank you for taking Emily for the Season. I give you my permission to deal with her very strictly if need be. What that girl requires is discipline." She smiled thinly at Alexandra. "Not unlike many willful young women these days."

Alexandra's eyes narrowed at the thinly veiled insult, but Grandmama merely gave Mrs. Hadley a measured look and then smiled encouragingly at Emily as they left the room.

Alexandra shook her head as they entered their carriage. "I hope Emily finds an eligible husband, Grandmama. I don't believe she can ever return to Hadley Hall."

"I think you're right." Her grandmother's mouth set in a grim line. "If anyone needs rescuing from a dire situation, young Emily Hadley does."

CHAPTER TWENTY-ONE

Away from the domineering presence of her stepmother, Emily blossomed in the congenial atmosphere of the Longmore household. Alexandra took Emily firmly under her wing, and as the days passed, the already close friendship between them deepened. Being of a less energetic nature than Alexandra, Emily was content to live life at a slower pace, generally choosing to work on her embroidery or playing the pianoforte instead of accompanying Alexandra and Letitia on their shopping and riding expeditions. However, she was eager to assist Alexandra in the garden and woke up early every morning to accompany her friend outside.

John became a frequent visitor to Longmore House, as well. After a while, Alexandra began to suspect that his presence owed less to familial duty and more to his evident appreciation of Emily's charms. He treated her with unfailing gentleness and courtesy, and she responded to his attention like a flower opening to the rays of the sun. Alexandra watched their blossoming courtship with hope in her heart. How wonderful it would be if her dearest friend married her beloved brother!

Grandmama also began to believe that a betrothal was in the air, and she chided Alexandra about it when they were comfortably ensconced in the Rose Salon one rainy day. "At this rate, your brother will be betrothed before you are."

Alexandra laughed. "Oh, Grandmama! You must not concern yourself over my unattached state. I am perfectly happy, I assure you."

"You are far too independently minded." Her grandmother pursed her lips a little.

"I prefer it that way. It makes my life less complicated."

"But why are you still so intent on remaining unmarried, my love?"

Alexandra considered the question. "I grew up with a father who treated me as an intelligent individual, Grandmama, which ill-prepared me for the attitude so many gentlemen have toward women in our society. I cannot bear to be treated as if I have no mind of my own."

"Your father was certainly an exceptional man, my love. But not all men believe women are inferior beings. You must not think that. Your dear grandpapa, for one, treated me with the utmost respect and consideration." She paused for a moment before continuing delicately, "What of your friendship with Stanford? The two of you seem to converse easily."

She smiled but refused to be baited into admitting affection. She had to be stern enough with her own thoughts about the duke. "That's true. But you, yourself, warned me against him, Grandmama. I would never be so unwise as to take his attentions seriously. I know he is merely amusing himself by keeping me in fashion. I do enjoy our interactions—and who doesn't enjoy a little flirtation at times? But that is all."

"So you are in no danger of losing your heart to him?"

"I would be a fool to do so."

"Then your defenses are much stronger than most women's, my child. Stanford's deadly effect on impressionable young ladies is legendary."

One morning soon after their conversation, Alexandra had just put the finishing touches to her toilette when a housemaid tapped on the door to inform her that her brother and Lord Denville had called and were awaiting her downstairs.

Alexandra received the message with pleasure. The duke had scheduled an urgent meeting with the bailiff of Stanford Court, who had traveled up to London to see him, and she had been obliged to skip her ride in the Park for lack of an escort. She had thought to do some extra weeding this morning, instead, but it would be much more pleasant to spend some time with her brother.

Emily, unfortunately, had developed a slight chill. She was confined to her bed and had sent a message to Alexandra by way of her maid, telling her that she was not desirous of receiving any visitors today for fear of infecting them as well. Poor John would be so disappointed. Alexandra hurried downstairs to the morning room and was about to push open the door, which had been left slightly ajar, when Lord Denville's voice, raised in speech, gave her pause.

"By gad, John. Charles Fotherby is the last man I would have expected to call someone out. I believed him to be a peaceable man."

"You would not have described him as peaceable last night," John replied. "Winters made some disparaging remarks about Lady Letitia Beaumont. Fotherby, who I believe is a close friend of the Beaumont family, took exception to the remarks and demanded Winters retract what he had said. Winters refused to do so, so Fotherby called him out. The meeting is tomorrow on Putney Heath."

Alexandra stood frozen outside the morning room. After a moment, she recollected herself and entered the room. John looked up and, after seeing her face, said uneasily, "How much of our conversation did you hear, Alex?"

"Enough." She greeted Lord Denville and then turned back to her brother. "John, this is dreadful! Can anything be done to stop the duel?"

"In an affair of honor? Nothing can or will be done. Winters was extremely offensive in what he said about Lady Letitia. I don't think the seconds will even attempt to bring about a reconciliation."

Alexandra frowned. "But something must be done. Either man could be killed in the encounter. And the damage done to Letty's reputation will be considerable if it becomes known that a duel was fought over her. Besides, dueling is against the law."

John met her gaze squarely. "This is a gentleman's affair, Alex, and doesn't warrant any interference. Try to forget what you overheard."

Alexandra rubbed her forehead. She knew that gentlemen took their Code of Honor very seriously and that, once a challenge was issued, it was rarely retracted. But it was pure folly for a man to risk his life in such a way.

John, however, was reluctant to discuss the matter further with her. So, after asking him to call on her tomorrow morning with any news he might have about the duel, she told him about Emily's indisposition and then listened with half an ear to the men's conversation as she wondered what to do.

When her brother and his friend left half an hour later, Alexandra went straight into the garden. As she wandered along the path, she turned the problem over in her mind. If only there were something she could do to prevent the duel from taking place. Alexandra came to a sudden halt, and, turning on her heel, rushed inside and up the stairs to her bedchamber, where she asked Hobbes, who was setting the room in order, to bring her writing materials.

A short while later, Alexandra hastened downstairs again and handed a sealed letter to Leighton, with the direction that it was to be taken to Stanford House at once and that the footman who delivered it was to wait for a response.

Twenty minutes later, Leighton entered the morning room, carrying a letter on a silver salver. Alexandra eagerly broke the seal and read the brief missive:

> *Dear Miss Grantham, I will call on you in half an hour. We can discuss any urgent business you choose in Hyde Park.*

Yours etc.
Stanford

Alexandra sighed in relief. It would considerably lessen her burden if she could share what she knew of the proposed duel with the duke.

Within the hour, Alexandra was seated beside him in his high-perch phaeton. This equipage had enormous hind wheels, and its body was suspended fully five feet from the ground. Alexandra, who had never driven in such a carriage, looked around with interest. It was a novelty to regard the world from such a high viewpoint.

The duke glanced down at her when they entered the gates of Hyde Park. "Now, what is this urgent matter you wish to discuss with me? Your note seemed quite unsettled."

Alexandra quickly related what she had heard about the proposed duel. "I know ladies are not even supposed to know about such things, but I could not sit idly by without doing something. Sir Charles is my friend, and I would not see him hurt or arrested." Her voice was impassioned.

"I am glad you had the good sense to come to me. Naturally, no one has spoken to me about the affair."

"Can you do anything to prevent the meeting from taking place?"

Stanford, concentrating on maneuvering his horses around a tricky bend in the road, took a while to respond. "I will do what I believe to be necessary, Miss Grantham."

Much to Alexandra's disappointment, he did not elaborate on these words, and when they had traveled around the Park once more, he took her back to Longmore House. Then, after escorting her to the door, he bid her farewell and drove away.

Alexandra watched the phaeton disappear around the corner with a perplexed expression on her face. Then she walked past Leighton, who held the door open for her, and went upstairs to her bedchamber. She had done the best she could in a difficult situation. Hopefully, the duke would somehow manage to put a stop to the duel.

Early the following day, John called at Longmore House. Alexandra, partaking of a solitary breakfast in the breakfast parlor, looked up eagerly when he entered the room.

"Well?" she asked after he took a seat opposite her at the table. "Do you have any news?"

John broke a roll and chewed a piece of it thoughtfully. "Winters failed to arrive. I had the news from Arthur Rigby, who acted as Fotherby's second, half an hour ago."

She smiled. "What wonderful news, John!"

"Rather surprising, though, Alex," her brother said slowly. "Winters, I believed, was in deadly earnest about the duel. Rigby is astonished that he cried off. As am I."

Alexandra nodded in agreement, though John's news did not surprise her at all. The Duke of Stanford, she was sure, was a man who rarely failed in his objective when he put his mind to doing something. And he would not have wished a duel to be fought over his sister's name.

An hour after John took his leave, the duke himself called to take Alexandra riding in the Park. As they rode down the street together, she said, "My brother informed me at breakfast that the duel was called off this morning because Mr. Winters failed to present himself at the appointed rendezvous."

The duke glanced across at her. "News of this nature spreads very quickly, it seems. Your brother spoke the truth. Winters was unable to arrive on Putney Heath on time."

"You did something to prevent his arrival, I suppose?"

He bowed from the saddle. "You suppose correctly, ma'am." He paused and, after a few moments, continued deliberately, "I know I can trust you not to speak of my part in this affair to anyone, Miss Grantham."

She inclined her head. "Of course I won't. You have kept my secrets after all. And I would not have either Letitia or you injured by such gossip."

"I am pleased I can trust your discretion. Just one of the many qualities I appreciate in you."

The blood rushed to Alexandra's cheeks at his warm glance. Then, rapidly changing the subject, she began a monologue about how turnips could be extremely productive in specific kinds of soil. She then went on to talk about the wheat crop that year, which was expected to be exceptionally fine. She managed to sustain this stream of chatter until they returned to Berkeley Square an hour later, where she thankfully escaped from his disturbing gaze.

AFTER HE TOOK his leave of Alexandra, Robert returned home and changed his clothes before driving to Sir Jason Morecombe's Brook Street residence. During his investigation into the altercation between Sir Charles Fotherby and Vernon Winters, he discovered that Winters had been in Watier's the night before last as Sir Jason Morecombe's guest. Although he could not yet be sure, he well knew the man's character and strongly suspected Sir Jason of playing some part in engineering the quarrel between the two men. He intended to find out precisely what had transpired.

He was shown into a salon by the manservant who opened the door. A few moments later, Sir Jason entered the room. He bowed when he saw his guest and said in a languid voice, "My, my, to what do I owe this unexpected honor?"

"I think you know the reason for my visit, Morecombe."

Sir Jason waved a pale hand. "My dear sir, pray be seated. I have a singular dislike of being loomed over. May I offer you some refreshment? A glass of wine, perhaps?" he said as Robert took his seat.

He declined the offer and then paused for a moment. "How well are you acquainted with Vernon Winters?"

"Vernon Winters?" Sir Jason raised his brows. "The name is

familiar, but I cannot quite place it..."

"He accompanied you to Watier's as your guest the evening before last."

"Ah, yes! That must be why it seemed familiar."

"Quite," Robert said dryly. "Do you have nothing more to say?"

"Oh, not at all, Your Grace. I believe we understand each other fairly well."

Robert leaned forward in his chair. "I am warning you this one time, Morecombe. Keep your distance from anything to do with my sister. And from Alexandra Grantham. If you attempt to harm either of them in any way, even by proxy, you will regret it."

Sir Jason's brows flew up. "I understand your concern for your sister's well-being, Your Grace, but Miss Grantham, as far as I can see, holds no claim to your protection. I think I should not promise, therefore, to... ah... 'keep my distance' from her, as you say."

Robert considered Sir Jason for a long moment. Then he rose from his chair and walked across to him. "I regard Miss Grantham as being very much under my protection. Remember that." His voice was soft.

With a slight bow, Robert turned and made his way to the door of the Salon. Before leaving the room, he turned back. "Ah, yes, Morecombe, one other word of advice. The next time you attempt to influence public opinion, do not rely on your sister-in-law to aid you in your task. She is tolerated in Society but will never be fully accepted. You made a simple tactical error in your campaign when you enlisted her aid. Good morning." With these words, he opened the door and quietly left the room.

Robert drove to White's, his mind preoccupied with the events of the morning. Sir Jason was a dangerous man with a vindictive nature, and it seemed as if the baronet was intent on making mischief, not only for Letitia but also for Miss Grantham. He wasn't surprised by Sir Jason's malicious intentions; he and the other man had been at odds for some years now, ever since Robert had refused to permit him to pay his addresses to his sister, Serena, some years back, when Robert had just come into his title. When the baronet had asked his permission to address her, Robert had cited Sir Jason's debauched way of life as the reason for his refusal to grant the baronet an interview with his sister.

The man's pride had been wounded, and Robert was aware that Sir Jason would welcome any opportunity that came his way to settle an old score. He would need to keep a closer eye on both Letitia and Miss Grantham from now on.

Upon entering the club, he relinquished his hat and cloak to the porter before walking up the stairs to the room overlooking the street. After greeting those of his friends who were present, he made his way to a seat by the window and settled down with a copy of the *Morning Post*.

Before very long, he was joined by Lord Wrothly. "Robert, dear fellow! Do stop reading that dull paper. I want your opinion on this new waistcoat of mine."

He glanced up from his paper and winced. "Edward, I find it difficult to understand this obsession of yours for everything striped. The cut of the waistcoat is very well, but the stripes, man, the stripes."

Lord Wrothly's face fell. "But, Robert! Schweitzer, himself told me that this waistcoat was in vogue."

"He lied."

"You wound me deeply. Very, very deeply. In fact, I am quite cast down."

"I am sure you will soon come about."

Lord Wrothly grinned. "I always do, you know. I always do." He tilted his head to one side and said in a contemplative voice, "Although I may never attain your level of sartorial elegance, I'll wager I cut more of a figure in the street than you do." He sighed. "How I long for the days before Brummell came along when a man could wear a flowered waistcoat with impunity." He regarded his shoes meditatively for a moment. "Oh well, times change, and we must change with them." He looked at the clock on the wall, and his face brightened. "I say, old fellow, I have a lesson with Fazio now. Come and have a bout with me."

Robert's expression was grave. "I think that if I were to fence with you, Edward, your waistcoat would distract me too much."

Lord Wrothly grimaced. "Damn you, Robert! You—you—" He laughed suddenly. "I'll change it on the way there. You'll come?"

"Certainly. But leave the waistcoat. It is sure to prove less distracting than some of the others I have seen you sporting."

The two men left White's and drove to the Italian fencing master's rooms situated in Bond Street. When they arrived, Signor Fazio's man showed them into a small apartment. "If you would wait here but a moment, gentlemen, Signor Fazio is presently engaged in instructing one of his pupils."

"Is he?" Lord Wrothly said jovially. "No matter, we'll watch."

Ignoring the servant's expostulations that his master would not like the interruption, he made his way to the door separating the two rooms. Robert shrugged and followed his friend at a more leisurely pace. Entering the large space a moment later, he came to an abrupt standstill. Signor Fazio and Sir Jason Morecombe were fencing in the middle of the room. The two men ignored the sound of the opening door and continued their bout for a few minutes longer before putting up their swords.

Signor Fazio turned to the newcomers and, leaning on his foil, smiled in welcome. "Milor', Your Grace. You have come to take a turn with the foils?"

Lord Wrothly nodded. "We have." He glanced at Sir Jason and bowed formally. "I am surprised to see you, Morecombe. As a veritable master of swordplay already, I wouldn't think you would take lessons from old Fazio."

Sir Jason smiled thinly. "I like to keep my wrist in practice." Glancing across at Robert, he murmured, "One never knows when one may be called upon to use one's fencing skills."

Fazio glanced sharply at the baronet. "You speak of the *duello*, Saire Jason?"

The baronet put on his coat. "I do."

Fazio shook his head. "With the new passes we have perfected today, Saire Jason, you will be able to win any duel. You are a rare Englishman—you appreciate the art of the *duello*. But you must use this knowledge with wisdom." He looked across at Robert, who was taking off his coat. "Only one other Englishman I have instructed understands the art of fencing, and that is His Grace."

Robert smiled across at the fencing master. "Coming from you, Fazio, those words are high praise."

The little Italian shook his head. "Me—I do not speak praise. I speak the truth."

"Who do you believe to be the better fencer? His Grace or my humble self?" Sir Jason regarded Fazio inscrutably.

He rolled his eyes. "You ask me a question that is impossible to answer, Saire Jason. Your styles are different—very different. You are cunning like your English fox. His Grace has great strength and a head that is cool under pressure. To say who is the better swordsman—it is an impossibility."

Sir Jason looked across at Robert again. "Perhaps one day we shall discover who the better man is, Fazio."

The small man smiled broadly. "Of a certainty, you two gentlemen must take a turn at the foils here, sometime."

Sir Jason made his way to the door, which stood open. Before he left, he turned around and bowed in Robert's direction. "I advise you to learn all that you can from Fazio, Your Grace. Some of the newest passes may come in useful to you one day."

Robert bowed in turn. "They may, indeed," he said quietly.

Nothing more was said, but a depth of meaning was understood.

Chapter Twenty-Two

Alexandra met Letitia in the Green Park the day after the averted duel. The two frequently walked in the hilly park together. Despite her enjoyment of the delights of the Metropolis, Alexandra missed the peacefulness of the countryside and felt quite at home here.

When she set eyes on her friend, she realized she was fairly bursting with news. Her cheeks were flushed a becoming shade of pink, and her eyes shone brightly. After she greeted Alexandra, she said in a breathless voice, "Oh, Alex! The most marvelously romantic thing has happened. You will not believe it. I can hardly believe it myself. To think that Charles would do such a thing."

Alexandra's voice was cautious. "What has he done?"

She sighed ecstatically. "A duel was nearly fought over me! I overheard Robert telling Cousin Amelia that Charles had called Vernon Winters out because he had made disparaging remarks about me. Charles was willing to risk his life for the honor of my name. The duel, however, did not take place. Vernon, being the dastardly coward that he is, failed to arrive at the agreed venue." Letitia hunched her shoulders in excitement. "I never thought such an exciting thing would happen to me! That Charles could be so—so manly has left me quite speechless."

Alexandra tactfully refrained from pointing out that, far from being rendered speechless, her friend had not stopped talking since they met. Instead, she said, "I have mentioned before that Sir Charles seems very fond of you, Letty. I am not at all surprised that he came to the defense of your honor."

"Oh, Alex! You know I think I may be in love with him. I have never regarded Charles as anything other than my brother's friend. But now! Well, the duel has changed everything."

"Do you love him, Letty, or are you merely succumbing to the perceived romance of the situation?"

She bit her lip. "I know my family thinks that I am a flighty featherbrain, and I am the first to admit that I have tumbled foolishly into love in the past. But what I feel for Charles is quite different from my other romantic entanglements. I believe I do love Charles. Only, I did not know it beforehand."

Alexandra smiled. "I am truly happy for you, then, Letty. Sir Charles would make a splendid husband."

"He would, wouldn't he?" Letitia said with satisfaction. After recounting the numerous virtues of Sir Charles—which would have astonished that gentleman had he been present to hear them—Letitia paused and looked inquisitively at her friend. "And you, Alex? I know you say that you wish to remain unmarried, but recently I have thought that perhaps you and Robert might make a match of it. I know several other people who think the same thing. And he is so very fond of you."

Alexandra felt the heat rising in her cheeks. "You—and they—are mistaken, Letty. Your brother has been very kind, setting his seal of approval on me in the way he has. But he certainly does not regard me in such a serious light, fond or not."

Much to Alexandra's relief, Letitia changed the subject, and they spoke of other matters until their return to Berkeley Square, including the thorny topic of the imminent birth of Letitia's sister's fifth child, which was expected any day now. After giving him four daughters, Selina's husband had made it abundantly clear that he hoped she would present him with a son this time. Letitia spent the entire walk back to Berkeley Square expounding indignantly on the entirely unfair pressure placed upon ladies to bear male heirs.

Alexandra agreed, but in the privacy of her bedchamber later, it was Letitia's earlier words that occupied her mind. How many other members of the *ton* believed nuptials to be in the air for her and the duke? It seemed as if she had been correct in questioning the wisdom of his decision to accompany her in Sir Charles's place during her morning rides.

Alexandra had thought that, at worst, people might suspect Stanford was setting her up as his latest flirt. But if rumors were spreading that he was intent on proposing matrimony to her, this was rather more serious. Something needed to be done to change the tide of talk again.

In Hyde Park the following day, she broached the subject with him. "Your Grace, it has come to my attention that gossip is now circulating about you and me. We may need to cease our morning rides together until it dies down. I could perhaps take my grandmother's groom along with me for a while instead."

He took a few moments to reply. "And what reason do you have for suggesting this?"

"The same reason you gave me when you suggested I cease my morning rides with Sir Charles. The *ton*, as I feared, have begun to link our names together. And a few misguided people even believe that you intend offering for me." Alexandra flushed slightly. "You and I know, naturally, that this is a ridiculous notion. But . . . well, I do not want people to speculate about us, Your Grace."

"I regret to inform you, Miss Grantham, that if we are no longer seen together, people will believe us to have fallen out. It will give rise to even more gossip than there may be at present, and that can only be damaging to your social career."

Alexandra's brow creased. "Oh. But—is there nothing to be done?"

"I am afraid not. People will continue to talk, whatever action we take. The best thing we can do is to continue as we have been going on."

Alexandra puzzled over his words when she returned to Longmore House. Why had he suggested accompanying her on her rides in the first place? Surely he had known the *ton* would be bound to speculate about them, as they had done about her and Sir Charles? His actions were mystifying. Feeling a trifle uneasy, Alexandra wondered what deep game the Duke of Stanford was playing.

AFTER BRINGING EMILY to stay at Longmore House, Lady Longmore decided it would simplify matters if Emily and Alexandra shared a coming-out ball. Their joint presentation promised to be an event of more than ordinary social importance, and nearly every guest who was sent a gilt-edged card accepted the invitation. It seemed that the whole of London would be arriving in force on their doorstep for the party.

The multifarious details that needed attention to ensure all went well on the appointed evening kept Alexandra's grandmother fully occupied during the week preceding the ball. The large ballroom and conservatory, which had not been in use for some time since Grandmama had not entertained on a grand scale since her husband died, were opened up, swept, and cleaned by the housemaids.

The crystal chandeliers were polished until they glistened, and furniture was removed from various rooms to create more space. Extra glasses, plates, and silver cutlery were found, and constables and linkboys warned of the large number of carriages that would be assembling in Berkeley Square on the evening of the ball. Musicians were hired to provide music for the dancing, and Grandmama decided, after a little consideration, to order supplementary refreshments from Gunter's so that her French chef could focus his attention on preparing the delicacies for which he was renowned.

Desirous of decorating her rooms in a manner quite out of the common way, Alexandra's grandmother decided to create an English country garden effect by making lavish use of flowers. "A garden is, after all, the perfect setting for you, Alexandra!" she said with a fond smile.

After spending a most enjoyable morning in consultation with the proprietor of a nursery garden in King's Road, they eventually decided on a blue, white, and silver color scheme. But Alexandra became so distracted by the beautiful blooms on display that her grandmother had to call her to attention to discuss which flowers she preferred. Finally, it was decided that the florist would make creative use of hyacinths, jasmine, and wood anemones in hanging baskets, which would create the perfect backdrop for Alexandra's ball gown.

Exquisite in its simplicity, this off-the-shoulder creation of figured lace over a cerulean-blue satin robe was described by Madame Bouchet to Alexandra when she went for her final fitting as *"ma pièce de résistance, mademoiselle."* Long white gloves, a length of silver net draped around the shoulders, a pair of dainty slippers of Denmark satin, and Alexandra's beautiful sapphire set completed the effect of classic elegance.

Emily, somewhat overwhelmed by all the preparations, retired into the background. She contributed very little to the animated discussions between Alexandra and Lady Longmore, and Alexandra, noticing her friend's reticence, confronted her about it one morning.

"Are you not looking forward to the ball, Emily?" she said in concern.

Emily drew in a sharp breath. "Oh no, Alexandra! I am sure it will be lovely. Only, I feel that I am imposing on you and Lady Longmore. It should only be your coming-out ball, not mine."

"Nonsense, my dear." Alexandra linked her arm through her friend's. "I couldn't ask for a nicer person to share it with."

She chewed her bottom lip. "Are you certain?"

"Of course I am, you goose! Now, tell me, what are you

planning to wear?"

"Oh, I'm not sure. I have my white evening gown. I could wear that, I suppose."

Alexandra shook her head. "But you have worn that on so many other occasions. Don't you have something else?"

"Stepmama provided more for Jane in the way of clothes than she did for me. I don't have many ball gowns." She lowered her eyes, as a flush rose in her pale cheeks. "That's partly why Stepmama left me at home so often, Alex. My wardrobe is very limited."

"Well, we must do something about that. I shall talk to Grandmama."

True to her word, Alexandra spoke to her grandmother later that evening about Emily's lack of finery.

"But that simply will not do," the older lady said firmly. "I shall ask Madame Bouchet if she can make up something for Emily to wear. We cannot have her looking or feeling out of place."

Madame Bouchet agreed to design a transparent cream lace gown, embroidered with silk sprays, over a cream satin slip for her new client. Since the ball was so near, the modiste arranged for three seamstresses to work on the dress so it would be finished in time. And even though the extra labor cost Lady Longmore a pretty penny, she did not begrudge the expense, telling Alexandra that she wanted Emily—who could be her future granddaughter-in-law, after all—to look her best on the celebratory night.

The gown was cut low and square in a straight line across the bosom, and when Emily tried it on for a fitting, she self-consciously covered her chest. "Don't I look a little fast in this, Alex?"

"Not at all! You look charming, Emily." The beautiful dress set off her friend's pale gold hair, grey eyes, and delicate bone structure to perfection. Alexandra considered her, a smile playing about her mouth. John would be enchanted.

"I don't think I will ever be able to thank your grandmother enough, Alex," she said, her lips trembling. "She has been so kind and generous toward me."

Emily had also been grateful when her hostess informed her that she had invited Major Rawlings to the ball. From what Emily knew of him, her uncle was a kindly gentleman, and she had told Alexandra that she would be pleased to have some familial support on this momentous occasion.

At his sister's request, John reluctantly agreed to take a few waltzing lessons from a well-known Italian dancing master so that he could partner Emily in the first waltz. "Although I'd rather not, Alex. Dancing is a cursed dull business, and I will more than likely tread on the poor girl's toes or embarrass us both by forgetting the steps." He said this with a chuckle and a teasing grin, but Alexandra, studying her brother's face closely, realized with a sinking heart that he was not well.

In recent days dark rings had formed under his eyes, and his skin had developed an unhealthy greyish tint. London air did not suit his constitution. And, although he tried to make as little of it as possible, the hacking cough that had plagued him since his early childhood had returned and was growing worse as the days of his prolonged visit to the Metropolis went by.

As much as she wished to tell her obstinate brother to return home for the sake of his health, Alexandra knew better than to do so. At heart, John was the archetypal country gentleman, but he was also a young man hungry for new experiences. Although he knew that the London air only exacerbated his asthmatic condition, this reality must be difficult for a young gentleman, suddenly exposed to the delights of city life and the charms of one young lady in particular to accept with equanimity. His frustration with his health made him disinclined to listen to any sisterly advice—no matter how well-intended. Alexandra, therefore, held her own counsel, but the problem continued to weigh heavily on her mind and cast a damper on her spirits in the days leading up to her ball.

CHAPTER TWENTY-THREE

ON THE EVENING of the grand occasion, just before it was time to go downstairs to help her grandmother greet the first of their guests, Alexandra paused in front of the long mirror in her bedchamber and regarded the image of the refined young woman staring back at her. She seemed almost a stranger, certainly very different from the carefree young girl who had once waded barefoot through a stream in search of unusual pebbles to add to an already large collection.

But this young woman was a picture of elegance and tasteful style, a model of ladylike perfection. Alexandra sighed, considering how her transformed physical appearance seemed to symbolize the different way in which she had begun to view life and love.

Being an innately honest person, she could no longer ignore her feelings for the Duke of Stanford, and the truth was that she was falling more and more under his magnetic spell.

Ever since the evening of Lady Rigby's ball, when she had so foolishly informed Sir Charles, in the duke's presence, that she was wholly unaffected by his legendary charm, his attitude toward her had undergone a subtle yet distinct change.

She should never have said such a thing. She ought to have realized that Stanford's masculine pride would not allow him to overlook such a blatant challenge, and, in all likelihood, he had decided then and there to set her up as his latest flirt to prove she *was* susceptible to him.

Even so, knowing his attentions were not serious did not alter the fact that her heart began to beat a little faster whenever he walked into a room. And lately, any parties she attended which he did not had been interminably tedious affairs.

Her lips curved in a self-mocking smile. So much for her much-touted imperviousness to the charms of men. Drawing herself up to her full height, she stared challengingly at the figure reflected in the glass. She would take a firm hold on herself and be careful not to reveal her budding feelings to anyone, least of all to the *ton*'s foremost breaker of hearts. Although in imminent danger of losing her own heart to him, she very much wanted to keep her self-respect. If her heart was going to break, she wanted it to break quietly.

Grandmama, John, and Emily were waiting for her when she descended the stairs. At the rustle of her skirt, they stopped their conversation and looked up at her, not saying a word.

"Oh dear, surely I don't look as bad as all that?" she said with a smile as she joined them.

Her grandmother cleared her throat. "You look enchanting, child—and so much like your sweet mother."

Alexandra embraced the older lady but made no response, understanding her grandmother's need for a moment's stillness to regain her composure.

Turning to Emily, Alexandra complimented her friend on her appearance before looking at her brother, resplendent in a new set of evening clothes. "What prime style you are turned out in, John. You *are* becoming a man of fashion."

Smiling self-consciously, he said, "I took Peter's advice and got Swindon to make up some new clothes for me. You're dressed up as fine as fivepence yourself, Alex."

"Hmm . . ." her lips twitched. "Perhaps I shall throw caution to the wind, talk of nothing but Latin verbs and crop rotation all evening, and rename myself 'The Dashing Bluestocking.'"

John was still chuckling at this remark when Leighton opened the door to admit the first of their guests.

Surrounded by a host of gentlemen later that evening, Alexandra smiled disbelievingly at the excessive compliments they seemed intent on paying her. Somehow she could not quite swallow Sir Richard Brampton's assertion that she reminded him of a "mystical woodland nymph" or Lord Hawthorne's declaration that her "eyes outshone the stars in their brilliance, and diamonds in their brightness," but she was enjoying their creativity.

She was happy to escape from her admirers' excessive attentions to dance the first waltz of the evening with Peter Denville, who had valiantly shared her brother's dancing lessons so that he could stand up with Alexandra on this special occasion. But when the chords for the second waltz struck up, she looked around uneasily. Stanford had arrived at an unfashionably early hour to secure this dance with her. But how successfully could she partner him in this intimate display after so recently admitting her feelings for him to herself? She would be bound to give herself away.

Just as she thought the duke had decided to forego their waltz, he made his way toward her. Bowing over her hand, he said quietly, "My dance, I think, Miss Grantham."

Sir Richard, who had also approached after the first waltz, straightened his shoulders and shot an accusing look at Stanford. "It was devilish inconsiderate of you, Your Grace, to steal a march on the rest of us by claiming a waltz from Miss Grantham before we had even arrived."

The duke smiled gently. "A little foresight, Brampton, and it would have been you, and not I, who would have the honor of leading Miss Grantham out."

Alexandra, feeling unusually shy, stepped silently into his arms. Fortunately, her numerous dancing lessons paid off, and she executed the well-rehearsed steps of the waltz without giving them a thought. All her attention instead was focused on the feel of Stanford's embrace as he held her close. So achingly close.

"My dear, you look beautiful."

Combined with the duke's devastating smile, this simple compliment affected Alexandra in quite a different way from her other more elaborate tributes. Blushing slightly, she thanked him, privately thinking he looked quite handsome himself in his expertly tailored clothes. A coat of black superfine perfectly fitted his muscular form, and pantaloons showed his fine legs off to advantage. A fob hung to one side of his plain white waistcoat, and a single diamond winked from the intricate folds of his necktie.

Sporting none of the affectations of the dandy-set, Stanford somehow made these gentlemen appear horribly overdressed. He simply took one's breath away. She straightened her spine and mentally shook herself. Such thoughts were dangerous. She must attempt now more than ever to put a guard on her susceptible heart.

The duke spoke again, and Alexandra met his intent gaze. "I am surprised to see your brother still in London. From what you said, I was under the impression his constitution would make a visit to the Capital impossible. Or has he only come to London for a short while to lend you his support at your coming-out ball?"

Alexandra shook her head. "I am afraid John has decided to remain in London for an unspecified period of time. Now that he has had a taste of the pleasures the Metropolis has to offer, he is reluctant to return too soon to Grantham Place. One cannot blame him for wishing to remain here for the duration of the Season. However, I must confess to feeling some concern over his well-being." She sighed, but not wishing to burden him with her worries about John's health, she forced a smile to her lips and changed the subject. "Your Grace, I must admit to feeling somewhat guilty that you have been obliged to attend the coming-out parties that I remember you once castigated as being 'interminably dull affairs,' merely to keep me fashionable!"

"No party you grace with your presence, Miss Grantham, could ever be described as a 'dull affair.' In any event, I can assure you that I no longer attend these affairs to keep you launched in Society. You must be aware by now that you are a success in your own right." He paused for a moment. "The reason I am in such frequent attendance is that I have become rather partial to your charming company."

Alexandra's heart sank at this proof that he was indeed attempting to set her up as his latest flirt. She wanted nothing of that doubtful honor. It would only bring her heartache. Once he succeeded in his objective of winning her over, he would no doubt tire of her company and focus his attentions on some other lady. And that she could not bear. It would be foolish to allow herself to be drawn further into a flirtation with him that would mean the world to her but very little to him. Therefore, it was in a cool voice that she murmured, "Your Grace, you flatter me."

"I can assure you, Miss Grantham, that I am not in the habit of flattering anyone."

She raised her brows. "The fact that London is littered with female hearts you have broken must have something to do with the smoothness of your tongue and your ability to turn a pretty compliment. Therefore, I am desolate to inform you that I do not believe you!"

"I never knew, until this moment, that I would come to regret my past."

"Poor, poor man." She laughed, determined to keep wading out of the deep and back into the shallows, where it was safer.

"Miss Grantham, you would try the patience of a saint. And I, as you should know, am certainly no saint."

"Rest assured, Your Grace, that I have never, ever since I have known you, mistaken you for one," she said reassuringly.

He chuckled, but as he looked down at her, the smile on his lips slowly faded. "Do you have any idea how utterly delightful you are?"

At the fervent look in his eyes, she glanced hastily away. The defenses she was attempting to erect against this man were woefully inadequate in the face of such a concentrated onslaught from him. She felt more helpless than a newborn kitten—and infinitely more vulnerable.

Because she wasn't merely in danger of losing her heart to him—she suddenly realized that she already had.

She only hoped she could somehow prevent him from realizing it as well.

The dance ended, and Alexandra, failing to meet his eyes, made a hasty excuse and escaped. Then, crossing the room, she approached Aunt Eliza, who had also traveled up to the capital for the occasion. She was staying with a sister, who lived retired from fashionable life in the village of Wimbledon, and Alexandra had not had an opportunity to speak to her aunt since her arrival a few days before.

"I trust you are enjoying your evening, Aunt Eliza?"

The older lady nodded, causing the enormous ostrich plumes in her headdress to bob back and forth. "Oh yes, my love. What a splendid occasion this is. And you look so beautiful, quite transformed! You cannot know what a relief it is that I have not failed your Grandmama in my duty." She dabbed at her eyes with a lacy handkerchief she extracted from her reticule. "It was such a weight of responsibility all these years taking care of you and your sisters. But I can see my efforts were not in vain."

"Abigail and Dorothea are returning to Grantham Place shortly, I believe? I received a letter from Thea last week."

"Yes, that is why I am only here for a short visit. It is a pity that I cannot stay for longer after enduring the jolts of that coach for so many hours on end. But I must return to welcome the girls home."

"I am pleased they have left the seminary at the same time, Aunt. It would have been lonely for Abby to stay on alone. I am so looking forward to hearing their news upon my return home."

Aunt Eliza patted her arm. "And they will be delighted to see you again, I am sure. Although I do not know when that will be."

She lowered her voice conspiratorially. "I believe nuptials to be in the air? I am so very proud of you, dearest, for snagging such a prize."

"You are mistaken, Aunt Eliza. I am not betrothed to anyone."

"It is only a matter of time, I hear. And this in spite of the fact that you never quite reached the desired level in all your accomplishments. However, you did persist with your embroidery, my love. I will grant you that, despite all those pricked fingers." She gave a shake of her head. "I only hope your sisters are more accomplished than you, particularly Dorothea, as she does not have your beauty."

Alexandra let out an indignant gasp. "Thea is lovely!"

"It is those spectacles. They make her look decidedly scholarly. And she is a little too shy and retiring. I hope that the seminary instilled some confidence in her."

"On that we agree, I suppose." Alexandra's smile was fixed. She also hoped that her middle sister had grown in assurance while she had been away, as instilling confidence in her nieces was surely not their aunt's forte.

"How delightful it will be to have a family reunion. You will all stare when you see the Duke of Stanford's improvements in the neighborhood, particularly Frobisher's Field, which has been quite transformed. It is no longer an eyesore, thank heavens."

Alexandra frowned. "What do you mean?"

"The duke has drained the field and enclosed it with a fence."

Alexandra opened her mouth and then closed it again. "But that is the only piece of land in the district where the poor can still gather firewood and graze their animals."

But her aunt was gazing over Alexandra's shoulder. "What a very odd headdress that woman is wearing. Do look. But be subtle about it and wait a few minutes."

"Aunt Eliza!"

The older lady brought her gaze back to her face. "Yes, dear?"

"Do you know what the duke plans to do with Frobisher's

Field?"

Her relative waved a vague hand. "The vicar informed me that His Grace plans to introduce some kind of new crop rotation method. But let us not speak of such a dull subject during your ball. Will you point out Lady Letitia Beaumont to me? Your grandmother informs me that she is a great friend of yours. I must say, that was a very clever move on your part to befriend the sister of the man you have your eye upon."

Alexandra let out a frustrated breath. It would be useless to try to find out more from her aunt. She made her escape a few minutes later, and the rest of the evening passed in a blur as she went through the motions of dancing with a variety of partners. She did not get the opportunity to speak to Stanford again that night, but she chatted with Emily and John during supper. They appeared to be in the best of spirits, although her brother looked far too pale for Alexandra's peace of mind. When he went off to procure a glass of lemonade for Emily, she took her friend aside and asked in a low voice if she could somehow contrive to get John to go home early.

Emily's forehead creased in concern. "He is determined to stay as late as possible, Alex, but I will do my best."

A short while later, Alexandra was relieved when John approached her to take his leave. As he left the ballroom, she wondered what magic spell Emily had cast on him that he listened to her suggestions without protest while studiously ignoring any advice given to him by his grandmother or sister.

After all the guests had departed, Alexandra dragged herself upstairs and crept into her bed, pulling the counterpane right up to her ears. She needed to hide away from the world and the dreadful discovery that she had given her heart away to a man who cared nothing for the things that mattered to her most.

How could she have been such a fool? The Duke of Stanford was an imperious aristocrat accustomed to shaping the world in the manner he saw fit. And clearly, he did not care about the poor the way he had led her to believe. He had utterly disregarded her concerns and taken away the last vestiges of dignity of the poor people in her own neighborhood.

It was true that the rich only got richer while the poor struggled along with less and less every year. And as a member of the upper classes, she was a part of the hierarchy that caused them such pain, but at least she felt the injustice of it and was trying to help.

How could she have believed herself in love with Stanford? He was a heartless wretch, and, in love or not, she wanted nothing more to do with him. Tears streamed down her cheeks, but she wiped them away defiantly.

The Duke of Stanford wasn't worth her tears.

CHAPTER TWENTY-FOUR

ROBERT LEFT LONDON the day after the ball at Longmore House. He drove his curricle to Stanford Court and spent most of the journey lost in thought, barely aware of the passing countryside as he welcomed the silence and solitude of his thoughts.

His relationship with Alexandra weighed heavily on his mind. After ten years on the town and having had more handkerchiefs thrown in his direction than he cared to remember, he had finally found the one woman with whom he wished to spend the rest of his days—if only she could be brought to take his attentions seriously.

Knowing full well his reputation placed him at a disadvantage in her eyes, he had set about courting her with circumspection, proceeding with decided caution in his attempt to woo and win her.

Never having fallen in love before, Robert had been unfamiliar with a state of being that he had always associated with sentimental young fools. But the more he saw of Alexandra, the more he was drawn to her. She offered him the respect of social politeness but seemed largely unaffected by his title and consequence, delighting him with her unconventional remarks and sparkling wit and humor. In a society where position and wealth seemed to take precedence over human warmth, she personified gentleness and kindness, thereby disdaining the airs and graces adopted by so many young ladies on the lookout for wealthy husbands.

But, although she appeared to enjoy his company, the minute he overstepped the invisible line she had drawn in their relationship, she became a wary, guarded stranger.

Perhaps she truly had no desire to enter the married state. He had not failed to notice the lengths to which she went to discourage her numerous suitors from believing she was open to receiving their addresses.

Remembering her pert assertion that she had "no desire to be saddled with a husband," a slight smile curled his lips. His beloved appeared to be uncommonly fond of the idea of becoming a spinster and disinclined to give it up willingly.

And yet, at times, he was almost certain that the beautiful girl he had fallen in love with looked at him with an expression in her eyes that could not be ascribed to mere friendship. She appeared to enjoy his attentions more than those of her other admirers, but the disturbing fact remained that he was unsure of her regard for him.

His mouth set in a grim line. Perhaps he had become spoilt. Having grown accustomed to women throwing out unmistakable lures to him, he had come to expect it from every member of the fairer sex like some contemptible coxcomb.

The only thing he could do was bide his time and continue to play upon Alexandra's defenses. He needed to go the long way round in winning her over. At present, he admitted wryly as he drove through the entrance archway of Stanford Court, it seemed to be the only way.

Looking around the familiar grounds of his ancestral home, bathed in the soft evening light, the tension holding him in its grip began to drain away. Returning to his childhood home had never failed to lift his spirits. His love for the magnificent lands he inherited upon his father's death ten years ago was deeply ingrained in him.

Contrary to what the gossip mongers implied, he had always intended to enter the wedded state to ensure his own son would one day inherit these lands. The only reason he had put it off for so long was that he had two younger brothers—one having sired a son already—which meant the impressive Stanford holdings were in no danger of passing out of the family.

And frankly, up until quite recently, the very idea of becoming riveted to some clinging female had filled him with distaste—until he met Alexandra. A smile played about his mouth as he thought of the fiery young beauty. Marriage to her would be neither a duty nor a chore; only, he was convinced, a delight.

He drove the curricle up the long, curving drive bordered by magnificent parkland studded with ancient oaks. The carriage wheels clattered over a stone bridge, the arches of which spanned a gently flowing stream, and when he rounded the next bend in the road, an enormous house came into view.

The main stone structure rose to three stories in the center with expansive wings on either side, sweeping forward to create a sizeable, terraced courtyard. The extensive lawns surrounding the stately mansion led down to an ornamental lake with an island of poplars in the center and hanging beechwoods beyond.

Robert brought his curricle to a halt in front of the entrance. Then, leaving Jimmy to drive the vehicle around to the stables, he strode up the shallow steps to the immense front doors.

Wilson, the butler who had served three generations of Beaumonts at The Court, opened the doors to him, his broad smile revealing his delight at seeing his master again. He took his hat and gloves. "Welcome home, Your Grace. It is a pleasure to see you again."

"Good afternoon, Wilson." He smiled at his old friend, who had so often covered for him during the madcap days of his childhood. "How is your rheumatism?"

"Much better, thank you, sir." He removed Robert's greatcoat. "Her Grace informed me that although she is at present resting in her bedchamber, she will be pleased to receive you in the Little Drawing Room immediately you arrive."

"Did she now?" he murmured. It was the unwritten law at Stanford Court that the Dowager Duchess of Stanford, once resting in her rooms, was under no circumstances to be disturbed. And, although she was the fondest of mamas, it was not her wont to order her offspring to visit her the minute they arrived. "Pray inform Her Grace that I shall wait on her in twenty minutes. I must change out of all my dirt first."

Exactly twenty minutes later, Robert entered the Little Drawing Room, the beautifully decorated apartment leading on from his mother's bedchamber. Due to the crippling nature of her arthritic condition, her mobility had been limited for many years, and she used this apartment as her private sitting room rather than the grand drawing room downstairs. A fire burned cheerfully in the grate, dispelling the chill from the air, and she sat nearby in a comfortable armchair, a warm rug spread over her knees.

His mother had, in her younger days, been considered a remarkable beauty. Ill-health and time had etched their inevitable mark on her flawless features, and silver now touched her lustrous mane of dark hair, but her exquisite bone structure and dark eyes gave her a timeless magnificence that neither age nor illness could ravage.

He bent down to kiss her proffered cheek. "You look as charming as ever, Mama."

"Thank you, Robert. You are too kind." Indicating the sofa across from her, she invited him to sit down.

After he had allayed her concerns about the well-being of her youngest daughter, she said in a carefully neutral tone, "What news do you bring me from London?"

He raised his brows. "Your cronies must be slipping up in their correspondence, Mama. They are usually most diligent in their efforts to keep you abreast of the latest London gossip."

She gave him a speaking look. "Is it true that you are to marry Alexandra Grantham?"

He brushed a particle of dust off his coat sleeve. "If Miss

Grantham will have me."

"*If* she will have you?" His mother sat up straighter in her chair. "What in heaven's name do you mean?"

"Miss Grantham is averse to the idea of marriage. On several occasions, she has informed me that she has no desire to wed. I have been . . . trying to overcome her objections in recent weeks but am, as yet, uncertain of her regard for me."

She burst out laughing. Then, wiping her streaming eyes, she said in a choked voice, "How vastly amusing, Robert!"

"Your maternal feelings do you credit, Mama. May I inquire as to why you find my predicament so marvelously diverting?"

She bit a quivering lip. "Well, dearest, it is only that for the last decade, every silly chit in London has tried to entice you into marriage. You are the most eligible bachelor in England and have been odiously courted and flattered by every lady you meet. And now, after all these years, the one girl on whom your fancy has alighted, you appear unsure of."

"It is probably doing me a world of good," he said dryly.

She laughed again. "I am even more eager now to become acquainted with your Miss Grantham. She must be a remarkable girl."

"You will find her quite out of the common way." He leaned back against the sofa, his arm resting along the top. "Perplexing, though."

"In what way?"

"Alexandra lost her mother when she was only thirteen, and she became a real mother hen to her brother and sisters as far as I can tell." He sighed. "But this role of caretaker led her to sacrifice herself for others to the extent that she does not seem to believe she also deserves such care."

"Hmm." She tilted her head to one side. "Rather like you." She hesitated a moment. "I know when you first appeared on the London scene so soon after your father died, you sought to enjoy yourself as a sort of temporary counterbalance to the heavy ducal responsibilities thrust upon your shoulders when you were not quite ready for them. But I think setting off on that path led you to become quite distant from yourself, Robert—your true self, I mean. Perhaps Miss Grantham has seen that part of you? The part you don't reveal to Society?"

He bowed his head but did not reply. In truth, he could not. He hadn't seen the similarities between himself and Alexandra before, but now they were set out before him in stark relief. Just as Alexandra had lost herself in her role of rescuer to her family members and those around her, so he'd experienced something comparable when he took over the burdens of the estate and the numerous people who relied on him.

As he studied his mother's delicate features, he suddenly realized that he and Alexandra also shared another concern—constant apprehension about the state of a close family member's health. He stilled. No wonder he felt so at ease with her. Even though they were from vastly different worlds, they had walked along connected paths.

"I received a most interesting letter from Anne Longmore the other day," his mother said finally as she adjusted the rug on her knees. "She is of the decided opinion that her granddaughter is head over ears in love with you."

Robert rose slowly to his feet. "Is she indeed?" Crossing the distance between them, he pressed another kiss to her cheek. "Mama, you are a jewel."

Chapter Twenty-Five

Alexandra sighed as she watched fat raindrops chase one another down the bay windows of the morning room. The dismal weather perfectly suited her downcast mood, and she released another long breath as the door opened and her grandmother bustled into the room.

Settling herself on the chaise longue across from Alexandra, she arranged her skirts about her. "I would advise you, my love, *not* to wear your heart on your sleeve."

Alexandra's gaze flew to her grandmother's face. "I am not sure what you mean."

"Last night at the Barton's ball, it was obvious to all who cared to look that you were not in spirits. People are not blind, Alexandra. They are bound to notice your downcast attitude and correctly attribute it to the fact that the Duke of Stanford is absent from town."

Alexandra sat bolt upright in her chair. "I am not pining over Stanford!"

"Then what is the matter?"

She folded her arms. "Aunt Eliza told me that the duke has fenced off Frobisher's Field. The people there use it for pasturage, and he took it away from them. After I *told* him there was limited land for common use in the district."

Her grandmother raised her brows. "Have you spoken to His

Grace about this?"

"No. Aunt Eliza told me of his plans at my ball, and Stanford left London the very next day. I haven't seen him since, and I don't wish to either."

"Ah." Her grandmother's gaze was pensive. "Plenty of problems can be resolved through a simple conversation. I would speak to Stanford before jumping to conclusions."

She straightened her shoulders. "I don't see why I should! He has shown me clearly that he does not value what I hold dear."

"Has he?"

"He doesn't care a jot about me."

"Hmm." Her grandmother wagged her head. "How diverting that Stanford has managed to convince the whole of Polite Society of his intentions toward you and yet has, ostensibly, failed to convince you. You must surely be the very last person in London not to know he has fallen in love with you."

Alexandra simply stared at her.

"You must have been blind not to have noticed that he has been seriously courting you."

"I believed he was merely attempting to set me up as his latest flirt—that he saw me only as a challenge. He is so very much above my station in life."

"His own mother wrote to me the other day to ask me if he was serious about his intentions toward you. I assured her that he was. And I can assure *you*, Alexandra, that you have him well and truly captivated."

"Do not speak thus, Grandmama." Alexandra grimaced. "You make me sound like one of those designing creatures, only intent on securing an eligible match."

"Forgive me, my love—that you most certainly are not." She paused a moment as she settled herself more comfortably in her seat. "You are a fortunate young lady to have won Stanford's affection, though. I would speak to him of your concerns about the field and hear what he has to say. I am sure he would not set out to do something calculated to displease you. Give him the benefit of the doubt. Sometimes, it is easy to allow your emotions to run away with you when it comes to matters of the heart. And I suspect you do love Stanford?"

The color rose in her cheeks. "I thought I did. Until I heard about that field."

"Falling in love can be a frightening experience. So frightening that we can sometimes look for reasons to push away the object of our affections. Think about that for a moment."

Alexandra sighed. "John said something of a similar nature to me recently. He believes I am afraid of marriage as I have refused every offer I have received thus far."

"I am glad he spoke to you, Alexandra, and I hope you will pay some heed to him. You should not push love away from you forever." A shadow suddenly crossed her grandmother's face. "I am sure you must have noticed your brother does not look in prime form. I have not voiced my concern to him because I know how much he dislikes being fussed over. But perhaps he would listen to you if you advised him to return home?"

Alexandra shook her head. "The only time I tentatively suggested to him that the London air might not agree with his constitution, he snapped at me very sharply." She raised her shoulders. "John is usually the most sensible of people, but when it comes to matters of his health, he can be infuriatingly obstinate. He resents the fact that he has a frail constitution and prefers to ignore his condition by burying his head in the sand. It appears that he has no intention of departing London in the near future."

"But he has always professed that he far prefers living in the country."

"That may well be. But for the first time in his life, he is enjoying the association of acquaintances of his own age. I think he is loath to give up his newfound friends—and Emily—and return to Grantham Place."

"Yes, and well do I know that stubbornness is a characteristic common in my grandchildren." Her grandmother's voice was acerbic. When Alexandra merely smiled at this, she continued:

"Now, if you will excuse me, I need to discuss the dinner menus for this week with Mrs. Watson."

Alexandra barely noticed her grandmother's departure as she let her mind drift back to Stanford, and the significance of her grandmother's words about him slowly sank into her consciousness. Alexandra had little experience of men, and in truth, she was alarmed at how swiftly and completely the duke had come to occupy her heart and mind. Perhaps her anger about the field did have something to do with the extreme confusion she felt at falling in love with him. She resolved to ask him about the enclosure when she next saw him and give him a chance to explain his actions.

She slumped back against her chair and allowed her chin to sink into her neck. She was in such a muddle. If this was what love did to one, she wasn't sure she liked it very much.

An image of a slightly younger, somewhat less experienced Alexandra flashed across her mind, and she groaned. How dearly she wished the disparaging remarks she had made about matrimony unsaid. Not that she was contemplating marriage now, was she? She let out a breath of frustration. She felt completely thrown off balance.

Thankfully, her grandmother would not tease her about her previous stance against the wedded state. She would be too happy to see Alexandra wed. But John would enjoy reminding her of how she had once scoffed at men and marriage. That was if her brother recovered. Alexandra frowned as she gazed unseeingly out of the window. Of late, his ill-health in London had had a decidedly poor effect on his usually sunny temper, and their easy friendship was beginning to become slightly strained.

The door of the morning room opened, and Alexandra glanced up. How surprising that someone had ventured out on this miserably dreary day. Her instinctive welcoming smile faded quickly when Edward Ponsonby walked into the room, clutching a bunch of daisies in his hands.

Espying her, he sidled forward, thrusting the flowers at her.

"My charming Miss Grantham, you look as bright and lovely as these blooms that I present to you."

Alexandra accepted his token of appreciation. She must look a very sorry sight to be compared to the most bedraggled bunch of flowers she had ever seen. "Mr. Ponsonby, it is good of you to call on us. My grandmother—"

Before she could complete her sentence, Mr. Ponsonby interrupted her: "Miss Grantham, we have no need of a chaperone. What I am desirous of saying to you does not require the presence of a third party." Alexandra looked desperately at Leighton, still at the morning room door, who bowed and exited the room, hopefully with the intention of alerting her grandmother to the presence of her unwelcome guest.

"Pray be seated, Mr. Ponsonby." Alexandra indicated the chair across from her.

He remained standing. "I come to you, Miss Grantham, as a man bewitched by your beauty. I cannot sleep or eat for thinking of you."

With great restraint, Alexandra refrained from glancing at his paunch, which hung over his tightly fitting pantaloons.

He took a step toward her. "I shall not rest until I can call you mine. My dear Miss Grantham, will you do me the honor of becoming my wife?" Before Alexandra could open her mouth to refuse him, he added in a condescending tone, "It is not wise to wait too long in deciding such matters, Miss Grantham. Eligible gentlemen do not come along every day, you know."

Alexandra stared at him, quite at a loss for words. But, before she could utter the stinging set-down he undoubtedly deserved, he carried inexorably on: "It has not failed to escape my notice that you have shown a decided partiality for the company of the Duke of Stanford in the past few weeks. As we both know, young ladies are always most affable when an eligible member of the opposite sex pays attention to them. But, be warned, my dear—you may have beauty and fortune, but the Duke of Stanford would never marry a lady of little consequence. You would do far better to favor me with your hand in marriage. I have estates in Surrey, and I can offer you a most respectable position in Society as my wife. It would be foolish of you indeed to refuse my offer of marriage."

Alexandra raised her brows. "Sir, I find your comments not only in bad taste but insulting." Remembering Sir Charles's remarks about Mr. Ponsonby's encumbered estates and the dubious state of his finances, Alexandra felt the heat of anger rising within her. The impertinence of the man! She took a deep breath to contain her ire—she would not allow him to provoke her into losing her temper. "I thank you, sir, for your offer of marriage, but I cannot accept it."

Mr. Ponsonby frowned, no longer looking quite so self-satisfied. Then his expression cleared. "Ah, my dear young lady, I see everything clearly, now. Yes, yes, so I do! As a young lady, you are naturally indecisive and need some time to consider my generous offer. I shall return to ask you again."

Alexandra's stomach turned as he winked conspiratorially at her. She looked up in relief when the door opened, and her grandmother entered the room again. "Mr. Ponsonby was about to take his leave, Grandmama."

The older lady studied him with a beady eye. "Indeed."

"Your servant, ladies," he muttered before being promptly escorted out of the room by Leighton.

Alexandra did not utter a word until she heard the front door close behind him. Then she turned toward her grandmother and said in a choked voice, "He said that I was in danger of becoming an old maid if I did not accept his generous offer of marriage. Oh!" Alexandra succumbed to laughter as she recalled Mr. Ponsonby's words. What a despicable little man he was, to be sure.

Her grandmother studied her in concern. "Are you quite well, my love? If the weather weren't so dismal, I would suspect you had a touch of the sun."

Alexandra shook her head and said in a strangled voice, "If I did not laugh, Grandmama, I would surely cry. Because the only illness that I am suffering from at present is a touch of the odious Mr. Edward Ponsonby."

Chapter Twenty-Six

A WEEK AFTER her coming-out ball, Alexandra wandered down the stairs to the hall, lost in contemplation. The gloomy weather of the last few days had given way to a bright, clear day, and she was looking forward to the shopping expedition she had planned with Letitia. Although neither of them had anything they wished to purchase, Letitia had intimated at the Hamilton's ball last night that she had something of a significant nature she wished to reveal to Alexandra without her chaperone being present. Her friend had not revealed what this significant "something" was, but Alexandra suspected a betrothal announcement was imminent.

Sir Charles's attentions to Letitia had become decidedly marked, and Letitia seemed to return his affections wholeheartedly. It was to be hoped that two of her dearest friends in London would make a match of it before the end of the Season. And, of course, the duke would not object to his sister's suitor in this instance. With his easy address and charming manners, Sir Charles was a matrimonial prize and an ideal companion for Letitia.

The knocker on the front door sounded as she reached the hall, and Leighton proceeded in his stately fashion to open the door. Alexandra's lips curved in amusement. How surprising that Letitia was punctual, for once.

But the cheerful greeting that sprang to her lips remained unsaid when the Duke of Stanford stepped into the house. He was back in London—and a day earlier than expected!

He stepped forward and raised her hand to his lips. "Miss Grantham, you are looking very well this morning."

"Your Grace." Her voice was stiff. "Letty mentioned that you had extended your visit to your estates and would only be back tomorrow."

"I decided I had far more pressing matters in Town that desired my attention—all of my attention." The warmth in his green eyes was unmistakable, and Alexandra glanced away in confusion.

"I . . . I also have a pressing matter that I need to discuss with you, Your Grace. Perhaps we could meet after my shopping expedition with Letty? She should be arriving at any moment."

"I have come to convey my sister's apologies to you. She has a headache and thus will be unable to accompany you to Bond Street."

"Oh. Poor Letty. I hope she hasn't succumbed to the influenza that has so many people in its grip."

"I would not be too concerned. I believe she is merely suffering from a succession of late nights. Amelia informs me she has been burning the candle at both ends. But tell me, Miss Grantham, would you give me the pleasure of your company instead? I thought you might enjoy a drive to Richmond Park."

"Yes, I would." She turned to Leighton, who hovered nearby. "My grandmother is still abed, and I do not wish to disturb her. Pray inform her of the change of plan in my activities for this morning."

"Certainly, Miss Grantham."

When Leighton padded off, Alexandra decided to grasp the nettle. "May I have a word with you in private before we leave, Your Grace?"

"Ah, yes. That pressing matter." He studied her quizzically. "It sounds rather serious."

Alexandra led the way into the morning room and then turned around to face him. "At my coming-out ball, Aunt Eliza informed me that you have fenced off Frobisher's Field and that you are in the process of draining it."

"Yes. It is more of a bog than a field at the moment."

"I know the land is of poor quality, but it is the only common land. The people graze their animals there and gather firewood from the copse at the end."

He remained silent for a moment. "I am aware of this, Miss Grantham."

"And yet you have taken the field away?" Her voice trembled with anger.

"Do you honestly believe I would throw the poor to the wolves by not compensating them in any way? What a very low opinion of my character you must have."

"You made alternative arrangements for them, then?"

"Of course I did. You are not the only person in the world with a conscience, Alexandra."

Color burned in her cheeks. "No. Forgive me. I must seem like a prig. It is just that I feel it to be my duty—."

He took a step forward and frowned down at her. "Why?"

"Why?" Her forehead wrinkled. "Because I have always done charity work."

"It isn't just charity work. Your need to help people is extreme. You have regularly placed yourself in harm's way to do so."

She shook her head mutely, unable to give voice to the strength of her protective instinct.

"Why is that?" he persisted.

She gave a helpless shrug. "I—I don't know."

He searched her features for a long moment. "You were forced into a position of responsibility at a very young age. That must have been difficult—taking on the duties of a parent as a child."

"I managed."

"Did you?" He took a step closer. "Think about it, my dear. You have grown so accustomed to taking care of others—your brother, your sisters, and the families your mother once cared for—that I think you came to believe it was your only role in life. But you are not the savior of the world, Alexandra. You cannot be."

You are not the savior of the world. And hadn't both John and Mrs. Simpson said the same in their own ways? He was right. They all were. She had tried to take on that role, using all the means at her disposal to solve the problems around her. But no matter how hard she tried, she wasn't able to rescue every soul in need. No human being was. And still, she had persisted in her endeavors to do so, carrying the heaviest of burdens.

She released her breath in a shuddering sigh. "I see sorrow around me all the time. I cannot ignore it." Her shoulders started to shake, and she folded her arms across her middle, trying to hold on to her composure.

He lifted his hand and touched her cheek, meeting her gaze steadily. Then, when she released a small sob, he drew her against his chest, holding her tightly. At first, she resisted the pressure of his arms. But then she sank into the comfort of his embrace as a tear rolled down her cheek. Soon another followed and then another until they poured down her face in a steady stream, washing away years of hurt, years of always trying to be a panacea to everyone and not succeeding.

Eventually, she leaned back in the circle of Robert's arms and drew in a couple of shaky breaths.

Withdrawing a handkerchief from his pocket, he pressed the fine linen square into her hand. She wiped her eyes and cheeks and then stepped out of his embrace to blow her nose.

"Feeling better?" His voice was kind.

She nodded. "I haven't wept like that in years."

"A drive in an open carriage will do you good."

"I should like that. I don't think I can stay cooped up indoors today."

She placed her hand on his arm and accompanied him outside. After he handed her up into his curricle, he took his place beside her, gathering the reins in his hands.

As they moved off, Alexandra inhaled the fresh morning air. He must think her the veriest watering-pot—time for a change of subject. "Although I have enjoyed living in London, Your Grace, I like the countryside above all things. I have not visited Richmond Park, although I have been to Kew Gardens, which is nearby. Letty informed me it is possible to imagine yourself in the country while there."

He smiled. "The *ton* would be astonished if they ever learned that the dashing Miss Grantham was once a countrified girl—gardening in a dowdy gown, with hair all down her back."

She straightened her spine. "I am surprised you condescended to launch me into fashion considering you thought me such a frump."

"Diamonds of the first water are recognizable at a glance by their brilliance. All you needed was a little polish."

"Oh." Her color a little high, Alexandra turned away from him to survey the passing street. Her brother was across the road, and she waved at him. He raised his hand in greeting and tilted his hat as the curricle passed alongside him. Although she only caught a glimpse of his face, his health appeared to have deteriorated even more in the few days since she last spoke to him, and now he looked positively gaunt. If only she could think of a way to get him to leave the country.

You are not the savior of the world. The duke's words rang hollowly in her ears. But she wasn't attempting to rescue the world in this instance, only her brother, whom she had taken care of for so many years. What a fool he was to stay in London! She barely noticed the change in scenery as the curricle left the bustle and noise of the capital behind and entered the open country. She needed to come up with a plan to help him.

Robert glanced down at his companion and was on the verge of inquiring after Lady Longmore's health when he noticed

Alexandra's pensive expression. She appeared to be lost in contemplation, her equilibrium upset. Perhaps it had something to do with that brother of hers. Although he had been occupied with directing his horses through the busy London streets when they passed him, he had glanced up when Alexandra waved at Sir John and had not failed to observe that the young man looked decidedly out of sorts.

Perhaps John Grantham had landed himself in some trouble. The boy did not appear to be lacking in sense. Still, he was a green youth fresh from the country and an easy target for any shady character intent on luring a susceptible cub into the gaming hells for which London was renowned. Whatever the problem was, he was determined to get to the bottom of it. Alexandra should not be required to bear the weight of her brother's problems alone.

When they entered the gates of Richmond Park, Alexandra made a few desultory attempts at conversation before finally falling silent.

He looked down at her. "Is something the matter, Miss Grantham?"

She bit her lip and paused before answering. "It's John. He looked dreadful when we passed him earlier. I confess it has quite upset me."

"I would like to help you if I may. I suggest that we walk a little way on the grass. Jimmy will take charge of the curricle."

He took her arm and led her onto the lawn, and soon, the whole sorry story of Sir John's deteriorating health and his refusal to return to Grantham Place came tumbling out. "And he is so stubborn—he refuses to listen to reason."

Robert's brow creased. "And you think that his principal motivation for remaining in London is that he is loath to give up his friends and Miss Hadley?"

Alexandra inclined her head. "He has led such a lonely life up until now, you see."

"If he retired to the country with a group of his acquaintances, surely he would not be averse to the idea of leaving London?"

"Perhaps. Although I doubt any gentlemen could be prevailed upon to accompany my brother home to Grantham Place at the height of the Season. And, even if they were willing to do so, John would not wish to invite a group of near-strangers to his home. Besides, I don't think he would wish to leave Miss Hadley. Their attachment, although of brief duration, seems very strong."

"Not to Grantham Place, but to my hunting box. It is situated quite near your home, so the clime should agree with John's constitution. My brother, Gerard, and a group of his friends depart London for the country on Friday morning. Peter Denville is, I think, one of their number—I believe he is a close friend of your brother's, as well. I am sure Gerard would be amenable to extending the invitation to John. And if your brother is serious about his attachment to Miss Hadley, this will provide a perfect opportunity for him to approach Squire Hadley to ask for her hand in marriage."

Alexandra's eyes shone. "If only that were possible, it would be the perfect solution!"

"I am sure I shall be able to make the necessary arrangements. And a word in Gerard's ear about the precarious nature of John's health will not go amiss. I shall inform my brother of the situation so that no undue pressure is placed upon John to partake in any vigorous activities."

WHEN JOHN CAME into the drawing room a few days later, Alexandra was seated alone, attempting to work on some embroidery. She had neglected the task since she had arrived in London and was trying valiantly now to do some stitches.

She set the frame aside with a sigh of relief and focused her attention instead on her brother, who was smiling from ear to ear and said without preamble, "Emily has just agreed to marry me,

Alex!"

She rose swiftly to her feet. "Oh, John! I am so happy for you!" She hastened across the room to press a kiss on his cheek. "When are you planning to marry?"

"As soon as the banns can be read. And I must first request permission from Squire Hadley, of course. Gerard Beaumont has asked Peter Denville and me to join a small hunting party he's putting together, so we'll be leaving for the Duke of Stanford's hunting box in the next few days. But, as the box is quite near Grantham Place, it ties in very nicely. I'll travel home to speak to Squire Hadley afterward."

"Emily must be over the moon!"

He grinned. "She does seem happy. I've just left her in the small parlor with Grandmama."

The drawing room door opened again just then, and their grandmother entered with a quick step. "Has John told you his news, Alexandra?"

"He just did. It is the best thing I have heard in an age."

John checked his pocket watch. "I'm afraid I cannot stay. I have a mountain of arrangements to make today. But I shall return to bid you farewell before we leave."

When the door closed behind him, Alexandra sank onto the sofa again, clasping her hands together. "Such good news! And John seems quite happily settled on the hunting scheme, Grandmama."

"Yes, I was beside myself with concern until you told me Stanford's plan. You must remember to thank him for his kindness when you next see him."

"We certainly owe him a debt of gratitude that will be difficult to repay."

"I am sure the only payment he expects from you is an acceptance of his offer of marriage," her grandmother said comfortably.

Alexandra smiled but made no reply as she gazed out of the window. She still had a difficult time believing that he wished to marry her. And her own thoughts on marriage were a jumble. The duke had not called since the day he had driven her to Richmond Park, and she wasn't at all surprised. She hadn't exactly covered herself in glory that day. But he had been remarkably kind. Repressing a sigh, she stood up and left the room to seek out Emily, to find out how she was bearing the news of John's departure.

Any concerns about her friend's well-being were swiftly put to rest when she entered the parlor. Emily's eyes shone with joy, and a tinge of color pinkened her cheeks. "Oh, Alex, I have never been so happy in my life. As soon as John arrived this morning, he requested a private interview with me, and he asked me to marry him. I said yes, of course. He is planning to speak to my father soon."

"It is the most wonderful news," Alexandra said as she embraced her. "I am so happy for you both!"

"I love him so much, Alex. I am counting the days until I see him again." She frowned a little. "John told me more about his illness and how the London air does not suit his constitution. Do you think he will be content to live in the country again after having enjoyed his time here so much?"

"John is a true countryman at heart. I am sure he will be more than happy to remain at Grantham Place with you at his side. One of the main reasons he was reluctant to leave London was that it would require leaving you."

"I must make it clear to him, then, that I have developed an uncommon aversion to Town." Emily's eyes twinkled.

"Then you will earn the entire family's undying gratitude! Grandmama was on the verge of ordering him to go home. How much more effective will your persuasion be!"

ALEXANDRA HAD THE opportunity to thank Robert for his actions at the Ashtons' ball on Friday evening. To her delight, he arrived early in the evening, as was his custom, and secured the first waltz with her.

As the opening strains of the music sounded, she stepped into his arms and smiled up at him. "I am much obliged to you for what you have done for my brother, Your Grace, and I sincerely thank you."

He studied her with a mischievous glint in his eyes. "Does this gratitude denote a softening of your opinion of me as an unprincipled blackguard, ma'am?"

She stared resolutely at his white shirtfront, keeping her silence.

"What—for once, no reply?" Laughter threaded his voice.

She raised her eyes to his. "Your Grace, as a gently bred lady, it would be the height of impropriety for me to disagree with the opinions of a gentleman no matter how much I might be tempted to."

He gave a low laugh. "That would be a change."

As the last strains of the waltz faded away, he drew her to the side of the ballroom. "I intend to visit you tomorrow morning, Alexandra, and I expect you to be at home when I call."

For once, she did not take exception to what was barely more than a veiled order on his part. Because she recognized the promise in his eyes, and it filled her with immeasurable joy.

Gazing up at him, she said quietly, "I shall be waiting for you, Duke."

Chapter Twenty-Seven

Alexandra looked up eagerly when the door to the morning room opened the next morning. However, Leighton entered alone and presented a letter to her on a silver salver. "A footman from Stanford House delivered this a few moments ago, miss."

"Thank you, Leighton."

Her face fell as she perused the note. The duke had been called away once again to one of his estates on urgent business, but he promised to visit as soon as he returned. She refolded the missive with a sigh as the door opened again. It was Leighton again with another letter on a tray. Perhaps Robert had changed his plans?

She quickly broke the seal but paled in fright as she perused the words on the flimsy piece of paper. Then, trying to still her shaking fingers, she read the note again:

Dear Miss Grantham,

This letter is to warn you of the danger in which you will place your brother, Sir John Grantham, if you accept a proposal of marriage from the Duke of Stanford. If you become betrothed to His Grace, your brother will meet with a most unfortunate end. Be warned: If you make this communication known to anyone, you may never see your brother again—shooting accidents have been known to happen during the course of a hunt. I am sure that you would never forgive yourself if your brother died such a sad and unnecessary death.

You shall hear further from me.

The unsigned letter was written in a carefully disguised hand. In shock, Alexandra released the page and it fluttered into her lap. Picking it up again, she perused the dreadful words once more. Who could be so averse to the possibility of her marriage to Stanford that they would go to the lengths of threatening murder to prevent it? A shiver of fear ran down her spine, and she hugged her arms around her middle, trying to calm her racing mind. Drawing in a ragged breath, she closed her eyes, sinking against the back of the sofa. Who would do such a terrible thing?

Her eyes shot open. It had to be a member of the *ton*, somebody who knew enough about the goings-on of Polite Society to be cognizant of the fact that John was a member of the party invited to His Grace's hunting box.

Her stomach clenched into a knot. Perhaps the note was from Lady Ballington? She had made it all too clear that she wanted to marry Stanford, and she seemed like the kind of malicious person who would delight in such underhanded dealings, but it seemed impossible to act until Alexandra received further communication from the author of the note. If the marchioness was behind it, it was highly unlikely she would be able to arrange for someone to shoot John at the duke's hunting lodge. The very idea was nonsensical. But, even if this was meant to be some sort of joke in poor taste, it was still a nasty threat.

As she rose slowly from the sofa, she decided not to say anything to her grandmother and Emily until she received further communication proving it was a genuine threat. Somehow, she contrived to put on a cheerful face for her grandmother and Emily during luncheon, but the effort of doing so left her exhausted, and she felt quite ill when she excused herself early from the table.

She made her way to the morning room and sat down. Letitia

would be arriving shortly to see her, though Alexandra had never felt less inclined for social conversation. The door opened five minutes later, turmoil notwithstanding, and her friend bounced in, taking the spot on the window seat beside Alexandra. She beamed at her. "I have the most exciting news, Alex. And finally, finally, I can tell you about it. Charles and I are betrothed, and we are to be wed at the end of the Season."

Alexandra was pleased to hear it in spite of her worries and embraced her. "How wonderful, dearest! I am delighted for you."

Letitia's smile faded a little. "I want to marry Charles before the end of the Season, but Robert insists we wait a while. He has not said as much, but I suspect he believes my affection for Charles may not remain constant." She grimaced a little. "I know I was mistaken in my sentiments for Mr. Winters—the despicable fortune hunter that he is. This time I know I am in love." She sighed dreamily. "Charles is the perfect gentleman—and so handsome. I am the happiest girl alive."

"I always thought you were an excellent match."

"As are you and Robert. Can you believe we will soon be sisters, Alex?"

"Your . . . your brother has not asked me to marry him."

"Oh, he will soon. He adores you, you know. And you do love him, do you not?"

There was no sense in denying it now. "Yes. Very much." Alexandra glanced down at her hands, suddenly a bit shy.

"When did you first know that you loved him?" Letitia touched her arm. "You have kept your feelings for him very well hidden."

Alexandra met her inquiring gaze. "At my coming-out ball, it struck me suddenly. I must say it came as quite a shock, as I have been denying my affections to myself."

Letitia gave a decided nod. "Love is unpredictable that way," she said in her wisest voice. "Sometimes it creeps up on one while at other times it springs on you completely unexpectedly, like a bolt of lightning."

"You make it sound rather alarming—like a predator stalking prey."

Letitia burst out laughing. "Well, I suppose it is a bit like that. And it can be just as vicious." Her conversation turned back to Sir Charles and to the arrangements he was making for their upcoming visit to Vauxhall Gardens. "You haven't visited the pleasure gardens yet, have you? They are quite splendid."

"I did ask Grandmama if we could visit Vauxhall, but she did not want us to go without an escort. I was delighted when Sir Charles extended his invitation the other day to include us."

Letitia rose to her feet. "I am afraid I must leave now—Cousin Amelia told me not to stay too long. But I shall see you at Lady Redham's rout."

"I am looking forward to it. And it will be lovely to congratulate Sir Charles on your betrothal."

ALEXANDRA RECEIVED A second note from the anonymous letter writer the very next day. She was seated alone in the drawing room, attempting to read *Pride and Prejudice,* when Leighton entered the room, carrying the letter on a salver. It had been delivered by hand once again, and although Alexandra had been expecting further notice from her adversary, it still came as something of a shock. She flung her book aside, and opened the message, the words blurring before her eyes:

Dear Miss Grantham,

It has come to my attention that Sir Charles Fotherby has invited you and your grandmother to be members of the party he has arranged to visit Vauxhall Gardens. If you desire to see your brother alive again, you will meet me there at half-past eleven by the statue of Milton, on the Rural Downs at the Cross Walk. Come alone, and do not inform anyone of your destination. Your brother's life hangs in the balance.

The script was once again disguised and the letter left unsigned. Alexandra released a shaky breath. She would like, above anything, to take her grandmother into her confidence. But she dared not do it because her relative would, in all likelihood, insist on informing the authorities, which could put John's life at risk if the threat turned out to be genuine.

If only she could go to Robert for help. Had he not been called away so inopportunely on business, she would have laid the matter before him. But he wasn't here, and as it was a situation of the utmost delicacy and potential danger, she needed to make the correct decision.

A crease appeared between her brows. How did Lady Ballington—for she was certain by now of the letter writer's identity—know Sir Charles had invited Alexandra and her grandmother to join his Vauxhall Gardens party? It was strange and fairly frightening that anyone could know the details of their lives so intimately as Alexandra hadn't informed any of her acquaintances about Sir Charles's invitation, and it wasn't common knowledge.

It seemed she must bide her time and wait for tomorrow night before she could clear up that mystery. It galled her that she was in the power of a woman whose sole reason for threatening her was jealousy, but there was very little she could do about it.

Alexandra's frown deepened as she contemplated the situation. Coming to a decision, she jumped up from her bed and rushed to the armoire. Opening the door, she removed a small, flat case and sat it on the bed, carefully taking out the silver-mounted pistol her father had given her.

When she was sixteen, John had taught her how to handle such a weapon. Her father, impressed by her superior marksmanship, surprised her on her seventeenth birthday with a small pistol of her own, admonishing her never to inform Aunt Eliza of the unusual present. "I shan't hear the end of it if you do, child," he told her.

The warning had been unnecessary. She would never be so foolish as to do such a thing. Aunt Eliza would be unlikely to recover from the ensuing fit of palpitations if she ever learnt her niece owned a pistol—and an eminently serviceable one at that! It had served Alexandra very well in the past as she rode the highways in her mask.

She loaded the weapon and placed it back in its case, suddenly feeling safer and more at ease. Now, should the need arise, she would be able to defend herself.

⸺⸺⸻

THE NEXT DAY, Alexandra decided to call on Lady Ballington. It would save her a great deal of trouble if she could sort the matter out during daylight hours instead of going alone to that statue in the middle of Vauxhall Gardens at night. Perhaps by paying a morning call on the other woman, she could confront her and thereby bring matters to a head. However, she would need to be careful in what she said. Alexandra did not want the marchioness to spread rumors about those letters if she happened to be wrong in her suspicions.

She rang the bell for her maid, and when Hobbes arrived, she said urgently, "I intend to pay a visit on one Lady Ballington this morning, Hobbes. You will accompany me."

Her maid shook her head. "But, miss, won't her ladyship wish to accompany you?"

Alexandra avoided her eyes. "No. I am going without her. Now, let us make haste. I wish to leave shortly."

Fifteen minutes later, they left Longmore House and walked the short distance to Grosvenor Square, where Lady Ballington's imposing townhouse was situated. The lofty being who opened the door to her knock looked even more imposing than the house.

"My name is Miss Grantham, and I wish to see Lady Ballington," she stated calmly.

The lofty being raised his brows. "Her ladyship is not at home this morning, madam."

"It is imperative that I see your mistress. Please tell her that I have called."

A voice came from behind him: "I will see Miss Grantham, Fairchild. Pray show her into the drawing room."

Alexandra peered over Fairchild's shoulder and saw Lady Ballington coming down a sweeping staircase.

The marchioness stopped on the landing and inclined her head. "I shall be with you directly, Miss Grantham."

Fairchild led her toward the drawing room, leaving Hobbes sitting on an upright chair in the hall. The butler gave a stiff bow as he showed her into the room, then closed the door quietly behind her.

Alexandra wandered over to a large, gilded mirror on the wall opposite the fireplace and frowned at her reflection. She needed to present an image of calm confidence. She arranged a wayward curl and determinedly straightened her shoulders before turning away from the mirror and gazing around.

A Récamier sofa dominated the room. Artfully arranged around it were a set of gilded armchairs covered in straw-colored satin, a shade that matched the room's ribbed silk curtains. An ugly Grecian-style vase was arranged on a mahogany table in the center of the apartment in front of some decidedly uncomfortable-looking chairs. Alexandra's mouth twisted in a wry smile as she wondered if the marchioness's more unwelcome visitors were invited to sit there—the hard-backed chairs seemed designed to drive callers away rather than detain them. Alexandra walked over to the side of the room and was contemplating a gilt-framed watercolor painting of a castle on the wall when the door opened, and Lady Ballington came in.

"Pray be seated, Miss Grantham."

Alexandra sat on one of the gilt chairs as her hostess took the seat opposite her. The marchioness spoke in her cool tones, "I do not suppose this to be a social visit, Miss Grantham. How may I help you?"

Alexandra looked across at her and shifted in her seat again. It was one thing to think of confronting the marchioness with suspected crimes in the privacy of her bedchamber but quite another to bring up the subject in Lady Ballington's own drawing room. Alexandra drew in a breath. "I have reason to believe you wish me harm, your ladyship."

Lady Ballington raised her brows. "Harm? I don't understand your meaning."

Alexandra fidgeted with her glove. "You have made it quite plain, Lady Ballington, since our first meeting that you hold me in dislike. And your dislike seems to extend to my family as well."

By not even a flutter of her eyelashes did Lady Ballington betray any discomfiture at Alexandra's words. She merely gave a tinkling laugh. "My dear child, what are you talking about? I regard you as a very slight acquaintance, nothing more. As to your family—well, your imagination seems to have run away with you." Her eyes narrowed suddenly. "Either that or you have allowed your naturally jealous feelings toward me to cloud your judgment."

Alexandra's voice was stiff. "I harbor no jealous feelings toward you, ma'am."

"Don't you?" the other woman purred. "Men of the world, no matter what the Gothic novels you have read might imply, far prefer worldly women to virtuous innocents like yourself."

Alexandra sprang up from her chair. "You are mistaken, your ladyship."

"I think not." Lady Ballington rang the bell for Fairchild.

She pressed her lips together. "Indeed, you are. I have always preferred reading the Classics to Gothic novels. Good morning, ma'am."

With her head held high, Alexandra followed Fairchild down the stairs to where Hobbes awaited her. When the door closed behind them, Alexandra released a sigh of frustration mixed with relief at being out of that drawing room and back outside. Her interview with the older lady had not gone well. Lady Ballington's barbed comments had found their well-aimed mark, throwing her off completely, and she had no new information as a result of the encounter.

Something else would need to be done.

The frown creasing her brow lifted as an idea occurred to her. At Lady Redham's rout this evening, she would do the unthinkable and seek out Sir Jason Morecombe. Very few social hostesses left the baronet off their invitation lists, fearing the sharp edge of his tongue.

If Sir Jason was in the marchioness's confidence, he might very well attempt to needle Alexandra as he had never been shy of voicing his offensive opinions in her presence. In this way, she might discover some pertinent information about Lady Ballington's plans. But she must be vague in how she broached the subject with him as there was a chance he might not have been informed of Lady Ballington's plans, and Alexandra certainly did not wish to be the source of any information he could use against her.

She pulled at the strings of her reticule as she strode along, frowning. Hobbes walked slightly behind her, puffing a little, and Alexandra slowed down immediately. "Forgive me, Hobbes, I am galloping away today, aren't I?"

"Is anything the matter, miss?" Her maid's sideways glance was concerned.

"It is only that I have a—a particular problem that I need to solve."

Hobbes nodded. "Well, I wish you all the best with it, miss, and hope that it isn't serious trouble." She hesitated before saying in a diffident voice, "Do you know—will we be much longer in London, miss? Only I received word this morning that my mother is very ill."

Alexandra came to a halt. "Oh, no, Hobbes. You must travel home immediately. I will arrange a ticket for you on the stage to wherever you need to go."

"But how will you manage without me?"

"I shall contrive. Never fear. Jarvis can assist me." She began walking again at a more decorous pace. "Besides, Lady Longmore decided this morning to leave London before the end of the Season as my sisters have returned home from the seminary. We are both eager to see them. I daresay we will not be long in London."

Emily was also eager to return to Grantham Place to be reunited with her betrothed, though Alexandra did not mention this to her maid. Hobbes probably already knew all about the engagement, but it had not yet been formally announced, so she ought not discuss the couple's plans. Lady Longmore wanted Emily to marry John as soon as possible—and the two were far from opposed to the idea—so the decision had been reached this morning to travel back to Grantham Place earlier than planned.

When Alexandra arrived at home, she went straight into the drawing room to inform her grandmother about Hobbes's mother. Lady Longmore instructed Leighton to purchase the maid's stagecoach ticket at once so that she could leave early the next morning. "For in matters such as these, Alexandra, I am afraid time is of the essence," she said with a sigh.

Later, as Hobbes helped her to dress for Lady Redham's rout, she expressed her heartfelt thanks for the arrangements that had been made.

"I am so pleased we can help you, Hobbes, and I hope your mother will make a swift recovery," Alexandra said quietly.

The dresser bobbed her head. "Thank you kindly, miss. I am praying for that as well."

When Alexandra entered the drawing room at Redham House that evening, she immediately spotted Sir Jason near the French doors, in conversation with a lady she did not recognize. She remained beside her grandmother until the woman left his side and then slipped across the room to him.

When she approached, the baronet raised his quizzing glass to one eye. "My, my, to what do I owe this honor?"

"Good evening, Sir Jason. May I have a word with you in

private? I have a matter I would like to discuss with you."

"How intriguing."

"I shall be obliged if you would grant me a few moments of your time."

Sir Jason lowered the eyepiece and said softly, "Who am I to deny the request of a lady? Let us repair to the antechamber off this room, Miss Grantham. We can speak there—in *private*."

Alexandra nodded and, hoping no one would see them leaving together, followed him into the small apartment.

She wiped her suddenly damp hands on the skirt of her gown. "I have reason to believe Lady Ballington wishes me and my brother harm," she began. "I suspect you are aware of this, sir?"

He regarded her inscrutably. "I fail to see what Lady Ballington's animosity toward you—and your brother—has to do with me, Miss Grantham."

"She has not confided in you then? I had supposed you to be her confidante."

"Oh, I am the confidante of many people, Miss Grantham, including your own fine self. At least for this evening, it would seem."

Alexandra pressed on. "If you are in her confidence, then it is your duty to speak to her about her misguided attempt to threaten and harm my family."

"My duty is it? And you have come here hoping that I would speak to her ladyship on your behalf? You cannot know me very well if you think I would raise even a little finger to help you." He opened his snuff box.

Alexandra swallowed past the constriction in her throat. "I doubt anyone has ever accused you of excessive gallantry, Sir Jason."

"Not as far as I can recall."

"But how can you approve of Lady Ballington's wicked schemes?"

"All is fair in love and war, my sweet. You should have learned that little lesson by now."

"But her ladyship's methods are despicable—and wholly unscrupulous."

He took a pinch of snuff and favored her with a knowing smile. "But most effective, wouldn't you say?"

Alexandra drew in a sharp breath. So it *was* Lady Ballington who had authored those letters. And she had taken the baronet into her confidence, just as Alexandra had suspected. She stood up straighter. "Surely, you cannot approve of her threat to murder my brother, Sir Jason? It is the act of a madwoman."

The drooping lids over his eyes lifted suddenly, and he looked at her with startling keenness. "You interest me very much, my dear. Do go on."

She studied him doubtfully. "You are not already aware of her plans?"

He snapped his snuffbox closed. "Oh, I am rarely unaware of anything. But why have you come to me with this? We are not precisely ... er ... friends."

"No, we are not. But you are Lady Ballington's friend, and I had hoped to prevail upon you to convince her to give up her scheme before it is too late. I cannot see what purpose it will serve for us to meet tomorrow evening at Vauxhall Gardens."

"Lady Ballington, I am sure, has her reasons."

Alexandra sighed. "Will you not speak to her on this matter?"

"No, I will not. I rarely help anyone and am disinclined to start now."

She glared at him. She had never met a more disagreeable man in her life. "Then, I have nothing more to say to you, sir." Her voice was stiff.

"I am desolate indeed. Good evening, ma'am."

She hastened out of the antechamber, almost stumbling in her desperation to escape from him. She was a fool to have attempted to speak to Sir Jason.

Everything now rested on that dreaded meeting tomorrow night.

CHAPTER TWENTY-EIGHT

THE NEXT DAY was filled with engagements, and Alexandra found very little time to contemplate her course of action for the evening. Only later, when she was in her bedchamber, changing her gown for the Vauxhall Gardens party, did she have a moment to herself.

Perhaps it was better this way. Although she had never been of a nervous disposition, she had an uneasy suspicion that if she had been granted an hour or two for reflection today, she might very well have worked herself up into a fever of apprehension. As it was, she was worried about how she could contrive to give her grandmother the slip this evening.

When Hobbes finally left her, Alexandra sank onto her bed, her stomach clenching. The thought of her upcoming meeting with Lady Ballington weighed heavily on her mind, and she was becoming more and more doubtful about the wisdom of her decision not to inform anyone about the letters and her appointed rendezvous this evening. She glanced up with a start when a knock sounded on the door, and when it was Emily who entered, she made a sudden decision.

"Please sit down. I have something I would like to say to you. But first, I want you to promise that you won't tell anyone."

"I give you my word," she said gravely, taking the spot on the bed Alexandra indicated. "I hope nothing is amiss? You look rather drawn."

Alexandra jumped up and began pacing. "Several days ago, I received an anonymous letter from someone who threatened to murder John if I accept an offer of marriage from the Duke of Stanford."

Her friend gasped. "Oh no, Alex!"

"And then two days ago, I received another note from the same person, telling me to meet her at Vauxhall Gardens tonight at the statue of Milton."

"You believe it to be a woman?"

"I think Lady Ballington wrote the letters. She is the only person I can think of who could have such a motive and might be aware of our outing. Letitia has told me she is desperately in love with the duke and is determined to marry him."

"But how dreadful, Alex! That she would wish to harm John merely to spite you. Is there any way we can send word to him?" Her brow creased in anxiety.

"Lady Ballington is in London, and I sincerely doubt she has an accomplice who would carry out her nefarious designs at the hunting box without instruction to do so. So I don't believe John is in imminent danger."

"But what about you, Alex? You cannot go alone to that statue!"

"I must. If I fail to arrive, there is every chance Lady Ballington could enact whatever plan she has in place. I believe her capable of harming John, and she certainly has the means."

"Don't say so, Alex. No one could be so—so evil." Emily raised her shaking hands to her face.

"I am beginning to think the marchioness is of unsound mind. There can be no other explanation for such behavior."

Emily's eyes welled up. "My poor John. I cannot bear the thought of losing him—or you!"

Alexandra drew in a deep breath. "I am determined to meet Lady Ballington this evening and get to the bottom of this affair. But I know I could be placing myself in danger, so I wanted you to know where I am going."

"Perhaps we should tell Lady Longmore? I would never forgive myself if you came to harm."

Alexandra looked her friend straight in the eye. "You have given me your word that you will say nothing of this to anyone, Emily. You must keep it. My grandmother would certainly wish to be involved—and probably inform Bow Street, which could endanger John further if the woman is serious in her threats. Only say something if I fail to return within the hour."

"Oh, Alex—you are so brave. I won't say anything, but do be careful."

"I am sorry to have burdened you with this, my dear, but I know I can trust you to keep silent as long as necessary."

"How are you going to contrive to slip away on your own?"

"I am not sure as yet, but I will think of something."

Alexandra was still contemplating this knotty problem when their carriage drew up at the entrance to Vauxhall Gardens. After her grandmother and Emily climbed out, she descended from the conveyance and greeted Sir Charles, Letitia, and Amelia Beaumont, who had already arrived.

When they entered the spacious pleasure gardens, Alexandra momentarily forgot her troubles as they strolled along a wide, gravel walk lined with hedges and trees. Groves and grottoes, pavilions and porticoes were all lit up by thousands of lamps, and the effect was of such brilliance that Alexandra came to a halt and stared around in amazement.

"It is a splendid sight, is it not?" her grandmother murmured.

"Yes, Grandmama. I have never seen anything like it."

They took a turn about the gardens, and Alexandra kept a weather eye out for the statue of Milton. But it was nowhere to be seen, and a short while later, she turned to Sir Charles and said in a nonchalant voice, "I have heard that Milton's statue is a sight to behold. Do you know where it is?"

"Certainly. It is located in the Rural Downs near the Cross Walk. I shall take you past it on our way to the fireworks display later."

Alexandra released a breath of relief as he led them toward the supper-box he had reserved. That much at least was easier than expected.

A painting depicting a couple of milkmaids adorned the rear wall of the booth they entered, and glass lamps were suspended from the ceiling. As Alexandra took her place at the table, a band of musicians, installed on the upper level of a nearby orchestra box, began a concert.

A waiter brought a cold collation to their table, but Alexandra studied the spread on the table with very little appetite. She nibbled on a wafer-thin slice of ham and tasted a little of the rack punch Sir Charles pressed on her, but she found it impossible to do justice to the meal he ordered, merely toying with the food on her plate.

When he asked her if she found the meal to her satisfaction, she forced a smile to her lips. "It is delicious, thank you, Sir Charles. Only, I am suffering a little from a headache this evening, and I regret my appetite has deserted me."

"I am sorry to hear that, Miss Grantham. I hope that you will soon feel more the thing. Would you care for a glass of lemonade?"

Alexandra gratefully sipped the cool liquid. The beverage helped to revive her somewhat, and she began to feel slightly better. However, she suddenly had the strangest sensation of being watched. Turning her head, she spotted Sir Jason Morecombe in a nearby box. He caught her eye and smiled nastily at her before turning away to speak to a member of his party.

Alexandra went first hot and then cold as she tried to make sense of his presence. Perhaps it was only a coincidence that he had decided this night, of all nights, to visit Vauxhall Gardens? But that horrid little smile belied any such chance.

Her stomach dropped. Sir Jason was probably here tonight on Lady Ballington's behalf. The realization came to her like a bucket of icy water flung over her head. She remembered now a rumor of bad blood between the baronet and Stanford. Her conversation with him at Lady Sefton's ball would have given him more than enough knowledge to seize upon this opportunity to cause some trouble.

Well, she was ready for him. Alexandra straightened her spine. She would confront him and demand an explanation. Placing her hand on her reticule, she felt the reassuring butt of her pistol through its soft material. Hopefully, she would not have cause to use it tonight.

At eleven o'clock, Sir Charles informed them that they needed to leave their box if they wished to see the fireworks. Agitated at the lateness of the hour, Alexandra rose swiftly to her feet. Then, conversing with Letitia and Emily on trivial subjects, she walked beside her friends toward the Firework Tower at the eastern side of the gardens. As promised, Sir Charles took them via the lit-up statue of Milton, which they viewed for a short while before continuing on to where the firework display would be best visible.

Skyrockets of serpents and stars exploded in the night sky as the spectacle began, and Alexandra stared in fascination as a representation of the eruption of Mount Vesuvius drew gasps of admiration from everyone around them.

An enormous Catherine wheel lit up the sky after that, and Alexandra decided that now, while everyone gazed upwards in rapt admiration, would be the best time to slip away. Emily stood beside her, and she briefly squeezed her friend's hand before making her departure. She hurried along the walk, lit by dozens of lamps, and glanced nervously around.

It was quiet at this hour as people were, no doubt, still at supper or watching the fireworks. Alexandra passed a couple of young gentlemen who ogled her, and a dissolute-looking man stepped forward and called a greeting. She hastened away, keeping her head down.

When she reached the statue, the moon's silver rays illumined it, and she shivered in the cool night air as she waited. A few minutes passed, and she turned around when she heard someone behind her, but it was only a woman hurrying past, perhaps on a secret assignation of her own.

A few moments later, Alexandra heard another footfall. But before she could turn around, arms like twin iron bands encircled her waist, and the breath was knocked out of her chest as a low, rough voice growled in her ear, "Walk on ahead me as if nothing is the matter. I won't be walking too close to you so as to avoid arousing unpleasant suspicions. But if you try to scream or attract attention, my little lady, I'll blow a hole right through you."

Alexandra released her breath in a gasp as he released her. She froze for a moment, but when the man prodded her in the back with his pistol, she regained her senses and stumbled along. Beads of perspiration broke out on her forehead as she looked around. What on earth could she do? She passed a blue-coated man with a tipstaff patrolling the walk, but Alexandra dared not call for help, the thug's threat ringing in her ears.

Perhaps suspecting that she might try to attract the attention of the constable, the man came right up to her. Glancing back, she felt the blood drain from her face at the sheer size of the man. He wore a frieze coat and a battered hat, and although his face was shadowed, she could smell the foul stench of his breath in her face.

"Go on, go on. And don't try anything clever, little wench. This gun here is still pointed right at your back if you so much as squawk."

He directed her along a deserted walk at the far end of the gardens, which eventually came out near the entrance. Alexandra caught a glimpse of several carriages awaiting their owners. Her heart pounded in her ears. Surely someone would step forward to stop her captor? It could not seem natural for her to be walking with this man thus. But within a matter of moments, the thug shoved her into a waiting post-chaise—with an occupant already waiting inside—and shut the door after her.

The carriage moved forward immediately, and Alexandra

cursed herself for walking into the trap Sir Jason had laid for her.

But the man sitting in the carriage with her was not the baronet. Alexandra blinked in horror as she stared at her kidnapper. "You vile, despicable, contemptible cad!"

"Now, now, my dear," Mr. Ponsonby admonished with a titter. "That is certainly no way to speak to your affianced husband. You must treat me with the respect I deserve. It is, after all, your wifely duty."

"What are you talking about?" But, with a sinking feeling in her stomach, Alexandra already suspected the answer.

Her worst fears were confirmed when he leaned forward and pulled a loose cravat from his pocket. "We are off to Gretna Green," he said in a smug voice as he tied it tightly around her wrists, "where we are to be wed."

Chapter Twenty-Nine

ALL THE PIECES of the puzzle of the past few days began to fit together in Alexandra's mind, creating a picture that was far from pretty. "*You* wrote me those threatening letters. You deliberately led me to believe that my brother's life was in danger so that I would not become betrothed to the Duke of Stanford."

Mr. Ponsonby stroked his chin. "A masterstroke, was it not? I did not believe that Stanford intended to propose matrimony to you until the evening of the Ashtons' ball. The realization was borne upon me then that the *ton* believed the announcement to be imminent. I could hardly credit it, but it did seem to be the case, and naturally, I could not allow such a state of affairs to continue. It is far easier to abscond with Miss Alexandra Grantham than the future Duchess of Stanford if you take my meaning?" He wriggled his eyebrows. "So, I set my plans in motion, and—"

"Succeeded in kidnapping me—fool that I am. Your actions are not only despicable but cowardly as well." Alexandra's voice dripped with scorn. "An honorable man would never attempt to rescue himself from his financial embarrassments by kidnapping a woman in order to marry her for her fortune!"

"It is not only your fortune that I desire but yourself as well. You must know, Miss Grantham," he said patronizingly, "that you are considered to be a very beautiful woman."

Alexandra gritted her teeth, itching to slap the self-satisfied smile off her kidnapper's face though she knew how foolish it would be to do so. At the moment, she was totally within his power. A thought occurred to her, and turning her head to look at him again, she inquired, "How do you know the details of my daily life so intimately, Mr. Ponsonby? You knew that Sir Charles had invited my grandmother and me to Vauxhall Gardens, even though I had not mentioned the invitation to any of my acquaintances."

Mr. Ponsonby puffed out his chest, clearly proud of his cunning. He reminded Alexandra strongly of an extremely vain peacock she had once seen parading around the grounds of her grandmother's country estate. This popinjay was not nearly as well feathered, she noted acidly. His cravat was poorly-tied, and he wore a dreadful puce coat, which clashed hideously with his pink complexion made even more florid by the evening's exertion and, by the smell of him, drink.

"My dear young lady, I am a man of remarkable powers. Many of my acquaintances do not credit me with genius, but that is because they do not know me well enough." He spread out his hands. "A footman working in my household is engaged to be married to one of your grandmother's parlor maids, and my how servants like to talk. It was simplicity itself for me to gain access to some quite useful information. A few coins in the hand of my large friend with the pistol and I had all I needed for my purposes."

"Your nefarious purposes." Alexandra's voice dripped icicles. "Has it not occurred to you, Mr. Ponsonby, that you cannot force me to marry you? You can carry me across the border to Gretna Green, but you cannot coerce me into saying my wedding vows."

"But, my dear Miss Grantham, think of the unfortunate consequences if you do not consent to marry me. You cannot come back to England unwed after being alone with a man for several days. Mothers will drag their daughters across the street when they see you because you will be a fallen woman. So you see, if you wish to save any scrap of your reputation, you have no other alternative but to agree to become my wife and then enjoy the position of remarkable consequence in Society that holding that title will bring you."

Alexandra gazed at Mr. Ponsonby in disbelief, stunned by the conceit of the man, though she recognized the truth of what he had said about coming back from Scotland unwed. No lady of good standing would invite a ruined woman into her home. Her position in society would be untenable. And although she would not mind being sent home to Grantham Place to live in seclusion, it would be a terrible disappointment to her grandmother. And, more importantly, her sisters. Because the scandal would not only impact Alexandra, it would also affect Dorothea and Abigail's chances of making successful matches.

Mr. Ponsonby was a despicable oaf. Still, he was cognizant, as she was, of the rules of the *ton*, and he had played a very clever hand by snatching her up in this manner. Alexandra bit her lip as she contemplated her predicament. If she hoped to avoid social ruin, the only possible thing she could do was escape from her captor tonight and make it back to Longmore House before her absence was noted.

Thank goodness she had brought along her pistol. Now, all she needed to do was find the opportunity to use it. She frowned down at her bound wrists. "Please untie me, sir. There can be no reason to keep me bound as I could not possibly escape from you while we are in a moving carriage."

He stroked his chin again as he considered her in silence.

Forcing a note of conciliation into her voice, she cleared her throat. "Please, Mr. Ponsonby. It is vastly uncomfortable sitting tied up like this. It is a very long way to Gretna Green, after all, and my hands are starting to feel numb."

He let out a heaving breath. "Very well, very well. I am a generous man, after all. But don't try anything silly."

When he untied her wrists, she turned away and stared out of the window. Soon, the post-chaise would leave London behind.

And with every yard they covered, she was traveling closer and closer to a frightening future.

The carriage lurched its way over the rutted road, and soon they came to a heath, eerie in the bright moonlight. They had passed some way through this deserted stretch of land when the faint sound of horses' hooves came to Alexandra's ears. She glanced at Mr. Ponsonby and noticed with some surprise that he was lost to slumber. He lay back against the seat of the carriage, his head lolling to one side. She wrinkled her nose as she sniffed the unpleasant odor emanating from his prone form. He had clearly imbibed far too freely tonight, perhaps in a bid to gain courage for his dastardly deeds.

Her heart began to pound. This could be her only chance to escape. Shifting closer to the window, she removed her pistol from her reticule while readying herself to wave at the driver of the other vehicle in a desperate bid to alert him to the fact she was in danger. If she had help in her escape from someone outside the carriage, she might be able to avoid shooting anyone inside the carriage. Hopefully.

The other carriage would pass by at any moment now. Alexandra extended her hand just as a loud shot rang out. She released her breath in a sharp hiss and quickly drew her arm back. Was it a bandit holding them up? It must be. There could be no other explanation for that shot. Was she now to face another threat to her life, or would the thieves perhaps be sympathetic when they realized her plight? Either way, the irony of being subjected to a robbery while carrying the very pistol she'd used to perpetrate her own was not lost on Alexandra.

Their chaise came to a shuddering halt, the door jerked open a short moment later, and a gentleman—a very familiar gentleman—leaped inside.

Her heart soared so high she feared it was in danger of flying out of the carriage. How had Robert found her? It was a miracle. An utter miracle.

Alexandra blinked at him in amazement and then hastily

trained her pistol on her kidnapper, who had woken up from all the commotion and was gazing blearily at her. He looked foxed, truth be told, but his expression became far more alert when the duke sat across from him and stretched out his elegantly sheathed legs as much as the cramped confines of the coach would allow. Finally, raising his quizzing glass, he studied Alexandra's kidnapper through the lens. "Explain yourself, Ponsonby."

Mr. Ponsonby's already flushed countenance suffused with even more color as he cringed back into his seat. Eventually, he opened his mouth, but he appeared to be at a loss for words. Finally, Alexandra, tired of waiting, said in a low voice: "Mr. Ponsonby kidnapped me from Vauxhall Gardens this evening. He planned to flee with me across the border to Gretna Green, where he intended to coerce me into marriage."

Robert glanced down at her. "I had gathered as much."

Mr. Ponsonby, regaining the use of his voice, said in a high-pitched tone, "It—it is not as it seems, Your Grace. I can explain. Miss Grantham has developed a *tendre* for me. Although she refuses to admit it to herself, she is head over ears in love with me."

Alexandra looked at him blankly. "What did you just say?"

"You have a *tendre* for me, my dear. We both know that."

The insolence of the man! "I refused your proposal of marriage, Mr. Ponsonby. That clearly illustrates that I am not—and have never been—enamored of you."

"You only did that to make me even keener to pursue you," Mr. Ponsonby said, warming to his theme. "Since time immemorial young ladies have been using that ploy to ensnare men."

"You are delusional, sir."

Mr. Ponsonby pursed his lips. "Indeed, I am not. You love me but are intent on marrying the Duke of Stanford for his fortune. Admit it, Miss Grantham. Your heart is torn in two—between your mercenary needs and your desire for me!"

The breath caught in her chest. "Mr. Ponsonby, I have a fortune of my own—as you well know—and I have no need to marry. Moreover, if I do ever marry, it will be for love, not for security. You are saying these things merely justify your reprehensible actions to His Grace."

She shook her pistol at him threateningly, and he cringed back against his seat. "No, no, Miss Grantham, we both know—"

"Silence, Ponsonby! You have said enough." The duke's mouth set in a grim line. "I shall give you until the end of this week to settle your affairs in England. Then you will leave for the Continent, never to return. I trust I make myself clear?"

"But—" Mr. Ponsonby stopped short when he saw the menacing look on Stanford's face.

"I have not called you out because I desire no breath of scandal to attach itself to Miss Grantham's name. You can count yourself fortunate in that regard. But if you do not leave the country, you will answer to me."

The duke helped Alexandra down from the chaise, but when she gazed around, no carriage awaited them. Instead, Robert's stallion was tied to the branch of a nearby tree. The post-chaise postilions were calming their frightened horses while keeping a wary eye on a slight youth who sat atop another horse with a pistol trained directly on them. Jimmy.

The duke threw Alexandra up into the saddle before settling himself behind her. The ride back to London passed in silence as she was gripped against his chest, the wind whistling past her face. She could not think while she was held within the circle of his arms. She could hardly gather her thoughts at all. But as the miles flew past and they neared London, Alexandra's stomach started to ache. What would Robert say when he learned that she had walked straight into Ponsonby's trap? She blocked the disturbing thought from her mind, and soon, in what seemed like no time at all, the duke was escorting her into Longmore House.

Alexandra's grandmother rushed out of the morning room, her face as white as a sheet. Then, mindful of the servants, they repaired to the morning room, where Sir Charles, Letitia, and her cousin Amelia were seated. They looked up in concern when

Alexandra entered the room.

Closing the door behind him, the duke walked over to the mantelpiece and stared down at the fire smoldering in the grate, only looking up when Alexandra took a seat beside her grandmother on the sofa.

Amelia Beaumont rose to her feet then and shook out her skirts. "I believe we shall take our leave of you now, Lady Longmore. I am pleased we have been able to bear you company while you awaited your granddaughter's return, but you must desire a few moments alone with her."

Letitia ran over to embrace her before returning to Sir Charles's side. The baronet then escorted the two ladies out of the room, leaving Alexandra alone with her grandmother and the duke.

Chapter Thirty

Her grandmother spoke first. "My dear child, what ever happened? After you disappeared, Emily told us some tale about some threatening letters and some crazed notion of a plot to murder John. But when I tried to question her more closely about it, she was quite overcome and nothing of sense could be gotten from her. I had to send her straight to bed when we arrived home."

"It was Mr. Ponsonby, Grandmama. He kidnapped me at Vauxhall tonight," Alexandra said wearily. "He wanted to carry me across the border to Gretna Green to force me to marry him."

In the stunned silence that followed that pronouncement, Alexandra rummaged in her reticule and removed the two, now somewhat crumpled letters that Mr. Ponsonby had sent her. She handed them to her grandmother, who paled even further when her eyes skimmed over the words.

Then, with a shuddering sigh, Lady Longmore handed the letters to the duke. After he had perused them, he glanced up, his face like a thundercloud. "Why did you not come to me with these?"

She swallowed past the tightness in her throat. "You left the morning the first letter arrived. John's life was in danger and—"

"And you foolishly believed you could solve the matter on your own?" His face set in even harsher lines. "You should at least have told your grandmother, Alexandra. Instead, you went alone to that statue, utterly defenseless."

"I was not defenseless. I took my pistol along with me."

"Your pistol, child?" Her grandmother stared at her. "What are you talking about? Surely you don't own such a thing?"

She looked away. "Papa gave me a pistol for my seventeenth birthday. I did not tell you because I thought you would disapprove."

"I do disapprove. Very much. Your papa always was an eccentric man, but to give you a pistol of your own! I find it difficult to believe."

"I am a good shot, Grandmama."

Her relative sat up straighter in her chair, her lacy cap askew and her eyes wide in her stricken face. "I am struggling to take any of this in. Young ladies should not own pistols, Alexandra. It is not at all the thing. Besides, Mr. Ponsonby managed to kidnap you despite your superior marksmanship. What happened?"

Alexandra sighed. "Unfortunately, I was overpowered from behind."

Her grandmother gazed at her for a long moment and then raised a shaking hand to her forehead. "My head is spinning quite dreadfully."

"Perhaps it would be best if you retired for the evening, ma'am." The duke's voice was concerned. "You can speak to your granddaughter in the morning."

"Yes, yes . . . I believe that would be best. I cannot think." She turned to Alexandra. "Goodnight, my dear. And Stanford, I shall never be able to thank you enough for rescuing Alexandra. We are forever in your debt."

He bowed his head. "Should I ring for your maid, ma'am?"

"No, no. I shall be quite well. But I should like a word."

Leaving Alexandra alone with her thoughts in the morning room for a moment, Robert escorted Lady Longmore to the foot of the staircase. She turned to face him, a frown marring her brow. "I plan to take Alexandra back to Grantham Place. Her sisters are there now, and she can remain at home until the scandal blows over."

"I doubt there will be any talk, ma'am. I have informed Ponsonby that he is to leave the country immediately."

She nodded. "That is a relief. But I still think it would be best to take her out of Town after suffering such an ordeal. Fortunately, I told several of my friends at Lady Redham's party that we planned to leave London shortly, so no one should remark on our early departure. My grandson has just become betrothed to Miss Hadley, you see, and we need to arrange the wedding."

"I agree that it would be best to leave Town at this juncture."

Her brow wrinkled. "There may yet be whispers. These things tend to get about somehow. Without fuel for the fire, any lingering gossip will die down quickly. Again, I cannot thank you enough for your swift actions."

"Your thanks are unnecessary, ma'am. I have always regarded Alexandra as being under my protection." His gaze was intent. "I would be obliged if you would grant me a private audience with her."

"Yes, of course, Stanford. And it is about time too!" Her voice was stern. "You should have asked Alexandra to marry you ages ago. But not now. You cannot be alone with her at this hour of the night."

He inclined his head. "I will send her straight to bed once she has had a sip of brandy."

At her weary nod, he turned away. Then, catching sight of Leighton hovering nearby, he instructed the butler to bring two glasses and a bottle of brandy to the morning room before walking back inside and closing the door behind him.

Alexandra looked up as he entered. "I have been wondering how you discovered my kidnapping, Your Grace."

He moved to the chaise-longue and, possessing himself of her hands, drew her to her feet. "I arrived back in London this evening and was told when I called at Longmore House that you were spending the evening at Vauxhall Gardens. I did not wish to wait until tomorrow to see you, so I went straight there and found Charles, only to be informed that you had disappeared. It was then that Miss Hadley made mention of threatening letters before she yielded to tears. And then, Jimmy, who had been waiting at the entrance, came to tell me you had been kidnapped."

Her brow cleared. "So, it was your tiger who saw me."

"I think your distinctive hair color had something to do with that, my dear." A smile softened his features. "He heard the postilion mention he was bound for Gretna Green, and putting two and two together, he hastened to find me. Unfortunately, he took a while to locate our party, but when he did find us, I came *ventre à terre* to your rescue in the time-honored way." His lips twisted wryly.

"I was fortunate indeed, Your Grace, that Jimmy saw me. Had he not—" Her voice faltered.

The door opened, and Robert looked up. Leighton came in bearing a small silver tray with a crystal decanter and a couple of glasses arranged on it. After placing the tray on a side table, he withdrew from the room, closing the door quietly behind him.

Strolling to the table, Robert poured a measure of brandy into a glass and handed it to Alexandra. She took it from his hand and, eyeing the amber liquid, sniffed it suspiciously. "Is this brandy, Your Grace?"

"It is. You have suffered something of a shock, and it will do you good."

Alexandra took a cautious sip and pulled a face. "It tastes awful."

At that moment, someone scratched on the door, and Leighton entered yet again. "I apologize for the interruption, Your Grace, but there is a gentleman here—a Sir Jason Morecombe—who desires speech with her ladyship. I informed him that Lady Longmore had retired to bed, but he insists that I wake her up. He refuses to leave. I am unsure how to proceed."

Robert frowned. "You may show him in here."

"Thank you, Your Grace." The butler withdrew, and a few moments later, he ushered Sir Jason inside.

The baronet's usually impassive face registered surprise when he saw Alexandra. "The kidnapped heiress has returned, then, no doubt rescued by His Grace, the Duke of Stanford." He bowed in Robert's direction. "My compliments to you, sir. Your gallantry is to be admired."

"You—you know I was kidnapped?" Alexandra sat her glass on the table.

"Indeed, I witnessed the whole shocking affair. You were a trifle foolish to allow yourself to be overpowered from behind."

Robert viewed Sir Jason through narrowed eyes. "How did you come to witness this?"

The other man shrugged. "After our dear little lady here told me of the supposed threats made to her by one Lady Ballington—and their planned meeting in Vauxhall Gardens—I decided such sport could not be missed."

Robert's jaw tightened. "You told him about the letters, Alexandra?"

"At the time, I thought Lady Ballington had written them and that Sir Jason was aware of it," she explained. "I sought Sir Jason out about what I perceived to be Lady Ballington's threats to me, hoping he cared enough about his friend to intervene."

"I see," Robert said quietly. Then, looking across at Sir Jason, he bit out in quite a different voice, "And you did nothing to prevent Miss Grantham's kidnapping from taking place, Morecombe."

"Er, no. I saw no reason to interfere in an affair that was not my own."

"Yet you have come here tonight." He spoke through clenched teeth.

Sir Jason's eyes glittered beneath their heavy eyelids. "I was intent on seeing how Lady Longmore was bearing up after the disappearance of her granddaughter—to give this little tale a proper ending. You see, although I have no desire to interfere in this affair, I have no objection to speaking about it. A more delectable piece of gossip has yet to come my way." A smile curled his lips as he glanced at Alexandra. "When the *ton* hears of tonight's happenings, you will be the talk of the town. And when I elaborate further on your illicit highway activities, Miss Grantham, which I know all about, they will be sure to be even more intrigued."

The silence that followed this extraordinary statement was complete.

The baronet took a step closer to Alexandra. "You stare at me so. Don't you wish to know how I discovered your part in those highway robberies?"

"I don't know what you mean!" Alexandra said in a breathless voice just as Robert stepped forward to shield her from the man.

"Well, let me tell you anyway." Sir Jason steepled his fingers together. "When I was visiting your esteemed neighbors, the Hadleys, I heard a rumor that the poor were not only receiving food parcels from Miss Grantham—such a charitable young woman—many of them also had more coins in their pocket than usual. My esteemed host believed the peasants were merely thieving, but when I became curious and spoke to one of Hadley's tenants, he was quick to tell me that Miss Grantham helped him out of her own pocket. And when I discovered—quite by accident—that a post-chaise had been robbed the day before he received a sudden windfall, the picture became clear." His voice hardened. "Criminally clear."

"You have no proof of this," Alexandra said in a shaking voice.

"Don't I? I'm a very thorough man, Miss Grantham. When I arrived in London and approached the Bow Street Runners who had been sent down to investigate the highway robberies. You see it pays to have friends in all walks of life. And they told me a very odd story about the Duke of Stanford's tiger, who had wasted the time of the law by pretending to be a highwayman. I do not suppose you know anything about this, Miss Grantham?

Should we ask the boy what he remembers?" His eyes narrowed, giving him the air of an inquisitor. "I am sure the Runners would be very interested when I bring these fascinating details before them. I have been biding my time, but I believe the time is now right."

Alexandra gasped, but before she could say anything, Robert said curtly, "You will not speak of this nonsense to anyone, Morecombe."

"But I shall, Stanford. I shall. You seem to forget that you do not have the ordering of me. The *ton* will be most amused to hear of Miss Grantham's adventures this evening. And Bow Street will be even more amused at her highway activities, so unexpected as they are. Our dashing little lady is soon to become a disgraced little lady."

Robert's voice was deathly quiet. "Do you choose swords or pistols?"

"My, my—chivalrous to the end." He gave a mocking bow. "I choose the small sword, of course."

"This affair will not go beyond the walls of this room," Robert said grimly. "I propose we settle this here and now."

"Without the presence of seconds, my dear man?"

"Without the presence of seconds. I shall send my tiger to Stanford House to collect the swords."

Sir Jason yawned. "Your proposal is quite irregular, Duke, but I shall indulge you. The defense of a lady's honor is a delicate matter."

Robert strode to the door and called for Leighton. When the butler appeared, he requested the presence of his tiger. Jimmy entered the morning room a short while later, and his eyes widened at his master's instructions. "'Tis to be a duel then, sir?"

"Yes." He divested himself of his coat. "But you are not to say a word about this to anyone, Jimmy."

"Course not, Your Grace." His henchman shot him a reproachful glance as he left the room.

Alexandra, who had been standing frozen all this time, took a hasty step toward him. "Robert, you cannot fight Sir Jason! You may be injured—or even killed! Please don't fight him. I couldn't bear it if you were lost to me."

Robert took her hands in his. "Sweetheart, there is no other choice. I shan't allow your life to be destroyed."

"But what if you are hurt?" She searched his face. "I know very little about fencing, but even I have heard that Sir Jason is a master swordsman."

The baronet bowed gracefully. "I am honored you have such confidence in my ability."

Alexandra glared at him. "I am not speaking to you. My concern is for the *honorable* man in this room." Then, turning back to Robert, she said, "Oh, please, please take care!"

"I am an experienced swordsman, so do not fret." He released her hands. "I believe it will be best if you leave us now."

"But this duel is being fought over me. I must stay!"

"Your presence will only serve as a distraction, Alexandra."

She looked gravely up at him. Then, with a small sob, she turned and hastened toward the door. Was there anything she could do to stop this? Her brain raced frantically, but she knew it was impossible. Robert would never draw back. Not when Sir Jason had it in his power to ruin Alexandra completely.

She turned back and studied the duke's sternly handsome features. And his eyes... those green eyes filled with such warmth and care for her. In an agony of fear, she realized this might be the last time she saw him alive. The thought made her feel dizzy, but Alexandra determinedly fought the darkness threatening to engulf her as she moved away and opened the door. Just before she left the room, she turned around and said, "I love you, Robert."

The words, however, came out only as a scratchy whisper, and Alexandra knew he had not heard her. She attempted to say them again, but her throat was too constricted, and no sound came out. Shivering uncontrollably, she took one last look at the duke, who now had his back to her, before leaving the room. It was the first time she had told him she loved him—and perhaps the last. And he hadn't heard her.

THE DOOR CLOSED behind Alexandra, and a few minutes later, Jimmy returned, bearing a pair of matching small swords. The chairs and tables had been pushed back by this time, and both Robert and Sir Jason had taken off their shoes and waistcoats and were in their stockinged feet. They tested the flexibility of their blades. "You agree they are evenly matched?" Robert's voice was curt.

"Yes. I am entirely at your service."

After a quick salute, their blades rang together. Sir Jason circled cautiously before opening the attack, lunging swiftly. Robert countered and delivered a thrust which Sir Jason parried.

The two men were also evenly matched. Sir Jason was of much slighter build, but what he lacked in size, he more than made up for in agility, the baronet's habitual languidness noticeably absent tonight as he skillfully fought his opponent. But Robert had the advantage in reach and power, and his wrist was firm and steady. Time and time again, he parried the cunning thrusts of the other man, careful not to drop his guard.

The fierce battle wore on, one man fighting for the honor of a lady he was prepared to lay his life down for, the other attempting to finally avenge a slight on his pride he had never been able to forgive. Beads of sweat, by this time, were rolling down Robert's face. It seemed that he would never find an opening. But then his opponent lunged forward, and, seeing his opportunity, Robert flashed his blade above the other man's guard, sinking sword into flesh.

The baronet stumbled, then dropped his weapon, clutching his arm. Stanford stood back, breathing heavily, as a bloodstain spread over Sir Jason's sleeve.

"You cur, Stanford," he whispered venomously as he swayed on his feet and crumpled over.

The door burst open, and Alexandra rushed inside, her gaze fixed on Sir Jason's prone form. "Oh, thank goodness, Robert! I heard someone fall and feared it was you. He . . . he's not dead?"

He wiped his sword. "No, he is not. I merely pinked him in the arm."

Leighton, who had seen Alexandra waiting in the hall and entered the room behind her, stared in horror at the scene. "Your Grace, I must protest! If Lady Longmore knew of tonight's goings-on—"

"She won't. What you have seen tonight must not be spoken of. It is understood?"

The manservant bent his head, but his gaze kept returning to the man on the floor.

"Bring me some strips of cloths, please. I shall bind up the wound, and then we will help Sir Jason to his carriage."

As the butler left the room, Sir Jason stirred. A few minutes later, he sat up and clutched his arm. "Damn you, Stanford, you've all but severed my arm."

"It's nothing but a scratch," he said impassively, eyeing the injured man. "Ah, Leighton has returned."

The butler bore some bandages and a pair of scissors. Robert moved across to Sir Jason and, ignoring the man's feeble protests, cut away his shirt sleeve. Then, after swabbing and binding the wound, he made a sling out of one of the cloths.

"I think that will suffice." He stood back and surveyed his handiwork before turning to Alexandra. "Leighton and I shall help Sir Jason to his carriage. You must retire now to bed, my dear. The hour is too late and the day too full for any further discussion."

Her eyes were wide with distress. "But, Robert, I hoped to speak to you tonight—"

He walked over to her and dropped a gentle kiss on her mouth. "I promised your grandmother I would send you straight to bed some time ago." He brushed her cheek with his fingers as he gazed into her eyes for a heady moment. "Goodnight, sweetheart."

Chapter Thirty-One

"But..." Alexandra trailed off, releasing her breath in a long sigh. Robert was correct. The hour was too advanced for conversation, especially as she was unchaperoned. A numbing tiredness began to spread through her limbs, and the thought of retiring to bed suddenly seemed most appealing.

Smiling tiredly at the duke, she bid him goodnight before leaving the room and making her way upstairs. The evening's adventures had left her feeling completely exhausted.

On the way to her bedchamber, she stopped outside Emily's door, but the room was in darkness when she peeked inside. She would wait until the morrow to speak to her friend.

With the aid of her grandmother's maid, Jarvis, who awaited her in her bedchamber, Alexandra undressed and slipped into a nightgown as images of the evening flitted relentlessly through her mind. The instant her head touched the pillow, she fell into a restless slumber, her confused thoughts merging into uneasy dreams.

Alexandra arose early the next day and went for a brisk walk in the small walled garden in the futile hope that it would help her clear her thoughts. She returned to her bedchamber a short while later and allowed Jarvis to dress her hair, her mind still in turmoil. As she studied her reflection in the mirror, she wondered if Robert would call on her today. What would he say to her now that she was out of danger? He had been very kind to her last night, but he must be annoyed with her for placing herself in harm's way yet again. Would she never learn? She bit down hard on her lower lip, clenching her hands together in her lap. She wouldn't be surprised if the duke did not wish to propose to her after last night. She had caused him so much trouble since their first disastrous encounter, and although her grandmother and Letitia were convinced that he wanted to marry her, he had yet to speak of marriage himself. Perhaps now he never would. Although he had kissed her on the lips last night. She released a little sigh—a memory to treasure forever.

After Jarvis placed the finishing touches on her toilette, Alexandra stood and moved to the door. Just as she opened it, she turned back and said softly, "Thank you for not asking me any questions about last night, Jarvis. I cannot speak about it."

"I know. Lady Longmore told me something of the sort." The maid smiled at her. "Now get yourself along, Miss Grantham. His Grace will be calling soon, I'll be bound."

Alexandra's eyes widened as she shut the door behind her. How did servants always seem to know every last detail of their employers' lives? She walked across to Emily's bedchamber and knocked on the door. When her friend bid her enter, she stepped inside to see Emily sitting up in bed, sipping a cup of chocolate.

Placing the cup back on the saucer, she said, "Oh, Alex! Thank goodness you are safe. Lady Longmore gave me some laudanum last night before you returned home, and I am ashamed to say that I fell asleep before I could find out if you had returned home safely. Forgive me."

Alexandra sat on the bed. "You mustn't apologize, Emily. I should be the one doing that for putting you in such a difficult position."

"I am not very good in a crisis, I'm afraid." She sighed. "I lost my head completely when you failed to return and went all to pieces. I knew it was dangerous for you to meet Lady Ballington on your own."

Alexandra smiled a little ruefully. "My adversary wasn't Lady Ballington after all. Edward Ponsonby wrote those letters."

"Mr. Ponsonby?" Emily hurriedly set the tray on the bedside table, causing the cup to rattle.

"He was intent on carrying me off to Gretna Green to force me to marry him. Thankfully, the Duke of Stanford's tiger witnessed the kidnapping and told him about it, and he managed to come to my rescue."

"How utterly awful, Alex." Emily's eyebrows drew together in alarm. "You don't think Mr. Ponsonby will try to murder John now to get revenge?"

"Those were empty threats meant to lure me into a compromising position. Mr. Ponsonby is nothing but a coward. He looked terrified last night when Stanford stopped his coach. I don't think we need to fear anything more from him as the duke has ordered him to leave the country." Alexandra stood, twisting her fingers together. "I wonder if His Grace will call on me this morning. I wouldn't be surprised if he decides to wash his hands of me after this affair. I have been such a trial to him. He was forced to fight a duel over my name when Sir Jason Morecombe called last night and threatened me."

"What?" Emily's eyes were as round as saucers.

"Sir Jason witnessed my kidnapping, you see, and came to taunt Grandmama. Only she had gone to bed, and so Robert fought for my honor."

Her friend's mouth dropped open. "A duel? I can't believe I slept through all of this. Was anyone injured?"

"Sir Jason was. But not mortally."

"My poor dear. That must have been a harrowing experience."

"Well, let us just say that it wasn't pleasant. I only hope Stanford hasn't developed a disgust of me."

"That would never happen, Alex. The duke loves you. It is clear to anyone who sees you together."

"Oh, Emily!" Alexandra leaned forward and embraced her. "I

hope you are right."

Alexandra made her way downstairs to the breakfast room, where she consumed her meal alone. She felt dreadful at having been the cause of so much anxiety for her grandmother and wouldn't be surprised if the older lady gave her a sharp scold when she emerged from her bedchamber later.

But it wasn't as though Alexandra had known Mr. Ponsonby was intent on kidnapping her. How could she ever have guessed at such a thing? And, besides, it was always easy to see in retrospect what one should have done.

Her grandmother came downstairs much earlier than usual. When she entered the morning room, Alexandra sprang to her feet, setting aside her copy of Elizabeth Blackwell's *A Curious Herbal,* which she had been attempting to read without much success.

"My dear child." She advanced into the room. "How are you feeling this morning? I still cannot believe that that man tried to kidnap you. Such wickedness."

"I am well, thank you, Grandmama. But I feel dreadful for having caused you such anxiety."

"You should have come to me with those letters, Alexandra." Her grandmother's tone was grave. "I cannot understand why you didn't."

"I thought I could manage the situation on my own."

"I have never known a young girl to be so fiercely independent. I daresay it stems from assuming so much responsibility for your brother and sisters at such a young age." She sighed as she sat down. "I wish I could have been more present in your formative years, my love, but your papa was determined to keep you at home, and I did not wish to separate you children after your mama's demise. It would have only added to your distress."

"We did rely on each other very much."

Her grandmother folded her hands in her lap. "I have decided to take you home even earlier than planned. Just in case rumors start swirling around. And you need some rest."

"Yes." Alexandra agreed, staring straight ahead. "When—when would you like to leave, Grandmama?"

"Tomorrow morning." She rose to her feet. "I have a great deal to see to today. And I need to make our excuses for all the engagements we can no longer attend. But my acquaintances will soon discover that I need to plan John's wedding, so they won't be surprised at our departure."

When her grandmother left the room, a core of ice seemed to settle in Alexandra's chest. Robert hadn't called as yet. And when she left London, she wouldn't see him again—not unless he came to Durbridge Hall.

Her grandmother had told her that the duke was on the verge of proposing matrimony to her. And he had, only last night, fought a duel to defend her honor and called her sweetheart. But what if he were having second thoughts about her suitability as his future bride after all her foolish behavior? The role of duchess was a position aspired to by only the most proper and gracious ladies in Society. And Alexandra wasn't proper at all. In fact, she was quite the opposite and would probably make Stanford a dreadful duchess.

As a peer, he had to consider more than his heart when he married. Men in Stanford's position frequently made dynastic marriages with ladies from other noble families, where love rarely came into the equation. Why would he risk the honor of his name on a woman who threw convention to the winds at every opportunity?

She sat in the window seat, gazing out into the square. But Robert did not come. How perverse to finally be able to see a future for herself that contained both love and marriage, and to know the man she wanted to share that future, only to have that vision disappear like a mirage.

Her grandmother bustled in to inform her that she needed to start her packing, and she hauled herself up the stairs to assist Jarvis with the monumental task. She had such a massive wardrobe now. It was actually quite bizarre. What would she do with all those clothes when she returned home? They would not be needed at Grantham Place.

She picked up the *Transactions of the Horticultural Society* to pack it away with her other books and then set it back down as she recalled her conversation weeks ago with Robert in the library. Her breath caught in a small sob as she hurried across to the window. But there was still no sign of him. He wasn't coming.

The day dragged on and on, and Alexandra's worst fears were realized the following morning when she eventually climbed into her grandmother's coach. Up until the very last minute, she had hoped to hear the sound of the knocker on the door. But the duke hadn't called.

The desolation that swelled in her heart was like a physical weight, but she did her best not to reveal her feelings to her grandmother or Emily. She had caused enough anxiety for them over the past few days.

The effort of putting on a reasonably cheerful front was difficult, to say the least, and Alexandra was relieved when they finally turned in at the gates to Grantham Place after all those hours together on the road. Naturally, Emily had travelled with them and would be staying at Grantham Place until the wedding. Grandmama had not mentioned the duke during the trip home, no doubt due to Emily's presence in the carriage. But her gaze, whenever it came to rest on Alexandra, was ominously speculative.

Emily had not raised the subject either. She must know that Stanford had failed to call at Longmore House before they left, but, fortunately, her future sister-in-law was too diplomatic to say anything.

When they entered the hall, a babble of sound filled the air as Dorothea and Abigail rushed into the hall to greet them. A short while later, Grandmama and Emily disappeared upstairs to their bedchambers, leaving the three sisters alone to converse.

Abigail linked an arm through Alexandra's, her smile sunny.

"I have so much to tell you, dearest, that I don't know where to begin."

Alexandra returned her smile, forgetting the ache in her heart at the joy of being reunited with her sisters. As they walked into the drawing room, she squeezed Abigail's arm before drawing Dorethea onto the window seat beside her. "How are you, Thea? I have missed you both so much."

"I am delighted to be home," Dorothea said in her soft voice.

"Thea is delighted to have her laboratory back." Abigail sat in a chair across from them. "Miss Mason strongly disapproved of her interest in chemistry."

Alexandra stared at her middle sister in dismay. "Why did you not let me know?"

"The other girls warned us that they suspected Miss Mason read our letters before they were posted. I dared not complain."

Abigail shook her head slowly, her expression pensive. "Miss Mason was determined to make proper young ladies out of us both. I have never had to abide by so many rules and regulations in my life. You would have hated it, Alex."

Alexandra gazed at her sisters in sympathy. "It sounds perfectly horrid."

Aunt Eliza and Grandmama walked into the room at that moment, and the conversation became more general until her aunt turned to Alexandra and said in a gratified voice, "The Duke of Stanford arrived at Durbridge Hall yesterday, you know. Your Grandmama has told me that the announcement of your betrothal is imminent. I cannot wait to tell Mrs. Hadley about it."

Alexandra opened her mouth and then shut it again when her sisters stared at her, eyes wide. Something in her face must have alerted Abigail to the fact that Aunt Eliza had broached a delicate topic, however, as she swiftly changed the subject and asked Grandmama about their journey.

Alexandra's mind spun with the knowledge that the Duke of Stanford was in the district. She barely ate a bite of dinner, much to Abigail's astonishment. But perhaps sensing that Alexandra's lack of appetite was due to more than the exhaustion typically experienced by travelers after a long journey, her sisters kept their silence, accepting without demur her early departure from the drawing room.

After she had undressed, Alexandra stared up at the canopy, feeling a stir of something akin to hope in her heart. He was here. *He was here.*

It changed everything.

Chapter Thirty-Two

Alexandra had just taken her favorite seat at the drawing room window the next day when Higgins ushered the duke inside. She gazed at him in silence as he crossed the room toward her, studying his beloved countenance as if she were learning it by heart. She couldn't quite grasp that he was actually here, and she blinked when he took her hands in his and drew her slowly to her feet. "Good morning, Miss Grantham. I am pleased to see that you appear none the worse for wear after your recent adventures. I have come to take you for a drive if you would care to join me?"

Alexandra met his searching gaze, her heart pounding in her ears. "Yes. Yes, I am very well. Thank you, Your Grace. I should love to drive out with you."

He offered her his arm and led her outside to his waiting curricle. After he helped her into it, Alexandra held her breath as he climbed up beside her and took the reins from Jimmy. How odd it was to be seated beside him after thinking she might never see him again. "I did not know that you had left London until we arrived yesterday, and Aunt Eliza informed me that you were staying at Durbridge Hall."

"I had a few matters to see to on my estate. But right now, I have something I wish to show you."

She turned in her seat, her brows knit together, as he set the horses in motion. "You do? Pray tell."

He glanced down at her, the affection in his eyes quite taking her breath away. "Patience, my dear."

He drove in the direction of the village. Alexandra was about to warn him that they would probably get stuck in the muddy road that led into the parish when she noticed it was no longer in disrepair. Indeed, it was much easier to traverse up until the outskirts of the village, where the duke skirted around some men who were working to repair that section. And the village, once a scene of dismal poverty, was being transformed. Several of the tumbledown cottages had been put to rights, and a number of new dwellings were being constructed. Moreover, each cottage now had a fenced-off plot, which was in the process of being cultivated.

Alexandra gazed around in wonder. "Are all these plots going to be developed into gardens?"

"Yes. The cottagers will be able to grow vegetables and keep a small quantity of livestock."

"Oh! What a wonderful idea."

"As you no doubt know, donations of money and food, although beneficial, are only short-term solutions to the problem of poverty in the countryside. What is needed is for the laborers to become more self-sufficient and less reliant on charity. This system will not only improve their living standards, but it will also increase their sense of independence and self-worth."

"It will make a difference to the lives of many families." Her eyes shone as she turned to him. "Oh, thank you, Your Grace."

They left the village and took the road that led to the Durbridge estate. When they entered the gates, the duke brought his curricle to a halt and helped Alexandra to alight. "I want to show you the improvements I have made to the cottages. We might as well walk as the weather is fine."

He handed the reins to Jimmy, who drove off at a smart pace, and tucking Alexandra's arm into his, they strolled in the direction of the dwellings. The sun shone down, warming Alexandra's skin, and she breathed in the scent of freshly-turned soil. When the cottages eventually came into view, she came to an abrupt halt. They had all been beautifully repaired, and, on one side, a large section of land had been fenced off.

"Is this to be another garden, Your Grace?"

He led her across to the plot, which was enclosed with palings. "This has been set aside as a community vegetable garden for the cottagers." He smiled at her. "I thought you might like to oversee it? I have also set aside fuel and grazing allotments, and the heath will be planted with turnips."

Alexandra caught her breath. "You have done more than I ever expected. Thank you. Thank you so very much." She leaned her arms against the palings gazing across the field, her heart so full she was sure it would burst.

He came up beside her. "When I arrived here, I fully intended to make changes to improve the lives of my tenants and laborers. However, I had not sufficiently taken their dignity into account. It was you who pointed that out to me." He paused for a moment. "I hope these changes will go some way to restoring it."

"I am sure they will." Her lips curved into a tremulous smile, and then she turned away to study the nearby cottages. "I see Mrs. Hind's roof has been repaired. Perhaps, now that I am here, I should pay her a visit."

"Er—later. Let us walk down to the stream."

He returned her hand firmly into the crook of his arm and led her down a path that eventually came out at an old oak tree, which overlooked the water. Alexandra had spent many hours fly-fishing here as a young girl. Now, she barely glanced at the familiar view as Robert took her hands in his and turned her to face him.

When he did not speak and merely beheld her in a way that made her pulse race, she said in a rush: "I am so concerned about Sir Jason's threats to spread the news about my kidnapping, Your Grace—and my highway activities. Do you think he will do so?"

"Morecombe is very proud. He won't wish for it to become known that I defeated him in a duel. He knows that if he speaks, so will I. I doubt he will say anything at all." He drew her closer. "But enough of him, sweetheart. I have brought you here, as I think you must have guessed, to declare myself. I love you, Alexandra." He dropped a swift kiss on her parted lips. "You own my heart, and you always will, my darling lady gardener." He cupped her face with his hands, gazing into her eyes. "I want you in my life as my wife, until the end of my days. But not only that." His expression sobered. "I need you by my side as my duchess, as both my friend and my aide. Will you marry me, my love, and make me the happiest of men?"

The world began to spin. "Yes," she breathed. "Yes, of course, I will!"

His lips met hers in a heady kiss, which quite took her breath away. And then the world spun completely on its axis as she was caught in an embrace so passionate she floated upwards, unmoored, with no way of ever coming back to earth again. She clutched at Robert's shoulders in a bid to stay on her feet. But he did not allow her to fall, holding her tighter and drawing her ever deeper into this new realm contained entirely within the circle of his arms.

Eventually, Robert drew back, his breathing slightly labored, and rested his chin on the top of her head. He leaned back after a moment, his green gaze intent. "I shall do my best to make you happy, my Alexandra."

It was as if she were in a dream. "I love you with all my heart, my Duke," she said softly.

"You called me by my name the other night."

"I—I know. But I am only allowed to call you by your name when you invite me to do so. In the heat of the moment the other night, I forgot all constraints."

"I shall be happy for you to forget those constraints for the rest of our lives."

"Then I shall oblige you . . . Robert."

She sighed as his arms tightened around her once more. To be held in his arms like this was wonderful, glorious, especially after believing he was lost to her.

He drew back, his expression serious. "Do you realize how close we came to disaster the other night? You were foolish not to inform anybody about those letters."

"I know. With you gone, I did not know who to turn to. I was afraid of endangering John's life by making a false move. I was sure Lady Ballington had written the letters, and when I called on her the next day—"

"You called on her?"

At his swift frown, she glanced away. "Yes. Before I spoke to Sir Jason. Fortunately, though, I did not tell her about the letters. I merely asked her why she wished me harm." She looked up at him, searching his face. "Lady Ballington never liked me because of my connection with you, you know, and she made it very clear that she hoped to marry you. So when I received the first letter," she lifted her shoulders, "it all seemed to fit neatly into place."

His eyes narrowed. "I can see how it must have appeared to you."

Alexandra nestled back into his arms, determinedly turning her thoughts away from the other woman. The marchioness no longer had the power to hurt her with her words, and the best thing she could do now was to forget her.

"Oh, Robert, this feels so much like a dream that I am afraid I shall wake up and find you gone," she murmured into his shoulder. "I've been in agony these past few days, fearing you were lost to me. I still can't believe we are going to be married."

"Believe it, sweetheart."

She met his eyes, taken aback at the glittering light in their depths. He seemed quite fierce all of a sudden, and her cheeks flooded with warmth.

She was going to be Robert's wife. His wife. The word held a special significance for her now, no longer representing the loss of freedom but rather the gain of so much more. For was it not the security of her beloved's embrace that could anchor her to fly so much higher? She smiled up at him. "I must say I feel somewhat foolish when I think about all the derogatory things I used to say about marriage."

"You are happy, then, to be saddled with a husband?" His grin was teasing.

"Happier than I've ever been." She started to laugh. "Oh, dear—"

"What is so amusing?"

"I was thinking about Mrs. Hadley." Her voice was solemn.

"Mrs. Hadley?"

"The squire's wife."

"Ah, yes. A hatchet-faced woman with that scarecrow for a daughter." He frowned. "Why are you giving thought to something so unpleasant?"

"I recalled a particular conversation I had with her a week or so after I first met you. She entertained the highest hopes of securing you as a husband for her daughter and warned me in the friendliest possible way that I would be foolish to even consider casting my eye in your direction because I am only the daughter of a baronet. She thought Jane was in a better position to attract your attention because she is . . ." Alexandra cleared her throat portentously, "the great-grandniece of a viscount on her father's side."

"Good lord!"

"Hmm. I wished her joy of you. But when I found out later who you really were, I told Emily I was surprised Mrs. Hadley would even consider the match considering your reputation as a dreadful breaker of hearts. However, Emily informed me her stepmother was quite kindly prepared to overlook your dangerous reputation."

His eyes glinted as he looked down at her. "The important question, my love, is whether *you* are prepared to overlook my . . . ah . . . dangerous reputation?"

Alexandra slipped out of his arms and shook her head regretfully. "Why, that is not the question at all, Your Grace. If you regard our situation more closely, it is *my* reputation that I must beg you to overlook. I am the dangerous one, after all, being a highwayman . . ."

"You talk too much, Alexandra," he interrupted. And, pulling her into his arms again, he proceeded to silence her in a most effective way. Flinging her arms around his neck, Alexandra sighed with pleasure, barely noticing he'd had the last word in this particular conversation. She was far too happy even to care.

The End

References

Transactions of the Horticultural Society of London: Volume One

The Market Place and the Market's Place in London, c. 1160 – 1850 by Colin Stephen Smith

Maria's first visit to London by Elizabeth Sandham

Reassessing the influence of the aristocratic improver: the example of the fifth Duke of Bedford (1765-1802) by David Brown

Letters to a Young Lady: on a Variety of Useful and Interesting Subjects: calculated to improve the heart, to form the manners, and enlighten the understanding by Rev. John Bennett (published in 1798).

Gardening Women, Their Stories 1600 to the Present by Catherine Horwood

Acknowledgements

Many thanks to my agent, Julie Gwinn, for believing in this book and in my writing, and to Courtney Brown, my excellent editor.

About the Author

Alissa Baxter wrote her first Regency romance during her long university holidays. After travelling the world, she settled down to write her second Regency novel, which was inspired by her time living on a country estate in England. Alissa then published two chick lit novels, The *Truth About Clicking Send and Receive* (previously published as *Send and Receive*) and *The Truth About Cats and Bees* (previously published as *The Blog Affair*).

Many years later, Alissa returned to her favorite era. She writes Regency romances that feature women in trend-setting roles who fall in love with men who embrace their trailblazing ways... at least eventually. Alissa currently lives in Johannesburg with her husband and two sons.

These are my social media details:
Alissa's Instagram page: alissa.baxter.author
Alissa's Facebook group: Alissa's Regency Companions
Alissa's Twitter page: @alissa_baxter
Alissa's Facebook page: facebook.com/alissa.baxter.writer
Alissa's website: alissabaxter.com
Alissa's blog: alissabaxter.blogspot.com